ANYONE BUT THE BOSS

SARA L. HUDSON

Boldwood

First published in Great Britain in 2023 by Boldwood Books Ltd.

Copyright © Sara L Hudson, 2023

Cover Design by Head Design Ltd.

Cover Illustration: Shutterstock

A CIP catalogue record for this book is available from the British Library.

Paperback ISBN 978-1-83751-741-1

Large Print ISBN 978-1-83751-742-8

Hardback ISBN 978-1-83751-740-4

Ebook ISBN 978-1-83751-743-5

Kindle ISBN 978-1-83751-744-2

Audio CD ISBN 978-1-83751-735-0

MP3 CD ISBN 978-1-83751-736-7

Digital audio download ISBN 978-1-83751-737-4

Boldwood Books Ltd
23 Bowerdean Street
London SW6 3TN
www.boldwoodbooks.com

For Jack—
My impulse purchase. My money-pit. My bed-humping champion.
My girl-to-woman-to-mother companion.
I love and miss you.
Always & Forever.

1

THOMAS

I never understood the appeal of a hairless pussy.

'Here, hold him.' Chase thrusts said pussy in my direction, holding him out over the massive Persian rug in our father's office, like baby Simba over Pride Rock.

Except it isn't a cute and cuddly lion being offered up to the savannah as the heir to the animal kingdom. It's a bald, wrinkled adolescent cat.

'Absolutely not.' My arms remain firmly at my sides.

'Oh, come on, man.' He jiggles the cat, like that somehow makes him more appealing. 'Mikey's a good guy, you just need to get to know him.'

I watch as two skin folds morph into one as it twists in his owner's hands. I don't even bother hiding my disdain. 'I have no desire to get to know your cat.'

'Fine.' Chase huffs a defeated breath and lowers the feline to the floor.

As if knowing he was stoutly rejected, the cat levels me with a snide look then begins licking his balls. The visual is an eyesore in and of itself, but the noise... the noise is enough to make my morning protein shake churn in my stomach.

Pointing at the offending animal, I level my stare at my brother. 'If that stains the carpet, you will reimburse the company from your personal account.'

With a deep, offending sigh, Chase scoops up his cat and deposits it on the upholstered chair in front of my desk.

Like that's any better.

With the cat moved and the licking over, Chase throws what some female employees at Moore's refer to as a 'charming look' in my direction. 'Looking forward to cat-sitting while I'm on my honeymoon?'

I do not find my brother charming. In fact, a few months ago I might have said that I disliked my brother. Though that would've been a lie.

He leans over the back of the chair to pat his pet, looking like he's tenderizing a chicken breast.

'I thought Bell wanted him to come with you.'

He stops patting his pet long enough to look up at me like a kid who dropped his ice cream cone. 'Bell *always* wants Mikey with her.'

I'm not the best at social cues, but... 'Are you *jealous* of your cat?' Confused, I point at the beady-eyed, loose-skinned beast with more indecent exposure violations than Marilyn Manson – *and* less physical attractiveness. '*That* cat?'

Another shrug. 'Maybe.'

I'm not surprised often, but I *am* surprised that he'd admit to such a thing. But then again Chase has always been good about expressing himself. One of the many, *many* ways we differ.

But in the name of turning over a new leaf, now that our

father is in prison and Chase and I have begun mending our fences, I attempt to express myself. 'I don't like animals.'

See? Emotional growth. I can change.

Chase's expression falls.

'And I especially don't like ugly animals.'

He clutches his chest like an old lady would her pearls. The cat, as if understanding my words, resumes his licking.

'Ask Mother.' I'd rather not pass the buck, or the cat, as it were, but our mother lives in a six-thousand-square-foot mansion complete with a bevy of maids that will cater to Mike's every catnip desire. And I'm sure, if paid enough, one will even pet the damn thing.

'Mom's going on that singles cruise.'

To say that Emily Moore, the matriarch of the Moore fortune, is enjoying divorced life, would be an understatement.

'And Liz is...' Chase shrugs.

We don't actually know where our sister is. It's a point of contention in our family.

Especially with me. I still require weekly updates from the federal correctional institute in Otisville just to make sure our father is doing exactly what he needs to be doing – nothing.

Which means when Liz skipped town, Chase and I wanted to hire a private detective. I'd had one fully vetted and ready to go when Mother and Bell teamed up to stop us. They think Liz needs time and space to come to terms with the fact that she isn't the daughter of the man she'd always considered her father.

Personally, I would think knowing that I wasn't blood related to the man arrested for embezzling her inheritance would be great news. Hell, even if it wasn't my inheritance that was embezzled, I'd still welcome the news that Stanley Moore –

an irresponsible, mentally abusive crook with poor business acumen – and I weren't related.

But that's just me.

Chase leans against the built-in bookshelves. 'Trust me, I tried everyone else. George said he'd quit if I even asked him.' Seeing as George, Chase's, and now our, administrative assistant, runs the place, I can understand Chase's reluctance to push the matter.

He glances over his shoulder at the door, as if worried George heard him talking. Sighing in relief when George's perfectly quaffed and pomaded low-profile pompadour doesn't pop into the open door frame, he turns back to pleading his case. 'Bell even asked Alice, but her building doesn't allow pets.'

My gaze jerks away from the car crash that is my brother's pet. 'Alice?'

'Yeah, Alice. Your new marketing team's visual merchandiser.' He drops his head to one side, assessing me, an annoying smirk on his face. 'You know, dark-haired, slim and shy?'

'Yes, I'm aware of who Alice is, thank you.' Though I wish I wasn't. Much to my consternation, I am very much aware of Alice Truman.

'You do, huh?' The smirk grows.

'Yes.' I pick up my fountain pen from the desk and examine the personalized 'Moore's' written across the cap. 'She's the one with the unfortunate haircut. Formerly of the shoe department. Great eye for displays.'

Chase's smirk drops into an open-mouth gape. 'Dude...'

I quirk a brow at my brother's obvious reproach. Alice *was* hired out of the shoe department for her eye-catching and stellar floor displays a few months ago. She's in her twenties and yet the severely cut bangs she's currently trying to grow out make her look just out of high school.

Everything I said was true. And yet, it's obvious from my brother's reaction, that I was *not* supposed to say it.

My family likes to inform me that I'm rude. Though the words they use in place of rude are far more colorful.

I don't mean to sound that way. I just... do. Why spend time trying to cultivate words and phrases that soothe people's much too sensitive feelings when the unvarnished truth wastes less time with its lack of ambiguity. I have spent years honing my efficiency.

And if I'm honest with myself, which I try not to be when it comes to *feelings*, the way I am might also have to do with my upbringing.

Prior to my father's arrest, if I had mentioned how impressed I was that a shoe salesperson made the leap into marketing on their own merits, or if I noted how rare it is that a person with such an unfortunate haircut could still strike such a favorable appearance, my father would use it against me. Even just acknowledging that I knew a female employee's name would be cause for my father to feel the need to intervene. And as his intervening would be either to fire them or sleep with them – as if proving to me, his heir, that he still rules the manor – I began honing my poker face early on. Cutting away the superfluous.

Now fixed at forty years of age, my deadened demeanor elicits two outcomes: fear or anger. For my brother, before our reconciliation, it was the latter. While for most everyone else, especially employees, it's the former.

Alice is the rare exception. For someone as tiny and beneath me in terms of business hierarchy, she does not ingratiate. And to anyone else she's shy, polite and unfailingly kind. Just not me.

A fact that in itself isn't particularly noteworthy as I tend to make most people, not just employees, uncomfortable. However, for some reason, I feel the bite of Alice's cold shoulder and the sting of her sharp words whereas I remain impervious to others'. And even more disturbing than the fact that I note a difference, is how even after becoming aware of this sensitivity, I have yet to control it.

Which is probably why I'm unusually and annoyingly cognizant of her.

No other reason.

* * *

Alice

Thomas Moore – my boss and the most arrogant man in all of New York – is an asshole.

'Good morning, Mr Moore.' Chase jumps in surprise as I walk into the office. A glance at Thomas shows no reaction. 'Mr Moore.'

Typical.

The stiff, rude and prideful Thomas couldn't be more different than the charming, sweet-talking and socially astute Chase.

I hand Thomas my design proposal for the upcoming front window display.

'Alice, hi.' Chase runs a hand through his hair, a guilty look on his face. 'All ready for Vegas?'

As it isn't his fault his brother is a snob, I force a smile to my face. 'Yes. Can't wait.'

Chase cuts his eyes to his brother, widening them as if begging him to say something.

Thomas opens the folder I gave him, skimming over my display proposal. 'I'll make notes and get back to you.'

Chase runs a hand down his face. Mike, who I just noticed peeking his head over the chair, meows with more emotion than Thomas Moore probably has in his heart.

'Great.' My smile feels brittle, my words clipped. 'Thanks.'

I make my exit, walking stiffly down the hall.

George's eyebrows shoot up over the top of his horned-rimmed glasses as I pass by him standing in the break-room doorway. No doubt shocked that the usually perky and cheerful Alice Truman is seething. Because I am *not* a seether. I never have been.

I'm perpetually polite. I avoid confrontation. I'm a peacekeeper.

But right now, instead of making peace, I want to punch Thomas Moore in his ridiculously handsome face.

Thankfully, George gets distracted by the whistling and beeping coming from the complex espresso machine that he insisted Chase buy him, enabling me to turn the corner and slip into the office supply closet without explanation.

I need to collect myself. I need to forget Thomas Moore's dismissive words. And I most definitely need to forget the week I spent going from cologne counter to cologne counter during my lunch break trying to figure out how, in the rare moments that I was in the same room as him, the condescending jerk smelled so delicious.

It took five days and a lot of sneezing but I figured it out – money.

Thomas Moore smells so delicious because he can buy a cologne that costs more than the monthly rent of a three-hundred-and-eighty-foot studio in a kind-of-sketchy but not-so-bad part of town.

The part of town that I live in.

Maybe if I had expensive-cologne-buying money, I could afford a real haircut and not an at-home special where I, regretfully, thought I could copy the curtain bang trend, but somehow ended up with a heavy blunt fringe that made me look pre-pubescent.

But while it is not my best look, I resent the hell out of Mr Starched Shirts for pointing it out. Just because he gets his chocolate-colored locks routinely trimmed by the best barber New York City has to offer, not all of us were born with a silver spoon.

Taking a deep breath, I make the most of my hiding spot and rifle through one of the boxes until I find the multicolored packs of Post-it notes. Bell likes to say my office looks like a serial killer's hang-out. But sticking color-coded Post-it notes and Polaroid pictures on my walls makes it easier for me to organize ongoing projects and social media posting schedules, as well as brainstorm window and floor displays.

I grab more blue ones – the color I use for Moore's social media posts. I use a lot of those.

Moore's never had its own marketing team, let alone a visual merchandiser. Instead, they'd hired outside marketing firms for advertising purposes and let floor managers display whichever goods they wanted based on whatever sales numbers they wanted to hit that month.

It was an outdated system that left a lot to be desired both creatively and financially. It wasn't until the middle Moore sibling, Chase, took over last year that the lack of proper and current marketing strategies was rectified.

I may have come from the shoe department, as Thomas Moore so aptly said, but I'm now Moore's first hire for their internal marketing department. My official title is lead visual merchandiser and social media coordinator. Basically, when not posting pictures on my phone, I do a lot of dressing and undressing of mannequins.

Not bad for a former shoe salesperson who aged-out of the foster care system.

Cracking the door open, I glance down the hall. Coast clear.

I couldn't be happier with a job that will allow me to help the people who depend on me, I remind myself as I quick-step toward the elevator.

Well, no, that's a lie. I definitely could be happier.

When the doors open I jump in and keep pressing the close door button until I'm safely shut inside.

I could *not* have to deal with Thomas Moore.

2

THOMAS

'No strippers, no gambling, no nipple tassels.' I look pointedly at Susan, Moore's head of womenswear from across my office's sitting area.

For the past hour Susan and I have been hammering out the finer details of my brother's wedding. If Chase wanted the typical seedy and sad impromptu Vegas wedding, then he shouldn't have made me best man. Because I've taken the small amount of power and responsibility that came with the title and multiplied it ten-fold.

Case in point – I hired Susan, head manager of woman's luxury, to act as wedding designer and planner.

Susan, a woman in her sixties who doesn't look a day over fifty, crosses one leg over the other, her houndstooth Yves Saint Laurent trousers falling perfectly over her chocolate snakeskin Jimmy Choos. 'Do you honestly think I'd allow *any* of those things?'

'No, but...' I tilt my head at Chase who's been lying on my office couch between us, his cat sprawled out on top of him, lightly dozing during our entire conversation. He's still mad at me for my earlier interaction with Alice.

Susan's pink lips twist into a wry smile. She knows full well what kind of mayhem my brother can charm his way into and out of. She concedes my point and concerns with a nod. 'Noted.'

Another few minutes of double-checking that all facets of my brother's ceremony venue are in place, all while my brother naps, Susan stands to leave. 'I know you were worried about this wedding at the start.' She glances at Chase, arm draped over his eyes as if exhausted by his charmed life, then back to me. 'But with how you managed to talk the chapel into suspending services while you paid for renovations, renovations *we're* in charge of—' she places her palm on her chest, the forty years of service diamond bracelet I gave her three years ago glittering in the lights '—it's going to be fabulous.'

'Hmmm.' I hadn't talked the owners of the chapel into anything. I'd simply written them a check. They get a brand-new chapel facelift for their future weddings all for the low cost of a free week's vacation.

Nothing about this wedding is a good ROI. Well – I glance at my brother, his usual smile in place even as he rests, a smile that has looked far more genuine since he met Campbell 'Bell' King – at least not a *financial* ROI.

Rising from my chair opposite Susan's, I re-button my suit jacket and walk her to the door.

After closing it, I stride back to my desk, the foggy winter's day outside the floor-length windows behind it mirroring my mood.

Meanwhile, my new office does not. Gone are the dark navy and burgundy as well as the heavy ornate furnishings from when it was our father's office just a year ago. In their place is a mixture of honey-colored wood, emerald-green velvet and cream linen. It's bright, clean, modern, and annoyingly refreshing.

'It isn't too late to have a respectable wedding, you know?' I sit in my leather desk chair, its lines more streamlined and its cushion more comfortable than the previous throne-like monstrosity that it replaced.

Chase's eyes pop open. 'What could be more respectable than the King himself residing over our nuptials?'

'Anything.' I stare hard at the minuscule space between Chase's shoes draping over the armrest and the light neutral fabric of the sofa. 'Anything would be more respectable.' And easier to control.

People like to think that New York is chaotic. And it can be, but it's a chaos controlled by such power and influence. Power and influence the Moore family name wields. Even after last year's unfortunate public family drama with my father's incarceration. And to me, control is key.

Vegas is defined, both denotation and connotation, by its complete lack thereof.

I don't need to experience it to know I'll despise it.

Chase raises his knees toward him and curls up, dislodging Mike and coming perilously close to scuffing the soles of his shoes over my cushions. 'But what's the fun in that?'

'Meow.' With great indignation, Mike leaps onto the back of the velvet side chair I'd just vacated.

'Marriage isn't fun. It's serious.' Not that I'd know. I've never been married, but being the product of an unhappy, unhealthy and now broken marriage, I know it's definitely not to be taken lightly.

But, I remind myself, if Bell and Chase want to elope to Vegas and have a polyester-and-rhinestone-clad imposter pronounce them man and wife until death do they part, then who am I to say no?

I should be happy that my little brother has found the perfect person to marry. And considering he and I have only recently reconciled, I should be thrilled that he not only invited me but asked me to be his best man.

I am. Really. My fingertips pound my keyboard harder than necessary as I check on yesterday's earning reports, half of my brain running through the massive Vegas to-do list still left to accomplish before this weekend.

It's redundant of me, and I *hate* being redundant, but I can't help make one more appeal to common sense. 'You should get married at home, where you and your wife plan to live, amongst friends and family. You should enter this marriage with the seriousness in which the commitment should be taken.'

Chase blinks in time with Mike. 'Sometimes I think you time-walked from the eighteen hundreds.'

I give in to the sigh that's been brewing since Susan and I reconfirmed which Elvis officiant from the twenty-five applicants would officiate the ceremony. 'Sometimes I *feel* as if I'm from the eighteen hundreds.'

Mike, now at eye level, lifts his leg and licks.

George emerges from the 'secret' door Chase insisted on installing between our offices in one of his fits of whimsy. The secret door everyone knows about because Chase told them, so impressed with himself for coming up with the idea. 'Mr Moore the younger?'

I'd like to say that seeing my brother annoyed does not give me pleasure, but from the rare upward pull of my lips when Chase clenches his jaw, it would be a lie if I did.

'Really, George?' Chase picks up Mike and faces George. 'The younger?'

Our administrative assistant has found creative ways to maintain a formal work environment without resorting to a first name basis since Chase and I began working together.

To me, it's well-earned karma from Chase forever calling me 'dude' and 'T-money'.

Continuing as if Chase hadn't spoken, George walks through the doorway into my office, his usual three-piece suit perfectly tailored and wrinkle free. 'I've been informed that Miss King is in the shoe department.'

Momentary irritation gone, Chase beams and grabs his cat. 'I knew your mommy would come if I brought you.'

As if understanding him, the feline nuzzles his head against Chase's chin to which Chase raises one of its paws and high fives it.

Pinching the bridge of my nose, I decide to stop being derailed by wedding nonsense and get back to work.

Until George mentions Alice.

* * *

Alice

'Why are you in here when you have a perfectly good office?'

Blinking against the light pouring in through the open doorway, I shield my eyes with my hand. A woman, backlit, leans against the door frame of the shoe inventory room. 'Bell?'

'In the flesh.' Her heels click on the unfinished concrete floor as she gets closer to where I'm hunched over a low shelf, shoeboxes pushed to either side to make room for my laptop and camera equipment.

'I, uh, am focusing on the shoe department today.' I snag my phone off the shelf and wave it. 'Going to upload some more shots to social media.'

Bell purses her lips before shifting her gaze to shoeboxes on the shelves above me. Shoeboxes that are already decorated with a rainbow of Post-it notes. 'You're going to focus on the shoe department two days in a row?'

Dang it. I forgot that as the marketing consultant, Bell would be well up to date with Moore's social media account postings.

'Well...'

I can't tell her that I find surrounding myself with the familiar smells of freshly honed leather and new rubber soles from the hundreds of shoes stacked in a dusty oversized closet soothing.

That would be weird.

'Is someone giving you a hard time in the office?' Bell folds her arms across her chest. 'Do I need to smack some heads together?'

I smile at her fierce expression. Bell is a great boss. Too bad she's not my *real* boss. Her year-long contract with Moore's is sadly coming to a close.

'No one needs to be smacked.' I stand, stretching out my back, sore from bad posture. 'And why are *you* here?' Bell may be Moore's interim marketing manager while she searches for her replacement, but she's usually a virtual worker. She's based in Houston, and though that will change after the wedding, she

doesn't come into Moore's too often because, as she says, she's
more productive working from home.

Which everyone at Moore's knows is code for Chase not
leaving her alone long enough to get any work done.

She shrugs, eyeing a stack of Louboutin boxes next to her. 'I
finished what I needed to, and with Chase bringing Mike with
him to work, I decided to surprise them for lunch.' She slides
one of the boxes out from the stack.

Which is precisely why Chase brings the cat to work. He
knows that feline is her weakness.

Opening the lid, Bell lifts out a platform heel that looks like
you'd have to be a tightrope walker to wear and dangles it
between us from the ankle strap. 'Too much?'

I know the price of those shoes. Between that, the flashy
color and heel height, there is no way she'd be able to wear
them more than a few times a year. But I don't mention that. I
just shrug. 'Maybe?'

'Yeah.' She re-shelves them, sighing. 'I guess.'

In a flash, she changes gear, facing me and clapping her
hands together. 'Come on. While I'm here I'll help you pick out
your bridesmaid shoes.'

My overgrown bangs fall in my face. 'Oh.' I grab the head-
band I took off because it was giving me a headache and slide it
back in place, pushing my hair back. It's taken nine months for
my bangs to *finally* grow out long enough to become manage-
able. 'I keep for—'

'Forgetting? Yeah, I noticed.' Bell places her hand on my
back, ushering me out of the dimly lit storage room and into
the bright light of day. Or rather, Moore's shoe department.

The space, though huge and nearly windowless, is lit up
like a summer's day by the many crystal chandeliers hanging
from twenty-foot ceilings. Like a busker coming up from the

subway, it takes a minute before I can fully open my eyes to the light.

'Susan is waiting for you.' Bell eyes the new Saint Laurent display. 'I'll catch up in a minute.' She hustles off in search of more death-defying heel heights.

I only manage to take two steps before a woman dressed in cropped, raw-hemmed jeans, a silk blouse and shiny slip-on Gucci loafers hands me a Jimmy Choo, her Cartier watch glinting in the chandelier's glow.

'Can I see this in a size seven?'

Out of habit I take the shoe and note the inventory number on the sole's tag. 'Of course.'

Raymond, the head floor manager, seemingly comes out of nowhere to take the heel from me. 'Allow me,' he says to the woman, waving her toward an empty chair.

'Well now.' The customer brightens at Raymond's formal manner, and probably his silver-fox looks. 'Thank you,' she says taking a seat.

Raymond lifts his head in Clarissa's direction, my one-time co-worker, and the subtle nod has her scurrying forward to help.

'Sorry.' I'm not sure why I feel the need to apologize to Raymond about trying to help a customer, but I do. Or maybe I feel the need to apologize to myself when I catch my reflection in a mirrored pillar and realize I'm wearing the uniformed suit of all Moore's salespeople when I was hired to sell shoes here five years ago.

I thought by wearing a blue shirt instead of white, and sans name tag, I was making a smart economical decision on updating my wardrobe for my new position. But I guess not.

Thomas's words from all those months ago reverberate in my ears. *She's the one from the shoe department.*

Raymond merely gives me a small smile, then, as if I'm also an expensively dressed customer with money to burn, leads me a few display tables down, where Susan stands next to a stack of shoeboxes.

'Sit.' Susan points to the chair on the other side of the shoeboxes.

I sit. Though Susan and I were both on the sales floor – me in shoes and she managing women's luxury goods – I've spent more time with her since being promoted to an administrative department due to her involvement with Bell and Chase's wedding.

Unveiling the first pair, baby blue wedge sandals with thin buckle straps, she sits on a shiny new shoe-fitting stool, prepared to slide them onto my feet. 'Let's try these on first.'

I dutifully try on the sandals, being careful to take the shoe from her and slip them on myself. It feels weird being served where I once worked. In a place I can't afford. Bell is the one buying all the bridesmaids' shoes for the wedding.

'You are the only bridesmaid left to pick out shoes. And without shoes I don't know what dress to put you in. I had to order three different dresses in your size just so you'd have one in time for the wedding.'

I cringe. 'Sorry.'

Susan arranges the next pair, platform stiletto pumps with rhinestone details, next to the worn ones I slipped off.

I fiddle with the tiny gold buckle. 'I thought people usually pick the dress *before* the shoes?'

Susan shrugs, somehow still looking ladylike while perched on the low stool. 'Maybe, but doing it this way is more fun for me.'

I stand in the sandals, the straps making me feel more secure with the higher-than-normal-for-me heel.

'If Thomas is going to let me run rampant and choose whatever dresses my little heart desires for the bridal party, then you bet your skinny backside I'm going to pick as I please.'

I wobble in the heels at the mention of *him*.

Susan arches a brow as I steady myself, then gestures for me to walk. 'Just be glad I'm letting you have a say in your shoes.'

I've heard of a bridezilla, but never a stylezilla. I make a little turn between display tables, shut down the part of my brain fixated on why Thomas Moore is so involved in a wedding he seems to have nothing but disdain for.

My small circle takes me past the very table the shoes on my feet are displayed on. I wobble once more at the price.

I've spent my entire life living frugally, living paycheck to paycheck. And though I work at a store dedicated to expensive high-end goods, I've only ever spent what I absolutely had to on functional, long-lasting clothes. Part of the reason I loved my job as a shoe salesperson was the uniform. Clothes were one less thing I had to worry about.

My only vice, if you can call it that, is reading. And I thank the New York City public library system every day for making that addiction budget friendly.

'Those shoes look lovely on you.' Susan leans back, assessing me as I return. 'You have such pretty ankles.'

I'm not sure what makes ankles pretty, but I thank her all the same.

Once seated, I reach for the platforms, which are heavy in my hands. How I'm going to be able to walk in these, even if it's just a few feet down an aisle, I don't know.

At least my promotion came with excellent healthcare benefits in case I break one of said pretty ankles.

'No, no.' Susan pushes the remaining platform on the floor

away with her shoe. 'Now that I see them, they're all wrong for you. Too clunky.'

I wince as the expensive silk shoe slides across the carpet.

She hands me the box in her hands. 'Try these.'

Once more, the shoes are baby blue. But these... these are *lovely*.

At first glance they don't seem anything special, but the heel, the shortest of the three, is thin and delicate. And a large bow, which might seem ostentatious, lays flat and at an angle across the closed and pointed toe.

'I wish they were black.' No, I take that back. If they did come in black, I'd be hard-pressed to talk myself out of buying them. Because I could wear these with everything. Dresses, suits, pants. I check the label – Stuart Weitzman. Expensive, but well-crafted. With my employee discount maybe it would be worth the price... *if* they came in a more practical and versatile color.

I slip them on slowly, nervous they won't fit. But they do, and I can't help but turn my feet this way and that when I stand in front of the mirror.

'You like those.'

I can hear the smile in Susan's voice.

'And they *do* come in black.'

My head pops up from my admiration. 'They do?'

Walking a few steps away from our chaos of shoes and boxes, Susan returns with the shoe in black. *And* in red.

I've never owned a pair of bow shoes, let alone red shoes. Growing up in foster care, you got hand-me-down sneakers and functional, thick-soled Mary Janes in case the foster home you were placed in went to church on Sundays.

Ten years have passed since I aged-out, but frugality and

functionality have been too well-ingrained. Especially when you have people depending on you.

'Get them.'

I freeze, my hand outstretched toward Susan, the deep baritone popping goosebumps down my arms. Dropping my hand, I turn, coming face-to-face with Thomas Moore.

3

THOMAS

Alice's stare is unnerving. It always is when she looks at me.

'Do you like them?' Bell asks her, sauntering up wearing a pair of bright pink Louboutins that clash horribly with her burnt orange blouse.

'What?' Alice wrenches her eyes from mine. 'Like who?'

Frowning, Bell's eyes ping-pong between us. Settling on Alice, she points to light blue pumps adorned with asymmetrically placed bows. 'The shoes? Do you like the shoes?'

'Oh.' Alice's cheeks flush before she turns her back to me, removing the shoes she was just salivating over and grabbing a pair of blue sandals off the carpet. 'Here.' She holds them out to Susan. 'I pick these.' Then hustles off through the shoe displays without a goodbye.

Before anyone can say anything, Chase comes running up, Mike in hand. 'Babe.'

'Don't call me babe at work.' In her new shoes Bell only has to tip her chin to kiss Chase's cheek. 'And what happened to you?'

Chase turns at the last minute, locking his lips with hers.

'Mike tried to pounce on a kid drinking whipped-cream hot cocoa.'

'You really shouldn't bring Mike down to the sales floor.' Bell's admonishment, mirroring my own thoughts, lacks power when she lets the whipped cream glutton nuzzle her chest.

'She'll regret not choosing these,' Susan says, picking up the shoes Alice was smiling over a second before. 'The dress I chose for the sandals is, well...' She shrugs, her eyes sparkling more than they should, making me regret giving her cart blanche over the wedding party's outfitting.

My brother's cat moves his paws, as if trying to swim through air, toward Bell.

Susan laughs while gathering the selected footwear, and heads toward a saleswoman helping a customer a few sections down.

Chase wrestles for control of his feline, turning away from his fiancée. 'Dude, would you—'

Mike leaps from his arms, beelining back toward the jewelry case he is now facing. With a curse, Chase runs after him.

Only Bell remains. Her eyes don't sparkle, but her grin does rival that of a Cheshire cat.

Hands behind my back, I focus on her questionable shoe selection rather than her smile. 'Those are ridiculous.'

* * *

Alice

Ding.

I pause in taking a picture of the Valentine's Day display I'd just created in the children's department, complete with heart balloons and pink teddy bears, as the text notification bubble is blocking my view.

Chase:

Code Penis

Covering my phone screen with my hand, I step behind a clothing rack. It would be just my luck that a customer would see that on my phone as I'm standing in the children's department.

I have informed Chase, *multiple times*, that if anyone over-heard him or knew he talked to an employee like this, Human Resources would crucify him. But I also can't help but laugh at the code phrase he chose for all bachelorette party-related things.

Ding.

Chase:

Can you come to my office?

Pocketing my phone in my Moore's salesperson uniform blazer, I grab my tablet from my backpack. My bag isn't fancy, just plain canvas, but it's black and unobtrusive and I've had it since I began working at Moore's ten years ago. It's reliable.

Clicking on the screen with my stylus, I see that I'm ahead of schedule, having worked through lunch to distract myself from today's earlier failure.

Not only did I mention the thing I vowed never to mention, but in a pique of irrational anger at Thomas Moore for telling me to get the very shoes I wanted, I'd grabbed the sandals and immediately understood the phrase 'cut off your nose to spite your face'.

I've never been a clothes horse. I couldn't afford to be. But I understand the power of beautiful, expensive clothes. It would be hard not to working at Moore's for all these years.

Today's disappointment has made me yearn to start using my much larger paycheck to upgrade my wardrobe. Slowly transform my outside to reflect the professionalism of my new job title.

However, as satisfying as it would be to prove that condescending man wrong by wearing new, more professional-looking clothes that befit my more prestigious title, I still can't force myself to spend the money. I have responsibilities that someone like the arrogant and privileged Thomas Moore would never understand.

I sigh, remembering the pretty bow shoes. Maybe if Kayla – my de facto sister for nine months of my life when her parents fostered me – ever called me back about my offer to get a larger apartment so that all of us could live together, I'd figure out if I could splurge on them or not.

But then I eye the pretty spring dresses, neatly displayed in the little girls' department, and I think maybe I should spend that money on Mary. Give her the colorful, vibrant-clothed childhood I never had.

Leaning against a mirrored pillar, I check my text message and call log. Nothing but Code Penis.

Kayla is still ghosting me.

It's like I'm sixteen again.

Twelve years ago on my birthday, Kayla's parents asked if they could adopt me.

I didn't know what happy tears were until that day. It was the best day of my life.

Followed closely by the worst. A few days later Kayla's parents were hit by a car while crossing the street in midtown. They died on impact.

A great-aunt took her in while I went back into foster care. I tried to keep in touch, but she ignored my calls and letters. Years had passed before Kayla called. She was crying. And she was pregnant.

As much as it hurt to hear how scared Kayla was, I jumped at the chance to have a sister again. To have a family.

Thankfully, with most of the commission I made saved up from Moore's, and the inheritance Kayla received from her aunt, we were able to afford rent in a small one-bedroom in a dodgy part of town that Kayla and I could share.

And as much as I hated myself for it, I loved every minute of Kayla living with me again, even though she spent most of her time in the apartment depressed and tearful.

Then the baby arrived. My niece.

I was there, in the hospital room, when Mary came into the world. I heard her first cry. Changed her first diaper while Kayla stared vacantly out the small hospital window. Probably traumatized from going through childbirth at twenty.

Though I'd always thought of Kayla as my younger sister, something about a baby makes the feelings concrete. The three of us were a real family.

At least, until Kayla met Jack and she and Mary moved out a few months ago.

Ding.

Chase:

Code Penis?

Pushing my non-Code Penis related thoughts aside, I text Chase:

Be there in five.

* * *

'The penis party is screwed.' Chase flops on the love seat in the sitting area of his office, grunting when Mike Hunt jumps on his lap. It never fails to make me want to pat myself on the back whenever I come to Chase's office. As a favor to Bell, after Chase surprised her with a whirlwind Elvis road trip right in the middle of construction, I completed the redesign of Chase and Thomas's offices – turning their father's monstrosity of old money and archaic and criminal business practices into two modern spaces.

The time I spent anxiously working with interior designers and architects – things I had never done before – feels well worth it whenever I'm surrounded by the finished product.

Chase shifts, resting his loafers on the coffee table in front of us, making me frown. 'Say again?' Sliding the straps off my shoulders, I swing my backpack around to retrieve my tablet. With a few taps on my stylus, the wedding file I created for bridesmaid duties is opened and ready. 'Screwed?'

'Yes.' Chase absently pets his cat, the feline's pale skin shifting over his bony frame.

He purrs, but swats at Chase's chin with his paw, as if telling him to pay better attention.

Mike Hunt is *not* a cute cat, but he's got a great personality.

'Stop it, Mikey.' Chase places Mike beside him on the couch. Mike climbs back into his lap. 'Bell left for Houston after lunch.'

'What?' I drop into one of the nearby chairs, my bag dropping to the floor at my feet. 'But the bachelorette party is tomorrow.' I think of all the penis party favors Chase, Leslie and I have purchased to decorate the speakeasy bar in SoHo that we'd rented for the party.

'I know.' He rubs his face with both hands. Mike swats at him again. 'But it isn't like I can tell her to blow off her work emergency. The party is supposed to be a surprise.'

A surprise Bell was adamant she *didn't* want. She'd explicitly told Leslie and me, her two bridesmaids, that she did not want a bachelorette party. Especially one the night before the flight to Vegas. She didn't want to be hungover on the plane.

Hence, why Chase, just as adamant that Bell *did* want a party but was too shy to ask for it, decided to throw a 'low-key penis party' two days before the flight.

'Maybe this is a good thing.' I try and sound upbeat in the face of my boss's forlorn expression. 'I'm sure she'll be happy with the spa day you planned for her on arrival.' I pause. 'She can still do that, right?'

'Yeah.' Chase continues pouting. 'She'll even get in earlier now that she's flying in from Houston. Plenty of time for that.'

He stills and I brace myself for whatever new idea he's come up with.

'She's getting in earlier.' He stands and pulls out his phone. 'I can move up all her spa treatments.'

'Okay...' I tap on the Vegas day planner in the file.

'And move the penis party to afterwards.'

My stylus hovers over the screen. 'I'm sorry, what?'

'An afternoon bachelorette party.' He paces back and forth, scrolling through his phone. 'That way she'll be surprised – because who throws a lunch time bachelorette party – but will still be able to get to bed at a reasonable time for the wedding the next day.'

I glance at the schedule, already jam-packed. 'But then how will we—'

'She'll fly in and go straight to the spa.' He pauses, eyes on the ceiling. 'I'll add Leslie to all her appointments so she can keep an eye on her.'

I add Leslie to the spa treatments on my calendar. 'Okay, but—'

'Then while they're there you—' he points at me '—can grab the dildos and—'

'Stop right there.'

I jump in my seat, my stylus sliding across the screen and creating havoc on the schedule, my eyes flashing to the threshold where the *other* Mr. Moore stands. And has been standing for some time if the arch of one of his eyebrows is any indication.

Chase's head turns toward the door, finger still pointed in my direction. 'Tommy-kins?'

'It's Thomas.' His handsome face is expressionless, though his brown eyes seem to be burning a tad brighter than usual. 'And yes, stop speaking.' His bright eyes flick to me, and then, as if dismissing me, return to his brother. 'You cannot speak like that in front of an employee.'

Even though his words perfectly mirror the ones I've said to Chase, I bristle at being simplified to 'employee'.

'We're talking about the wedding,' I explain to him as if he's an overgrown, solidly handsome child. 'Not work.' I sniff, feeling quite snobbish myself at the moment. 'I'm a bridesmaid, in case you've forgotten.'

'I remember.' Focus still on Chase, he does not sound impressed. 'However, it is still inappropriate.'

Chase rolls his eyes as if he's used to his brother's lectures. 'Yes, yes. You're right.' Looking at me, he tries, and fails, to look apologetic. 'About the party favors—'

'Chase.' The warning in Thomas's voice is a shade more than annoyed. Menacing comes to mind. And though I should take umbrage over his high-handedness, I'm going to tactfully retreat. Because if I'm right, and I'm pretty sure I am, Chase is about to ask me to take a suitcase full of sex toys with me to Vegas for the recently rescheduled afternoon, low-key penis party.

No thank you.

'I better get going.' I stand, ignoring Chase's sullen look and Thomas's glare. 'I need to call everyone and tell them the change of plans.'

'Already on it.' George leans into the office, cell phone to his ear. 'Mrs Moore has been informed, calling Leslie now.'

Blocked by George, I stop just short of the doorway. Right next to Thomas.

When he turns to his eavesdropping executive administrator, his delicious, expensive scent wafts my way. 'Do you make a habit of standing by our office door?'

Goosebumps break out over my arms, but George shrugs. 'Only when it's Code Penis Party related.'

Thomas's nostrils flare and I duck out before anything else can be said.

4

THOMAS

'Give me one reason why I have to carry the bag of assorted phallic favors.'

'Because I have to hold Mike Hunt.' Chase jostles his cat as if I can't see the hairless creature wearing a blue and white striped sailor sweater with a red bow tie collar.

The elderly women in front of us in the airport security line does a double take at our conversation. *And* the cat.

Reluctantly, I roll my brother's carry-on full of sex toys forward. 'You should have checked it.'

'No way.' Chase nudges his empty pet carrier forward with his foot, needing both hands to restrain his mutated sailor companion. 'What if they lost it? Bell's bachelorette party would be messed up a second time.'

'And that's a bad thing?' We turn in the snake, heading back toward the ID check. 'Why are you so set on Bell having a bachelorette party, anyway?' He is weirdly obsessed with it, especially seeing as Bell said – multiple times – that she didn't want one.

'I'm going to ensure she has as close to her actual dream

wedding as possible.' Chase tries to guide the carrier with his foot again, but it gets caught on a divider pole. Sighing, I grab the handle and do it for him.

'Why don't you put him *in* the carrier?'

'I'd just have to take him out to go through the metal detector.' Mike tries to climb behind my brother's head. 'And I do not want to have that struggle twice.' He shivers, pulling a very disgruntled feline closer to his chest.

I'm not sure if it's the sweater or the chaos of air travel that's upsetting him, but even I can tell the cat is not happy. 'What do you mean about her dream wedding? All your Elvis-obsessed fiancée's friends and family are flying to Vegas so your sacred union can be blessed by a polyester-wearing imposter.' There's no hiding my sarcasm. 'Isn't that dream enough?'

'But that's just it – it may be Bell and my friends, but it isn't *her* family.' He ducks Mike's attempt to blind him. 'She never said it, but I know she's sad her parents won't be there.'

That makes me feel like an ass. Bell's parents died when she was in college. Having no fondness for our father and with our mother already coming, I hadn't thought about Bell's family.

'Also, Leslie would've killed me if we didn't have a party.' He snorts. 'Life is easier when she's happy.'

'I feel like you spend the majority of your time trying to make your life easier,' I mutter, once more rolling the bag of penis party paraphernalia forward.

Chase frowns at me. 'Why wouldn't I?'

'Next.' A TSA security guard motions us forward and I hand him my ID and ticket. Even with pre-check, the line at LaGuardia is long and slow. It's like booking an appointment at the DMV. You think it'll help, but it never does. I wanted to fly private, but Bell nixed the expense, especially with everyone flying at different times and some from different airports.

The woman in front of us walks to the left conveyor belt, so I move to the right, Chase following.

'Mommy, mommy!' A kid in front of me with tousled dark brown hair, jumps up and down pulling on his mother's shirt.

After she's loaded all of her and the boy's bags onto the belt she shifts her lavender headscarf back into place and sighs down at her son. 'Yes?'

I can feel the exhaustion pouring off her.

The kid points at Chase. 'Look at the sick animal!'

'He's not sick.' I glance back at my brother's pet. Well, not sick in the medical sense of the word, at least.

At my voice the young boy's head drops back, his joyous expression vanishing when his eyes reach mine.

'He's a sphynx.' Chase steps between us and crouches down until he's eye level with the kid. 'Wanna pet him?'

I'm sure if the cat could talk, as my brother seems to think him capable, he would have something to say about his owner whoring him around. Instead, he burrows his face in Chase's neck like an ostrich in the sand.

The kid's eyes flick to mine once, as if to make sure I haven't come closer, then widen at the cat. 'Can I?'

'Sure.' With effort, Chase peels Mike off of him. 'Go ahead.'

Slowly, as if petting a dangerous creature, the kid's small hand reaches out, his eyes lighting up on contact. 'Wow.'

'Come on, Mehmed.' His mother waves him forward toward the metal detector then smiles at Chase. 'Thank you.'

'No problem.' Chase remains smiling, but I catch the flinch when the cat's claws dig back into his chest. Retaliation for the petting, no doubt. 'Not too good with kids, are you?'

I hate when my brother asks questions he already knows the answer to.

Instead of replying, I heft the surprisingly heavy suitcase onto the conveyor belt.

'I'll go first.' Chase tilts his head at the metal detector. 'They always stop me because of Mike.'

And sure enough, after walking through without the beep, Chase is waved to the side by a TSA agent. 'Sir, if you'll step this way.'

He flashes her a smile. 'Sure thing.'

The bag of bones in his hands hisses.

The agent's long braids swish over her shoulder as her head swivels to check out my brother's rear end as he walks past her to the pat-down section. Not looking at me, she waves me forward. 'Next.'

After walking through, I reach to grab our bags, but only the pet carrier is waiting for me. No suitcase. Frowning, I look back down the belt.

'Sir?' the security officer manning the X-ray machine asks.

'My bag isn't here.'

'Ah, yes.' His nostrils flare like he's trying to hold back laughter and points to a separate table where the bag in question is laid out. Directly behind where Chase is busy being frisked, the nautical-themed cat held up over his head with his feline private business on full display.

A different security officer approaches me. 'If you'll come this way?' He waves me forward toward the hairless cat circus and the penis party favors.

'No.'

'No?' The officer's hands drop, his frown indicating that he's probably never been told no before.

I stare hard into his eyes, wondering what he'll do if I continue to refuse to cooperate. If I simply state that the bag in question is not mine.

He shifts on his feet but doesn't back down. 'Sir?'

I'm about to throw my brother under the bus and inform the officer that the bag in question is his when I glance over and see a very dedicated TSA agent pat my brother's backside with the back of her hands. She doesn't look like she'll be done with the search anytime soon.

And we have a plane to catch and penis favors to bring to my parentless sister-in-law's bachelorette party.

God damn it.

I straighten, preparing myself for public evisceration. 'Lead the way.'

My lone consolation is that I spared an employee this embarrassment. Alice may have transformed from polite to disgruntled when I overheard her voice from my adjoining office and interrupted my brother trying to plan penis-related things on company time, but she was smart enough to get out of there before Chase foisted this unsavory wedding task on her.

Although, *she* probably would've been smart enough to check the bag.

Nodding, the TSA agent walks me over to a different agent – one who is now elbow deep in dildos. 'Sir, is this your bag?'

Several people exiting security, including the elderly woman from before, stop and stare. I remind myself that I love my brother.

'Yes.' I say between clenched teeth. 'This is my bag.'

Flushed and slightly out of breath, Chase comes up beside me, his cat under his arm like a football. 'What's the problem?'

As if the tableau before him is not answer enough to his question.

The agent's face turns red. 'Um, something in here is vibrating.'

'They vibrate?' My brother looks at me. 'Cool. I thought they were just standard dildos.'

I pinch the bridge of my nose and imagine myself somewhere else. Anywhere else.

The TSA agent riffles deeper. 'Here!' Triumphant, he lifts the buzzing vibrator in the air like an Olympic torch. It's easily two feet long. Something like confetti erupts from the bag along with the dildo.

Instinctively, I step back.

'Oh no.' Chase, cemented to the floor, gapes in horror. 'The catnip.'

There's a flash of flesh and red, white and blue, like a flasher wrapped in an American flag. The dildo-wielding TSA agent screams, backpedaling away from the patriotically dressed speed racer cat until the line divider behind trips him and he falls, throwing the still-powered vibrator into the air.

The feline pounces, using the open suitcase as a springboard.

Dildos roll everywhere. One stops at the feet of the elderly woman from earlier.

If I wasn't so horrified, I might have been impressed when my brother's cat snags the tossed dick mid-air, landing with his treasure on the chest of the fallen TSA agent. All sprinkled with catnip.

Mehmed, having escaped his mother, picks up a neon green phallus. 'Is this a light saber?'

Chase chokes on a laugh, while Mehmed's mother smacks the saber out of her son's hand. Who then begins to cry.

Somehow, I remain calm in the eye of the dildo hurricane raging around me.

Mike begins a public tryst with his airborne captured silicone boyfriend – *on top* of the downed TSA agent.

My brother looks torn between grabbing his cat or collecting the scattered rainbow collection of sex toys.

When Mike hisses mid-thrust as the downed TSA agent tries to sit up, Chase chooses the action least likely to end with hand dismemberment, and sinks slowly to his knees to help the pat-down agent gather the roll-away dildos.

Most other agents continue to gape along with the rest of the international airport's passengers who are stalled in line behind us.

Turning my back on the whole charade, I hand Mehmed's mother a hundred dollar bill, with a nod of apology. At first too stunned to register the gift, she finally takes it, grabs her son, and hustles the hell out of security.

A new TSA agent, one that looks far more superior in rank, approaches me. 'Sir, I'm going to need you to come with me.'

I glance at Chase and his sphynx, each still dick-wrangling in their own way. 'Just me?'

The agent's eyes flick toward my travel companions then back. 'Better bring your whole party.'

* * *

Alice

'Promise me you'll send me pictures of the princess.'

I smile into my phone as I hurry past the check-in desks to airport security. 'I promise.'

My six-year-old pseudo niece started confusing brides and princesses years ago when we saw a bridal photo shoot in Central Park and I told her that brides were like princesses for a day. Even as she got older, she's still obsessed with royalty.

'Do you think she'll wear a tiara?'

'Maybe.' I love her. So much. I want to talk to her every day. Live with her like I did when she was first born. But I can't set that plan in motion, or even figure out why Mary isn't in school right now, when her mother, Kayla, is avoiding me. 'Can I talk to your mom?'

Mary sighs, clearly unhappy moving away from the subjects of princess brides. 'She's sleeping.'

'Sleeping?' I double check the time on my phone. Ten in the morning.

'Yeah...' Mary's voice, lower now than when talking about tiaras, jabs my chest.

Something isn't right.

I knew it when, this past Christmas, Kayla wanted to spend the holiday at my place. I hadn't asked why we were celebrating in my small studio apartment rather than the larger apartment she shared with her now ex-boyfriend, or even about how the job search was going since she'd been let go from her last place of employment after Thanksgiving.

I hadn't wanted to ruin Christmas by bringing up unpleasant things.

But now I'm angry at myself for missing my chance.

'You know not to leave the apartment, right?' I force enthusiasm into my voice as I hustle around a man with five suitcases stacked on a luggage cart. 'Be a good girl while you wait for Mommy to wake up.'

'I *know*.' Her exasperation makes me smile. 'I'm watching *Cinderella*.'

I bite back a laugh. Even when trying to act older than her six years, her all-time favorite movie is still Disney's *Cinderella*.

She's stayed loyal to the classic though it lacks the vibrancy of the current animation styles or the abundance of catchy tunes new releases have.

'Good.' I look wistfully at the shorter pre-check line as I pass it on the way to general security. 'When I get back, I'll come straight over and you can show me your new buildings.' And then I'll figure out what's going on with Kayla.

Mary cheers. She and I both love Lego. They're expensive, but Mary doesn't mind building then rebuilding the same set over and over again.

I double down on my promise for a building play date and hang up before showing my ticket to security.

'Wrong line, ma'am.' The woman in navy with the TSA badge points to the entrance of a line further down. 'You go there.'

I frown at my ticket and then where she'd pointed to. 'I can?' It's a much shorter snake to the metal detectors.

'Yes, that's the first-class line.'

'Oh.' I hadn't really looked at my ticket except to make sure my name was correct and check the gate number. But I should've known that Chase and Bell would've upgraded their wedding party. A thrill shoots through me.

I've been so worried about Mary and Kayla and all the bridesmaid's tasks that I haven't allowed myself to get too excited. But knowing that my first ever plane ride is going to be in first class sets me over the edge.

'Alice!' George, his loafers slapping fast over the polished floor, waves at me with one hand while rolling a monogrammed designer bag behind him in the other. 'Thank God I'm not late.' He throws the security guard a smile and waves me forward toward the first-class line.

I guess he already knew we'd been upgraded. Actually,

knowing George, he was probably the one who suggested/demanded/booked it.

'I had trouble deciding what encapsulated wardrobe to bring.' He glances at my duffle bag slung around my chest. 'Did you check luggage?' His expression making it clear that if I hadn't, I am woefully under-packed.

'Um, no.' A second ago I was quite pleased with my strategic weekend packing. This being my first vacation I'd googled biggest vacation pitfalls, and nearly every article said packing too much or too little.

I packed my toiletries, a swimsuit and a nicer than T-shirt top as well as an old, oversized Moore holiday shirt that PR handed out a few years ago for the plane ride back. I'm wearing a comfortable pair of sneakers along with a T-shirt and sweatshirt as I heard airplanes can be cold. The jeans I have on are my nice jeans that I plan on wearing to the bachelorette party tonight.

But now, under George's judgmental scrutiny, I feel like the carefully selected clothes, all wrapped around my flip-flops and flats, are woefully inadequate.

George distracts me from worrying with his ideas for entertainment while in Vegas until we reach the conveyor belt.

'Give me a hand, will you?' He tugs his trousers up at the knee before squatting down by his carry-on.

'Sure.' I reach for the handle to lift while he embraces the bag around the middle. 'Ooof.'

Though the proper size for a carry-on, I nearly collapse under its weight, even with George deadlifting it onto the conveyor belt.

I can lift my duffle with one hand.

We pass a group of TSA agents on our way to the gate, one gesturing wildly, the others nearly collapsing with laughter.

'I've never seen TSA agents so lively.' George slows his roll to give the laughing officers one last look before regaining our speed-walking pace toward our gate. 'I bet something good happened. Like those funny stories I read online about people smuggling stuff on the plane by stuffing it in their—'

I stop so abruptly at the sight of Thomas Moore standing stoically in front of the gangway that George's suitcase runs into the back of my heels.

'Oh, sorry!' George pulls his luggage back. 'But why did you—'

I don't even register the sting. 'What is *he* doing here?'

George, brow glistening from the effort of pulling his luggage, follows my outstretched arm to where I'm pointing. 'Huh. I have no idea why the bossmen are here.' Ignorant of my apprehension, he wields his way to the brothers through the crowd to the first-class pre-boarding lane. 'I thought you were both taking the early morning flight.'

'We were,' Thomas answers, not bothering to look behind him at George.

Chase bites his lip as if trying not to laugh. 'There was an incident.'

'An incident?' George perks up. 'What kind of incident?'

'The kind that you can't mention in your gossip blog until after the wedding.' Chase shakes his finger at his executive assistant.

George purses his lips, studying Chase's hand. 'Does this incident have anything to do with your arm?'

I'd been so careful to not look at Thomas that I failed to see the many red and painful-looking scratches up and down Chase's arms. 'Oh my God. What happened?'

Thomas turns around and my jaw drops. His tie is askew,

his top button unbuttoned, and his hair looks like many a person drove their fingers through it.

I have never seen the perpetually pristine man so unkempt.

Thomas's death stare lands on Chase. 'Mike Hunt happened.'

5

ALICE

I'm going to die.

Whether from the general awkwardness of having to sit next to Thomas Moore or from a plane crash, I'm not sure. But I'm certain this is the end.

The plane sways and I grab the armrest. 'Is it going to be this way the whole time?'

'Doubtful.'

My teeth grind together, this time having nothing to do with the way the aircraft is turning mid-air like a stunt plane. 'Thanks for the reassurance.' I flick my gaze from the window to him, then back. 'So *kind* of you.'

Sarcasm is not my usual. Silence and removing myself from the problem (aka retreat) are my normal tactics. But when I'm climbing to thirty thousand feet while the plane dips and swerves, I get snarky. Who knew?

The plane levels out and remains steady for the next ten minutes. I know it's ten minutes because I've counted each and every six hundred seconds of it. With my eyes closed. I'm no longer excited or interested in seeing the world from a bird's perspective out of my window. I no longer care about my roomy leather cushioned seat, my footrest bar or the complimentary blanket and slipper pouch the friendly steward handed me upon sitting down.

Instead, my focus is centered on the man who'd sniffed disdainfully when he reached his seat number then muttered something about commercial flights before hefting his roller bag into the overhead compartment and settling himself in his seat. The seat next to me.

If I hadn't been so nervous stepping onto the plane from the little tunnel connecting it to the airport with Thomas Moore at my back, I might have had the forethought to come up with an excuse to change seats with someone. Like Chase, who's sitting in coach. Apparently when the Moore brothers had to change their flight, there was only one first class seat available. A seat that Thomas, the best man, booked for himself, forcing his brother, the groom, to fly economy.

My stomach lurches once more, even as the plane remains stable.

Oh dear God, no.

My eyes pop open as heat creeps up my neck, sweat dotting my upper lip.

'I, uh…' I chance a glance at Thomas who looks as if he's relaxing at a private members only club. 'I think I need to use the bathroom.'

He doesn't speak, just turns his square jaw in my direction, one eyebrow raised.

I *hate* that eyebrow.

My stomach yaws like a boat in a storm and I shift in my seat, poised to hurdle over his large frame if needed. 'I don't feel so well.'

Looking at me like one would a wild animal, Thomas taps the seat in front of him. 'George.'

When there's no response from his executive assistant seated in front of him, Thomas reaches around the aisle seat and shakes George's shoulder.

'Huh, what?' George's head bobs into sight over his seat back. 'Are we there?'

'No.' Thomas's hand remains outstretched in the aisle. 'Dramamine.'

'You sick?' George sits further up in his seat. 'You never get sick.'

The woman to George's right jerks forward as if I'm about to projectile vomit.

Which, with the next swallow of excess saliva flooding my mouth, I might be.

'Not me.' Thomas's eyes return to mine. 'Alice.'

'Oh, shoot, really?' There's rustling and then George appears, on his knees facing us over his seat. His eyes are barely open. 'Here.'

When he holds out his hand, I automatically reach out with mine.

He drops two orange tablets, each about the size of a nickel in my palm. 'Feel better, Alice.' With a yawn, he drops back into his seat, presumably to fall back asleep.

Thomas thrusts a water bottle at me. 'Take it.'

I inhale deeply in through my nose, out through my mouth. 'I'm sure I'll be—'

'I'd rather not arrive in Las Vegas splattered with vomit.' He taps the bottle against my arm. 'Take the anti-nausea medication.'

Rather than his condescending expression, it's the plane pitching that has me tossing the pills in my mouth and chomping the orange-flavored chalk as if my life depended on it. Though the turbulence is infinitesimal, my stomach seems to think we're making loop-the-loops.

He shakes the water bottle in front of me and my annoyance only increases when the cold water notably washes away the fake orange flavor and cools my flushed body. I'm about to thank Thomas for helping me when he rests his index finger alongside his nose.

'In through your nose, out through your mouth.'

My eyes focus on his perfectly manicured finger resting on his perfectly straight Greek nose. 'Huh?'

He lowers his finger to the corner of his now slightly pursed lips. 'You have...' He taps.

The heat I feel in my cheeks has nothing to do with airplane sickness as I raise my hand to my mouth.

Just as my fingers wipe away the moisture leftover from the water bottle, I catch the slight pinch to his expression before he bends down to retrieve his valise from under the seat in front of him.

Any feelings of gratitude I'd previously felt vanish.

Excuse me for not having a handkerchief to dab at my lips like a lady.

Removing his laptop, he slides the bag back into place before raising the seat tray from the armrest between us. 'Close your eyes and breathe in through your nose and out through your mouth.' He doesn't even spare me a glance as he places his laptop down and opens it.

'Closing my eyes is what made me feel bad to begin with.' If my niece used a tone like I just did, I would've given her a stern talking-to.

Thomas says nothing, just powers on his computer, effectively dismissing me.

Jerk.

The plane veers again, yet my stomach remains calm.

I make a mental note to thank *George* for the Dramamine when we land.

Ignoring Thomas and his advice, I settle back in my over-sized leather chair and grab my phone. Bell gave me specific instructions not to bring my laptop this weekend, wanting me to have fun and not work.

I'm not off to a good start on the fun part.

Aiming to fix that, I open my reader application and tap on the new romance series I'd been saving to binge read on this trip. Vampires, shifters and demons – oh my.

In my peripheral, Thomas clacks away on his keyboard. Either Bell didn't bother instructing the high and mighty Thomas Moore to relax, or he's ignoring her wishes.

Typical.

Angling my shoulders so Thomas can't see my phone screen, should he even deign to look my way again, I begin my long-awaited binge.

I make it almost 20 percent through the first book before my body begins to weigh heavily against the leather and the words on the screen drift in and out of focus. It's not the book's fault. The tension is building between the two characters and I'm certain in just a page flip or two there's going to be a thigh-squeezing, page-turning scene. A scene that I probably shouldn't read next to my boss.

My eyes flick to my left, landing on his computer screen.

'Is that my proposal?' I shift closer, looking at the digital copy of the design board I'd given him.

His fingers pause, poised above the keyboard. 'Yes.'

Forgetting to keep my normal distance, I lean in. 'What are you doing?'

'Making notes.'

'Oh.' I blink a few times, trying to shake off the looming exhaustion and focus.

He makes a few more notes in the margins.

I lean even closer, pausing when his fingers stop typing mid-sentence. 'Ah.' I sit back once more. 'I just thought—' I fiddle with my phone, it nearly sliding out of my grasp '—I mean, I'm here, so we could, uh, discuss the display now.' Taking a breath, I force myself to meet his dark eyes. 'If you want.'

'Hmmm.' He holds my gaze for an uncomfortable beat before pointing to his screen. 'Before I give you my notes, explain your concept to me.'

'Okay.' I draw out the word, shocked that I initiated conversation with him and then shocked even more that he's engaging. 'Well... I want to make use of the length of windows on either side of the main entrance and create a timeline of sorts.' Two nine-hundred square foot windows flank the brass and glass turnstile entrance to Moore's.

When I pause, he looks at me as if to say, *And then?*

A fresh spike of irritation helps me continue, this time with more confidence. I explain the concept of a journey through spring. A rebirth after the home-bound winter months. Bright blues and greens with varying pops of colors like flowers sprinkled throughout Central Park. How I'd highlight the athletic department on both ends moving through career-wear, weekends out, vacation mode.

He nods when I finish, staring at the screen again.

My shoulders tighten. 'I know I don't have a lot of experience and this is my first solo design, but I paid very close attention when Bell called in that professional visual design team for the big Holiday display this past December, and I've been studying on my own after work and I really think that the story I'm telling through the various tableaus leading up to the entrance will make people take notice.' I'm dizzy after spewing that out in one breath.

No reaction, he just continues to stare at the screen. I take deep breaths and try to control my desire to fidget, remembering what Bell once told me about maintaining an air of confidence, even if it's fake.

'The storytelling is good.' He leans back in his seat, his thumb and pointer finger cradling his chin in thought. 'But the design is missing something.'

I'm too shocked by the compliment to be irked by the criticism. 'It is?'

He drops his hand. 'Height.'

'Height?'

'Yes. You're used to working and creating on the sales floor. You can't build too high there because you'll block the customer's line of sight to the surrounding merchandise. However—' his eyes lock on mine '—the front windows are enclosed. There's a solid backdrop. So while you'll want the majority of the merchandise at eye level, you still need to fill in the encompassing space.'

I stare at the screen, mentally arranging my design like chess pieces on a board.

His forefinger glides over the mouse pad. 'Here.' He minimizes my design board bringing up a rectangular blueprint of the window display case measurements. 'If you take into account the mannequins, signage, furniture and accessories you have listed, you're only using a little over half of the available height.'

My design slides into place, and it hits me. 'There's too much dead space.'

He flashes a small smile before flattening it out. 'Correct.'

I wait for the feelings of embarrassment or shame that I thought would come after having my boss, the man who thinks of me as a former shoe girl, point out my first big solo design's failure. But it doesn't come. He doesn't feel like some overlord throwing out criticism and demanding results. His smile wasn't one of condescension, but of approval.

Right now, Thomas Moore feels like a colleague, a collaborator.

I wonder if this is a turning point in our professional relationship or a side effect of the Dramamine.

Surprisingly, I hope it's the former. I've always fed off collaboration, my creativity often triggered by topical conversations. I find the act of saying the things I've been thinking aloud helps me solidify ideas.

I just never thought Thomas Moore would be the one listening.

'I, uh, had an idea for that, but was concerned it would be too expensive.'

'Speaking of, I didn't see a budget listed.'

'Is it okay if I...' I point at his computer.

He leans back to give me space. 'Please.'

Reaching over, I rest my phone on the tray and toggle over to the email Bell had forwarded him with my design board. I click open the last attachment that itemizes the display by cost.

He angles his chin up, as if trying to move further back, before reaching into his jacket pocket. His arm brushes against my hand resting on the armrest between us as he pulls out a pair of reading glasses. When he slides them in place, peering at the screen, it's hard to breathe. 'Is that right?'

'Hmm?'

When his eyes, now larger behind his reading glasses fix on

mine, I break out of my trance, focusing on the total calculation he's tapping on the screen.

'Uh, yes.' I roll my shoulders back, surreptitiously wiping the back of my hand across my mouth in search of drool.

I've always said that you learn something new every day. Case in point – reading glasses are sexy.

'That's only a third of the budget.'

'Well, no—' I focus on my hands, telling myself to stop acting like an idiot '—but I thought if I was prudent at the start of the year, it would leave for a larger budget later.' I have an idea for next Christmas that involved a snow machine that will cost quite a bit to run twenty-four/seven.

'The budget is proportionate to the expected revenue at any given season and holiday.'

I jerk my gaze to his. 'It is?' No one told me that.

'Yes.'

The idea I had at the start of spring design planning re-forms in my mind. Not only would it complement the design Thomas seems to like but it would fill in the dead space he's concerned with. However... it requires quite a bit of money.

His lenses reflect a glare from the window behind me, obstructing my view of his eyes. I angle my head to the side, blocking the window. 'Are you sure?'

There's an infinitesimal tilt to his glasses as he raises his eyebrow. 'Seeing as I made the budget, yes, I am sure.'

Heat crawls up my neck. 'Of course.' I'd almost forgotten who he is. And if I was anywhere else, this would be the point where I'd make up an excuse to leave.

But as that's impossible on an airplane, I settle for straight-ening in my seat, letting the sunlight reflect off his glasses once more.

No longer able to see his intense stare, I expel a long breath, fighting back a yawn that comes out of nowhere. 'I *did* have an idea that could solve the space issue.'

He answers by raising his eyebrow again.

Trying to keep my back straight, I reach out and grab my phone off his table, opening up my saved pictures and finding the ones I need. 'I'm not sure if we have the personnel required for labor and installation.'

He leans forward, staring at me over the rim of his glasses. 'Show me.'

* * *

Thomas

'... as we begin our descent into the Las Vegas...'

Alice, fast asleep beside me, stirs as the pilot continues his overhead announcement.

Five minutes into her pitch for the 'expensive' additional design element, Alice's eyelids began a slow downward trajectory.

She surprised me by lasting as long as she did. I've flown with George on numerous occasions for work, so I'm well aware of how quickly and efficiently Dramamine cuts motion sickness but puts you to sleep. It's why I thought closing her eyes and focusing on her breathing would help ease her into the medication's side effects.

Yet, before I could explain that my eyes had homed in on the drop of water clinging to the corner of her mouth and I had to make use of my seat's tray table to obscure my inappropriate reaction.

Thankfully, George is still asleep and Chase, in a rare apologetic action for the TSA dildo debacle, insisted on giving me the lone, first class seat, so neither can witness my latest distress.

Alice shifts in her sleep, her dark hair tumbling from her shoulder to mine. It smells of vanilla, with a faint hint of cinnamon. Vanilla is a fragrance I'd always considered common and unimaginative. Inhaling more deeply, I wonder why, when on Alice, the aroma makes me salivate for cookies.

I don't even like cookies.

Earlier, after one too many slow blinks, I told Alice to send me the information she had and that we'd discuss her idea later, thinking she'd fall right asleep. Instead, she'd frowned at me before retreating to her phone, where, from the text I can see on her still lit screen, she'd been reading.

I double take at the phone in her hands. Surely, I didn't read...

Alice slides farther down in her seat, her cheek resting on my shoulder, her phone threatening to fall to the floor.

Carefully, I lift the phone from her loosened grasp before it can fall. My good deed does not go unpunished when, without her phone, Alice snuggles deeper into me, both arms hugging the one of mine.

I'm not unaware of the warmth of her body against mine, my problem under the tray table is proof of that, but I'd be more aware of it if I wasn't so preoccupied with what I read on her phone.

His cock swelled, throbbing. With a roar, he found his release, his eyes rolling back in his head as each spasm racked his body. As the mindless passion began to fade, he was left with a sense of intimacy he'd never known before this woman. His mate.

This is what Alice reads? Sweet, polite Alice who wants to dot eighteen hundred square feet of space with a hundred butterfly neon lights to, as she put it, 'create a juxtaposition between the season of nature's rebirth and New York's urban lifestyle'.

Reaching up, I open the cool air vent wider, suddenly hot. The current blows the wisps of dark hair that have fallen out of her high ponytail across her pale skin. I'd always considered her looks to be youthful and innocent, but the words on her phone have my mind thinking anything but innocent thoughts as I stare at her parted full lips.

A passenger bumps my shoulder on their way to the restroom, causing one of Alice's hands to slide downward, stopping just as the tips of her fingers reach my thigh.

I clench my teeth, willing myself to ignore the few inches between her and my growing situation. A situation I'd previously thought under control after Alice fell asleep but that is going to start knocking on the underside of the tray table soon.

I'm about to try sliding her back across her seat with my free hand when the pilot comes back on to tell us the local weather. Alice's hand advances further under the tray table, stopping only when it encounters my current moral handicap.

My knee jerks and Alice lifts her head, peering at me with half-closed eyes. 'What...?'

My body freezes and my mind blanks. I seem incapable of doing anything but wait for her to move her hand that still rests on my fully fledged flagpole.

She doesn't. Rather, her eyes start to close once more.

Clearing my throat, I get her eyes to focus on me, but I can tell her brain isn't quite functioning.

'Your hand.'

The space above her nose pinches. 'My hand?'

I count five seconds before her gaze finally drops. First to the hand still upon my arm, then to the hand unseen beneath the tray table.

Eyes wide, she yanks her hand up, bashing it against the tray table, which then sends my laptop toppling over the edge and into the aisle. 'Jeezishhh!' She clasps her hand to her chest, her wide eyes watering.

I don't trust myself to say anything, nor do I want to invite conversation that might involve questions about why things hadn't been placid beneath the tray table. Exhaling, I retrieve my laptop from the floor.

A smiling flight attendant appears again. 'Everything okay?'

'Fine.' Alice voice is high-pitched, her cheeks bright red.

The stewardess taps the table. 'You'll need to store this for landing.'

'Ice.' I raise the lid on my computer.

The smile fades from the stewardess' face. 'Excuse me?'

'Can you—' I meet her eyes for a moment before checking my computer for damage '—procure an ice pack?'

'Yes, of course.' As the stewardess takes off on her task, my laptop screen lights up, the documents I'd been reading before its fall appearing as normal.

'Is your computer okay?' In the ensuing moments after impact, Alice's back has remained pressed against the side of the plane, as if trying to create as much distance between us as possible.

'Yes.' It's more grunt than word, but she nods, so I'm assuming she understood.

'Good. That's good.' She's still nodding.

'One ice pack.' The stewardess leaves the hastily wrapped linen napkin of ice next to my computer before moving past to tell a lazy passenger to bring his seatback to its upright position.

I hand the ice to Alice. 'Your hand.'

Alice's fingers brush against mine as she takes it. 'Thank you.' She lays the ice pack on top of her hand.

'Hmmm.' Lifting the tray table, I'm careful to place my laptop on my lap – to be used as both armor and camouflage – before dropping the tray into its slot in the armrest between us.

The jolt to my knee and the interaction with the stewardess may have helped settle my situation, but I'm not taking anymore chances.

The remainder of the flight is spent in silence. Awkward even by my standards.

6

ALICE

I never imagined a bag of dicks would be this heavy.

Or that I'd be carrying one inside of Thomas Moore's hotel suite.

After the plane ride I double timed in my sneakers off the plane and through the carousels of luggage, beelining for the man holding the Moore sign. No one questioned me. Probably because George had still been under the influence of Dramamine while lugging a fifty-pound-plus carry-on and Chase had been stuck waiting for coach class to deplane.

I had I-accidentally-touched-my-boss's-*thing* adrenaline shooting through my veins to shock me awake.

Thomas said nothing as I whipped past him on the gangway with my small duffle bag in hand. Nor did he say anything when I sat in the front seat with the driver, rather than in the back of the limo with him and the rest of the group.

He was no doubt relieved that I'd taken the initiative to create as much distance between us as possible.

The downfall to my plan became evident at hotel check-in where Chase informed me that he'd called Leslie, who had already arrived in Vegas with Bell, on the ride over from the airport while I was out of earshot on the other side of the limo's privacy panel.

Code Penis plans were solidified without my input. Plans that included me setting up the bachelorette party in Thomas Moore's suite whilst they kept Bell busy with spa appointments. Something about it being the last place Bell would suspect and keeping Mike Hunt away from the party favors.

And so here I am, standing in front of my boss's door. Asking him not to be here.

Taking a deep breath, I knock on the suite's door.

Nothing.

I knock again.

When no one answers for the second time, I pull out the card key Chase had given me, along with the roller bag of dicks, and beep myself into the room. 'Hello?' I pause in the open doorway, listening. Nothing.

Pushing the roller bag in front of me like a shield, I peek around the corner of the small foyer into the suite's living room. One, it's huge. Two, no Thomas.

Breathing a sigh of relief, I look around for one of those luggage stands. Not finding one, I realize it's probably in the bedroom. And since no amount of money or Code Penis alerts could make me willingly go into Thomas's bedroom, I swing it up onto one of the barstool seats.

I learn two things. (It's a banner day for self-education.)

One, I prove I'm lying to myself when I say being on my feet all day while rearranging mannequins, merchandise and lights is equivalent to actual exercise.

Two, unlatching a suitcase full of dicks with shaky muscles while it rests precariously on a barstool seat is not a good idea.

I stare in horror as the heavy case tumbles off the seat,

throwing brightly colored silicone penises about like confetti at a pride parade.

If Thomas could see his room now.

Thankfully, he's probably living his best life somewhere that only high-rollers can enter while I sprawl on the floor amongst silicone-coated wands of pleasure. My hand twitches as I remember the wool gabardine covered wand of pleasure I'd encountered earlier on the plane.

Don't think about that.

I've been trying, without success, to banish the memory of groping my boss. But it's kind of hard to do that when you're corralling room-temperature dildos and your hand keeps comparing them to the very warm and very real thing it held a few hours ago.

Something vibrates and I drop all the dildos I've collected, worried I might've turned one on. When the vibration continues, I realize it's coming from my phone.

It's either a bride update from Leslie, who's standing guard at the spa, or Kayla.

Unearthing my phone from my pocket, my hopes inflate when I see it's the latter, but sink as soon as I read the message.

Im good tlk latr

I get that it's a text, so grammar isn't particularly necessary, nor spelling, but Kayla's text doesn't put me at ease. Still, I send a thumbs-up emoji.

Clicking the phone closed, I catch a glimpse of my reflection in the dark screen before I slide it back into my pocket.

I took the time to curl my poker-straight hair before getting dressed for the party this afternoon. So while my bangs still haven't reached the length of the rest of my hair, the shorter strands blend in when curled. Between the time I took on my hair and my dressy-casual top I bought on clearance, I don't think I look all that bad.

A glint coming from the bags of penis-shaped glitter fanned out by the mini fridge catches my eye. I let out a little prayer of thanks that they didn't burst open.

On my knees, I shuffle forward collecting multicolored and sized dildos as I go, trying to distract myself by imagining how I'll hang the neon lights in the Moore's window display when I get back.

After hotel check-in, I checked my work email on my phone and found an approval letter for the lighting addition I'd pitched Thomas on the flight. He must have approved it while I was sleeping, *before* I groped him. Either that or after out of some sense of guilt or embarrassment – *if* the man can feel any of those things. I guess I'll never know, because I'm sure as hell not asking.

That way lies madness.

Soon, I've amassed a mound of sex toys and glitter bags any porn star would be proud of. Right before getting up, I catch sight of a dildo that's rolled all the way under a nearby console table in the reflection of the floor-length mirror across from me. I have to flatten myself on my belly, stretching my arm out until my fingertips nudge silicone and I manage to wrap my hand around the exaggerated girth of made-for-her pleasure.

At least, I hope it's exaggerated.

Laboring to my feet, I study the dildo with the words 'Trusty Thrusty' scrawled at the base. My fingers barely wrap around it.

How could *this* be enjoyable?

People say bigger is better, but the thought of thrusting Trusty Thrusty inside me doesn't make me horny. It makes me queasy.

Thomas's size would be much more enjoyable.

Don't think about that!

Pushing my whorish inner voice aside, I wrap both hands around the dildo. Curious, I lean down, mouth open, my jaw stretching uncomfortably wide. Even so, my teeth still graze the sides.

'Ugh.' My lips smack with distaste from the silicone flavor.

Out of the corner of my eye, something moves toward me.

'Ahhhh!' I whip the Thrusty around like a bat and whack whatever's there. Hard.

'Fuck!'

All I catch is a blur of white before I take off toward the front door. Growing up in foster care and living in New York City, my survival instinct is deeply ingrained – act first, question later.

Even so, I don't even make it two steps before my shoes, the soles a tad too worn, slide across the marble, one foot finding yet another rogue dildo, and I slip, falling back into whomever, it was I just dick-whacked.

'Ooomph.' Firm, hard arms wrap around me in the seconds before the person and I land on the floor with a hard thud.

Seconds pass, maybe a minute. I'm not sure.

The air has been knocked out of my lungs and oxygen deprivation may be skewing my sense of time. All I know is that the tiny shimmering crystals on the chandelier above me twinkle in and out of focus while my lungs fight their way back to working order.

The person's arms are still wrapped around my midsection, but loosely. Unfortunately, now that the adrenaline is wearing off, I'm too scared to move. I can only shift my eyes to the left, toward the floor-length mirror on the closet door. And when I do, my mouth drops open.

The oxygen I've been fighting to inhale, vanishes once more.

There, flat on his back, his brow pinched (but still looking every inch as though he belongs in the fabulously expensive suite), is the man who occupies an infuriating amount of my thoughts – Thomas Moore.

And though one of his eyes is fast swelling shut from Thrusty making contact with his orbital bone, the other is clearly fixed on me – eye-shouting, *What the actual fuck?*

* * *

Thomas

What the actual fuck?

I'd just finished rinsing off travel grime in the bathroom's steam shower when I heard a bang from the living room. It had taken a moment to dry off and grab the hotel's monogramed bathrobe before padding through the bedroom and down the hall to see what made the loud noise.

It took even longer to process what I found once I turned the corner.

'Oh-my-God-oh-my-God.' Alice rolls off me, her hipbone digging into my stomach, forcing a grunt from my lips.

I want to say something to calm her down, but honestly, now that I know she isn't injured from the fall, it's all I can do just to lay here and regroup while I internalize the pain from my face having exploded on impact from the hefty, nearly TSA confiscated, penile contraband.

Don't think about that.

Because even though I should very much welcome a distraction from the intense throbbing around my left eye, the image of Alice trying to wrap her plump, pretty lips around the tip of said monstrous phallus will start a different sort of throbbing. One below my robe's belt.

'Stay there,' Alice instructs me, though I don't know where she expects me to go. Her shoes clack rapidly across the floor.

What is she even doing here?

Trying to clear the tears from my one working eye, I blink, thinking back to mere seconds ago when I was pain-free and envisioning an evening with my brother. One last night to bridge the gap that our decades-long rift had caused, before he moves on into married life.

But when I'd walked into the suite's living area after hastily tying my robe, it wasn't my devil-may-care brother crashing my room early – it was Alice Truman.

Alice Truman, whose earlier accidental touch inspired a thousand fantasies that I exorcised moments ago in the shower, had been double-fisting a cock of gigantic proportions and opening her mouth wide as she attempted to take it in.

My memory is hazy after that. I think I moved closer. Whether to stop her, talk to her or just get a better look, I'm not sure. All I *do* know is that I ended up assaulted by a hefty dildo and am now lying down on the cold, hard marble floor of a Bellagio suite with the wind knocked out of me.

If I believed in karma, this would be it.

The footsteps return. 'Here.'

My face erupts in pain again, and then cold bliss.

Alice had grabbed a can of sparkling water from the fridge. One she's fumbled, as if in the last second she became afraid of actually touching me, and dropped it the last few inches on my injured face.

'I'm so sorry,' Alice says, flitting from spot to spot picking things up off the ground and throwing them into the open suitcase on the floor.

My vision isn't the best at the moment, even my good eye is still blurry, but I saw enough earlier to know she's collecting sex toys.

The realization sinks in and nothing can stop the only real phallus in the room from reacting. I adjust my robe with the hand not holding the soda can to my face, making sure I haven't offered up one more penis to the party.

Angry at myself for reacting, *yet again*, my voice comes out harsher than intended. 'What are you doing here?'

She pauses mid dildo reach. 'I-I was decorating.'

I have no idea what she's talking about. Maybe I have a concussion. I press the can harder into my eye socket.

At my continued silence, Alice starts tossing dicks in the suitcase again. 'Chase said you wouldn't be here.' She fists tiny bags full of sparkly things with both hands and drops them in after the toys. 'I *knew* I should've said no.' The last is said under her breath before she drops onto her knees to reach something that has rolled under the bar's overhang.

'Wait.' I take a breath, trying to regroup. 'Why are you decorating in *my* suite?'

'Because this is where the bachelorette party is going to...' Alice pauses, dildo in hand. This one a more average size than the one she swung at me, but electric purple in color.

My uninjured eye stays focused on the cock that Alice's thumbs are sliding up and down, like an absent-minded mating dance.

The throbbing *not* in my eye worsens.

'You *did* agree to host Campbell's bachelorette party here, right?' Her voice breaks at the end, helping me focus on something other than the purple dick in the room. 'Chase said that since Mike has a problem, with, uh...' She waggles the dildo in her hand.

'Chase?' I struggle to a seated position, one hand holding the can to my eye, the other keeping my robe closed. I move too quickly and the room spins while I fight the urge to vomit. 'Fuck.' I close my eyes and widen my nostrils, trying to take deep, calming breaths.

It isn't lost on me how the shoe is now on the other foot. Or nausea.

Remembering how Alice said closing her eyes made her nausea worse, I open them. Or try to. The swollen skin pinches. 'Dammit.'

'Should I call the front desk and see if there's a doctor?' She's resting on her haunches, as if poised to spring-load into motion at a word from me.

I wave away her concern. 'I'm fine.' Which is physically and emotionally untrue, but the truth is not something either she or I would find useful at the moment.

Because the truth is I've realized the reason why I've been so acutely aware of her these past few months.

It's why, though still a poor hairstyle choice, Alice's past bluntly cut bangs had made it near impossible for me to look away from her large, enchanting eyes. Why, when I should've been working in my office, I found myself circulating the sales floors, scanning for signs of her and her displays.

All these instances, which had initially confused and frustrated me, suddenly shifted together like pieces of a puzzle in the aftermath of spending far too long stroking myself to various detailed fantasies in the shower – all of which had centered around her.

The truth is, I'm attracted to Alice Truman. Sexually. And that makes me no better than my father.

* * *

'Swap the purple dildo with the green one.' I point to the putrid-colored dildo in Alice's hand.

Phallic candles, phallic drinking glasses, phallic plates and even phallic-tipped straws are arranged around the suite's living area, while serving dishes await the food and beverage's eminent arrival via room service.

'You think?' Alice clocks each dildo on the table, as if evaluating their size and color. Her demeanor a veritable one-eighty from a few minutes ago when I was sprawled out on the suite floor in my bathrobe.

When I retreated to the bedroom to dress, Alice threw herself into visual merchandiser mode, setting up for the party as if she was preparing a penis sale at the National Gallery. The work seems to have calmed her nervous energy.

I flip the hand not holding a cold canned beverage to my face, palm up, to Alice.

Passing me the lime baton, she steps back as I swap the dildos. 'Huh.' Her eyes move over the arrangement. 'You're right.'

'Indeed.' I try not to take offense at her surprise.

When she doesn't say anything more, I swivel my head around to look at her with my one good eye. Her top teeth are biting into her lower lip, her eyes focused on the purple pussy-eater in my hand.

She giggles.

It's the first time I've ever been laughed at.

Catching sight of my expression, she coughs to mask her amusement. 'Sorry.'

'Hmmm.'

She sobers and the mood shifts. 'I really am sorry.'

I turn away, somehow irritated at how often she apologizes. 'I'm fine.'

'Are you dizzy at all?'

Eyeing the row of shot glasses surrounding a double-ended dildo, I wonder just how much the bridal party plans on drinking. 'Not anymore.' It may be an afternoon party, but consuming too much alcohol before the wedding can't be good. Getting drunk at all is never a good choice. But a group of people hours before a carefully structured and planned event? I shudder at the thought of such an overwhelming loss of control.

'But even if you aren't dizzy *now*, just the fact that you *were* means you could have a concussion.' Her flats tap across the floor, coming closer. 'Are you sure you shouldn't see a doctor?'

I nearly laugh. 'Positive.' Having to explain to a medical practitioner that I was made nearly unconscious by an eighteen-inch vibrator, which was wielded by my petite female employee in my hotel suite, is something I refuse to experience.

In the silence, I chance looking at her, wondering how much of her concern is for me and how much is for her boss. Which is ridiculous. I am one and the same. There is no difference. I am her boss just as she is my employee – no matter how distracting I find her.

'Knock, knock!'

Alice and I start, heads swiveling toward the foyer where Chase holds the door open with one hand, his other cradling his sphynx.

He pulls up short when he sees the ice pack I'm holding. 'What happened to you?'

Surprised by the emotion rushing through me, I advance on Chase whose eyebrows jump to his hairline. 'Why did you send Alice to my room?'

Chase takes a step back, nearly colliding with the hotel staff arriving with trays and trollies of food and beverage. 'Dude, I came here as soon as I realized I forgot to tell you about the location change.'

When I don't pull back, Chase lifts the cat between us like a shield. 'I couldn't get here earlier because I was keeping Bell occupied until her massage appointment.'

The aluminum can crinkles under my grip as fight to retain control of myself. Especially in front of staff.

Our father had far too little control – of himself and his actions.

I refuse to follow in his footsteps.

'Sending an employee to my hotel room unannounced is inexcusable. Remember who you are and where you came from, for God's sake.' One of us needs to remember whose blood flows through our veins. I lower the can from my face before it bursts open.

A collective gasp resounds.

Well. That's never a good sign.

'Holy fuck.' Chase's jaw drops. 'What the hell happened to your face?'

Having dressed in a hurry and then kept the cold can pressed to my face since, I haven't looked at the damage inflicted by the comically sized dildo. Pivoting to face the mirror, I'm oddly calm as I take in the dark purple slash of bruising that runs from the middle of my engorged brow bone diagonally down and past the corner of my eye. Without having to squint, which I couldn't do if I tried, I make out the veining detail from Trusty Thrusty etched on my skin like pillow creases after a hard night's sleep.

Alice's complexion pales. 'I'm *so* sorry.'

'Y*ou're* sorry?' Chase gapes at her then back to me. '*Alice* did this?'

My reflection and the horde of sex toys easily visible inside my suite make my previous attempt at professionalism moot. Agitated once more, I level a look at my brother that promises future retribution.

For my eye, the airport and mostly for Alice.

7

ALICE

'You turned an extremely poor-taste penis-party paraphernalia into a Pinterest-worthy affair.' Leslie pauses for breath after that tongue twister, staring around in wonder.

A minute earlier, as planned, Leslie had escorted Bell to Thomas's suite after their massage appointments where Bell thought she was retrieving her fiancé's cufflinks before heading back to her honeymoon suite to relax. Instead, the bridal party surprised her at the door and engulfed her in a swarm of glittering penis confetti.

'It's bad enough that you ruined our original plan—'Leslie gives Bell a beleaguered look '—but now, even though we're in *Vegas*, today's party has gone from seedy sex club-esque to an Upper West side afternoon tea party with a side of dick.'

Bell chokes on her cracker while George snickers behind his champagne glass.

At the sound of his mistress coughing, Mike Hunt, wearing a pink bow-tie collar, leaps onto the counter to check on her. And by check on her, I mean motorboat her.

Unperturbed, Bell scratches behind his saggy, wrinkled head as he rubs his face across her boobs.

'I think it's enchanting, Alice.' Mrs. Moore, who arrived the day prior from the Bahamas to relax before her son's nuptials, smiles fondly at her flesh-colored penis straw. 'You found the perfect balance between tawdry and fun.'

I flush at the elegant woman's compliment.

Leslie spares Mikey an eye roll before returning to the matter at hand. 'Come on.' She jabs a finger at the charcuterie boards and drink trays I arranged after Chase and Thomas left. Each interspersed with fresh flowers, various-sized dildos, and a smattering of penis confetti. 'You made all the neon-colored dicks look artful and classy.' She grabs one of the glasses I'd filled with her requested whipped-cream-topped Blow Job shots off the Trusty Thrusty tray.

Shots I'd sprinkled with edible glitter.

'Who does that?' Leslie pouts over the whipped cream.

George, the lone male at the bachelorette party, wraps an arm around my shoulders, clinking his glass with mine. 'I love it.' With his free hand he waves his phone at us. 'Already uploaded to the Facebook group.'

Thinking of Thomas's reaction to that, I snicker. Maybe I should tell them that he helped. It would make for a great caption.

'That's why I scooped her up for Moore's new marketing team.' Bell places an assortment of meats, cheeses and fruits on her plate. 'Alice is going to do great things at Moore's. Her floor displays are already increasing sales.'

I can never thank Bell enough for not only pushing Chase to hire me for Moore's new marketing team but for becoming such a good friend and mentor.

'You weren't the only person wanting to scoop her up,' Leslie murmurs.

Bell jabs her with her elbow, turning Leslie's smirk into a wince.

I fuss with the peony arrangement situated next to the fruit tray, confused by what Leslie means but too embarrassed to ask. I'm pretty sure no one else was looking to hire me out of the shoe department, but it's nice of her to say.

My phone vibrates while everyone fights over which color penis straw they want. I sneak off to the bathroom down the hall knowing that there's only one person who would be calling me, seeing as everyone else I know is here.

Closing the door, I slip out my phone, unsurprised by Kayla's name and photo on the screen. It's the photo I took of her and Mary at the zoo three years ago. Back when we were much closer.

I slide the phone open. 'Kayla?'

'Hey girl, what's going on?' My one-time sister's chipper voice is nearly drowned out by loud, bass-pounding background music.

I do the time change math in my head. Even with the time difference it's only 6 p.m. in New York. 'Where *are* you?'

'I'm out!' she hollers, causing me to pull the phone away from my ear. 'That's why I called. Come meet me.' Glasses clink. 'How long has it been since we went out together?'

Never. We've never gone out drinking because she was pregnant and then we were raising her daughter. 'Where's Mary?'

'With the neighbors. No worries.'

The only neighbors of hers I know of are the single mom who works nights and an elderly couple. 'Which neighbor?' I'm hoping that in the time she started ghosting me someone new moved in.

'Stop worrying. Sometimes you just need a break, you know?' Her platitude is followed by the slurping of a straw sucking up remnants of a drink. 'Come out and have some fun with me.'

Now that I hear her voice, some of the worry melts away, making room for anger and frustration. 'When I called earlier Mary answered. Why wasn't she in school and why were you asleep?' I shove my free hand in my hair, my fingers getting caught in the curls. Questions I've held back these past months come pouring out. 'As far as I know you still don't have a job. How are you covering your rent?'

Kayla's silence is telling. I usually walk on eggshells around her. She's temperamental. Always has been.

At first, I thought it was typical teenage girl stuff when we met back when she was thirteen and I was fifteen. Then grief. Reconnecting years later, I blamed pregnancy hormones and then the stress of being a young, single mom.

But Mary's six now and I'm tired of making excuses for her. Kayla needs to grow up.

'This past week you left me all these crazy texts and voice-mails.' I lean against the door, my anger draining just as fast as it surfaced. 'What is going on with you, Kayla? I'm *worried*.'

She orders a new drink, a double gin and tonic, and though it seems like she isn't paying attention anymore, at least she hasn't hung up.

Taking a breath, I relax my voice. 'I was thinking, now that I have a decent paycheck, we could get a place together again. The three of us. Somewhere in a good school district.' It's the whole reason I've been living so frugally, even after my promotion.

When she still doesn't respond, I hurry on, hoping my news will put her in a better mood. 'If we're careful, I could support you and Mary while you figure things out. Just think, Kayla, if you stayed home with Mary we wouldn't need to pay for after-school care or day care this summer.' My voice speeds up, excited that I finally get to share my plan. 'With one less bill to pay and my new salary plus my savings, I could cover food and rent until the next school year. You could spend more time with Mary while you figure out what you want to do.' And I'd get my family back.

'You just love throwing your new job in my face, don't you?' Her voice, absent for most of the conversation, snaps back just as loud as when she was yelling in celebration a moment ago.

'What?' I frown in the mirror as if my reflection has the answer. 'No. I didn't mean—'

'You've always thought you were better than me.' Her words come fast and sharp.

I press my palm down on the cool marble countertop. 'I've *never* thought that, Kayla. I can't believe you'd think—'

'Well, you're not better than me, okay?' There's an edge to her words I've never heard before.

I bite my lip, trying to stop the sudden onslaught of tears welling in my eyes. 'Kayla... I never meant—'

'You never had parents and I did. My parents cared about me, yours just left.' Her words cut deeper than any knife, slashing my soul, exposing my greatest fears.

I stagger to the side, nearly falling onto the toilet. As much as I try to stall the emotions from welling up, a sob escapes.

'Alice...' Kayla's voice is softer now, as if spewing venomous words purged her of whatever mood she was drowning in. 'I... I didn't mean...'

Blinking rapidly, I let out a long breath, trying to stop the tears from pushing their way out. 'We'll—' I clear my throat. 'We'll talk when I get back, okay?'

'Get back from where?'

It takes me another deep breath before I can answer. 'I'm out of town, remember? At my boss's wedding.'

'Oh. Yeah. I forgot.' Sounding like a chastened child, Kayla is quick to agree. 'Sure, we'll talk later.'

Ending the call, I lower myself on the toilet seat lid, my energy zapped. I could blame it on the jet lag, or the glass of champagne, but I'd be lying.

Deep breath in. Deep breath out. Blink, blink, blink.

After one or two more inhalations, I have my emotions under control. Or at least pushed down far enough where I can smile at myself in the mirror. An unnatural smile, but still a smile.

Beyond the door, the music is turned up and the women (plus George) cheer.

'This is not a pity party,' I tell my reflection, awkward smile still in place. 'This is a bachelorette party for your friend and you will *not* ruin it.' Nodding at myself, I run my hands down my front, as if I can physically brush away Kayla's words. 'You're going to get back into that room and have fun.' Grabbing the door handle, I give myself one more nod and take one more deep breath before wrenching the door open and striding out.

'Take it off, take it off!' A piece of black fabric hits me in the face.

Pulling it off my head, I have time to register it as a man's shirt before Mike, barreling past at breakneck speed, nearly knocks me over.

'Mikey!' I grab onto the bathroom's door frame to stop my fall. I've never seen him move that fast. He looked like the Flash, only a cat and, you know, naked.

Holding the shirt, I turn into the living room only to be met with the cause of Mike's sudden departure.

Two half-dressed men are thrusting their hips faster than Shakira while surrounded by the small wedding party, all of whom have their arms up and their butts shaking, looking quite tipsy.

How long was I on the phone?

'Alice!' Bell dance-walks toward me and points over her shoulder. 'Liz came!' She smiles, her joy and the outrageousness of the situation making it easier to push aside my conversation with Kayla. 'And she brought strippers!'

'Get in on it, girl!' Liz air lassoes me and pulls me into the group. It's either draw unwanted attention to myself and my problems or play along.

Taking a breath, I force a smile on my face and pretend to be tugged onto the makeshift dance floor by the youngest Moore sibling.

* * *

Thomas

'I can't believe you're going to have a black eye at my wedding.'

My brother, laying on his back on the hotel suite's sofa, laughs while scrolling on his phone. He's been laughing on and off since we left my suite for his.

I school my expression under my newly made ice pack, which is more about trying not to aggravate my grossly swollen eye than maintaining indifference. 'I'm so glad you're amused.'

'Sarcasm, T-money?' He smirks at me. 'I thought that was beneath you?'

If looks could kill, I'd be wearing my custom-tailored tuxedo to his funeral tomorrow and not his wedding.

From the adjacent love seat, I stare longingly at the bar where my dark amber Pappy Van Winkle, a twenty-year old sipping Scotch, that I had brought with me sits, feeling like a starving man denied entrance at a buffet.

'Alice said no drinking.' He doesn't look up from his phone.

My one good eye narrows on him. 'Since when do you listen to an employee over your brother?'

The look he throws me rivaling even my best sneer. 'Since when are you such a dick about calling my friends employees when they're here as guests at my wedding?'

The barb hits. 'Hmmm.'

I drum my fingers on the arm of the love seat wondering how to explain that my repeatedly calling Alice an employee is more for me than any sense of archaic class distinction some might have. Out of everyone, I'm the one who needs the reminder. I was called 'my father's son' too often growing up not be acutely aware of how my actions are constantly compared to our lecherous paternal figure.

'Damn it.' Chase scowls at the phone screen, held up over his head.

'What?'

'George just posted a picture of Mike licking whip cream off a Blow Job shot.' He closes his eyes and sighs. 'The plane ride here was bad enough. I don't need Mikey having stomach distress during the wedding ceremony tomorrow too.'

Apparently his cat, on top of being an everyday unattractive nuisance, is a nervous traveler. Aka a veritable stink bomb. When Chase retold his coach flight experience it was the only time I felt a flicker of happiness over having to reschedule our flight after the TSA inquisition.

'Why is the cat still in my room, anyway? Wasn't the whole purpose of moving the party to my room to keep Mike here, away from sex toy temptation?'

His phone screen tapping turns aggressive. 'What was I supposed to do when he hid under your bed when the hotel staff unloaded the food? If we'd stayed any longer we would've risked blowing our cover.'

Condensation drips onto my dark green sweater. 'You shouldn't have brought him there to begin with.'

Chase spares me a narrowed look before shrugging. 'He gets separation anxiety. He's fine at home, but God knows what he'd do to the hotel room if I'd left him there alone.'

I've never been one for modern day colloquialisms, but the phrase 'I can't even' comes to mind.

More condensation droplets fall and the ice shifts under my palm, pain ricocheting around my orbital bone. After getting a look at my eye in the mirror earlier, I'd hoped that if I kept icing it, the swelling would go down. That doesn't seem to be the case.

Which means besides appearing uncouth for my brother's wedding, my ability to use my vintage Leica camera will be greatly hindered if I can't squint my left eye to make sure the aperture is in focus. I fight a shudder thinking and quickly dismissing having make do with my phone's camera.

My eye flicks to the whiskey bottle again. Seeing what the Leica's aspherical lens could do with the high-contrast environment of Las Vegas' neon-lit nights was going to be the one bright spot about this trip. You know, besides my brother's matrimonial happiness. I was going to take the free day I added to everyone's schedule after the wedding to treat myself to an all-day photo shoot while the rest of the wedding party did whatever ill-gotten things they wanted.

'Holy shit.' Chase levers into a seated position, eyes on his screen. 'Liz is there.'

At the mention of our sister who's been MIA for months following the aftermath of our father's legal and family downfall, I lower my ice pack. 'What do you mean, "*there*"?'

Chase stands, leaning over to show me a picture of Liz, Alice, and Leslie with their arms wrapped around each other. The caption reads, 'All bridesmaids in attendance'.

My eyes linger too long on Alice, wondering why her smile doesn't seem to meet her eyes.

'I sent her an invitation by email, but she never responded.' He looks at me. 'Did she tell you?'

I move to shake my head but stop when it pounds. 'No. She didn't.'

I may not be the touchy-feely brother that Chase is, but I care for my sister. It's taken a lot of self-restraint not to give the private detective Chase and I had vetted the go-ahead to track her down. I agreed to hold off only because both Mother and Bell made logical arguments about giving Liz space and time to get over the revelation that she's a love child from Mom's one-time affair.

We sit, two brothers stewing in mutual indignation for a few minutes, until Chase lifts his phone screen again, this time doing a double take.

'What now?' I lift my ice pack back in place.

He holds his phone up once more. I lean back, trying to bring the picture of the unfamiliar, bare-chested men into focus with one eye sans reading glasses. 'Who are they?'

He swipes right, and for the first time tonight I wish I'd been knocked unconscious by that dildo. Because no one should see their mother stuffing twenties in someone's G-string. Let alone a policeman stripper holding the weapon of my eye's destruction in front of him mid-thrust.

* * *

Alice

Someone turns the music up. The Village People of all bands. Ridiculous but perfect for the fireman and cop costumes the strippers are wearing.

I would never have thought 'YMCA' good hip-thrusting music, but I'm proved wrong. Very wrong.

My smile isn't as forced as it was. A Blow Job shot and a glass of champagne helped with that. Enough to have me raising my hands along with everyone else, shaking what little hips God gave me.

I bump butts with Mrs Moore, who, according to Bell, is fresh off her fling with the Bahamas cabana boy and is still making every minute of her matrimonial freedom count.

And by freedom, I mean tucking twenties into suspenders and G-strings.

I sweat. I laugh. I forget.

A song change later and a too-close encounter with the feel of the fireman's hose through his parachute pants, I escape for another drink.

Never a good drinker, I'd thought of holding back tonight. But, things having gone the way they have... I pluck a shot off a brass tray and try and mimic the others when they'd downed it in one go.

I get the liquid down but choke on the mouthful of whipped cream.

Eyes watering, I twist the cap off a bottle of water just as George emerges from a bedroom, arm up like a bespoke Statue of Liberty. 'I got it!'

I take a sip, the cool water calming my cough, as George bends down over an outlet. 'What do you have?'

'The perfect ambiance.' He straightens with an expression of victory on his face, only to frown as he looks around. 'Damn it. It's too light in here.' He waves his hand at me. 'Flick that switch behind you, will you?' He steps over to the door. 'I'll get these.'

The 'ambiance' George spoke of turns out to be a portable light projector, casting millions of lights around the room in various colors. Like a multicolored disco ball.

Almost everyone gasps in delight.

Who knew that turning off the lights would be the catalyst to penis party Armageddon?

As if he'd been waiting for the perfect moment, the fireman stripper yanks off his pants to reveal a Dalmatian-printed thong encrusted with diamond rhinestones. Rhinestones that sparkle tenfold under the new lighting.

A shadow streaks across the room.

'No!' Bell lunges toward it, but it's too late.

Everything plays out in slow-motion.

Mike leaps on the coffee table, surprising Mrs. Moore who stumbles backward into the counter, upending the tray of Blow Job shots and catapulting them into the air, causing glitter, cream and alcohol to rain down on the party.

Entranced by the lights, Mike continues jumping, this way and that, like a Mexican jumping bean, turning over champagne glasses and penis candles, which instead of being doused, ignite the spilled alcohol.

A trail of fire spreads out across the floor toward the discarded parachute pants.

Do you know how flammable polyester is?

Very.

'Shit!' Leslie grabs the ice bucket off the bar, the clang of her ring against the metal bucket acting like a bell before a fight. Mike freezes, looking up from the lights dancing across the coffee table and floor – and right into the fireman's reflective crotch.

Whose scream will give me nightmares until I die.

'Ahhh!' Turning this way and that, the stripper tries dislodging Mike, who has jumped, claws out, and attached himself to the glittering thong and, from the man's screams, the skin under it. 'My dick!'

The song changes to Nelly's 'It's Getting Hot in Here'.

George, behind me, mutters, 'Seriously?'

Leslie tosses the melted ice, in her haste getting more of it on us than she does the fire.

But the cold water trickling down my body and into my shoes kicks my brain into gear. 'Someone grab the bedspread!'

George jumps, but races to the bedroom. Bell and Liz dance around the stripper, trying to reach Mike without getting clobbered by the stripper's flailing arms.

I run to the sink and yank on the extendable faucet, thankful we're in a suite with all the amenities.

'Got it!' George runs back in the room, the duvet trailing behind him like a bridal train.

I hose him. Well, him and the blanket. And it's a testament to how freaked out he is that he doesn't complain about water damage to his suit.

'Cover the flames.' I drop the faucet spray and grab the wet blanket, tugging it and George toward the fire. In seconds the heavy, king-size duvet is spread out and without telling them to, Mrs. Moore and Leslie upend the water on top.

Bell yanks Mike off the fireman.

George turns on the lights.

Liz cuts the music.

The cop stripper makes a run for it in his G-string, his butt cheeks jiggling with each stride, a few bills floating to the floor in his wake.

And in the eerily silent aftermath, only the sound of our panting breath and the soft whimpering sobs of the fireman can be heard.

Then the smoke alarm goes off.

8

THOMAS

Vegas is costing me more than a wedding at Westminster Abbey.

A six-foot Bette Midler drag queen saunters down the sidewalk behind me belting 'Wind Beneath my Wings', forcing me to step closer to the group of hotel evacuees or risk being smeared with body glitter and pink feathers from her boa.

The Vegas equivalent of being tarred and feathered.

Chase is somewhere in the crowd with his fiancée, probably trying to ascertain the exact details of what the fuck happened.

Because I knew, *we* knew, as soon as the fire alarm sounded causing my skull to nearly split in two from the pain axing through it with each shrill blast, that the bachelorette party was the cause.

'Thomas dear—' my mother weaves toward me, unsteady on her two-inch kitten heels '—what happened?' Her hand, a place where the few wrinkles she's allowed to show her age reside, cups the side of my face.

The long, seemingly unending day must be getting to me. Because at the touch of my mother's soft skin against my five o'clock shadow, it becomes necessary for me to blink. Repeatedly.

I can't remember the last time my mother touched me so affectionately. That I allowed her to.

Air kisses, yes. Holding my arm as we entered a gala, yes. Resting this same hand on my jacketed shoulder to show public display of pride at my business acumen in a room full of employees, yes.

But affection?

Hoping any accumulated moisture can be excused by the swelling of my eye and not my unnerving emotional state, I clear my throat.

'The shape of the bruise...' Mother squints, tilting her head to the side as if that will help her make out the phallic impression on my face. And what with the various neon signs, spotlights, glitter and rhinestones to rival the Hope Diamond's reflective facets, it might actually work.

I tilt my head to the left, my injury out of her line of sight. 'Why did you lie about Liz?'

She drops her hand. 'I didn't actually lie.'

I let my lack of expression speak for itself.

Mother sighs, looking far more her age than she had minutes earlier as she danced out of the hotel unconcerned with her damp outfit, the crowd's general displeasure or her complete lack of propriety as she specifically asked the concierge for more Blow Job shots to be handed out to the guests as a way of apology. 'She needed time, and I knew you wouldn't give it to her if I told you where she was heading.'

'And where was that?'

'You'll have to ask her.' She raises an eyebrow in return of my own. 'I'm not lying. I am saying I *do* know where she's been, but I don't feel it's my place to say.' She pats my arm, back to the distant warmth that we're used to. 'She's okay, Thomas. I promise.'

'Hmmm.' I scan the sidewalk looking for a blonde female sporting French braid pigtails, as only my sister would do in Vegas, but while my eyes land on Chase clutching Mike to his chest in a stranglehold while throwing I-love-you-eyes at Bell and then on George patting a tear-streaked stripper on the back, Liz is not to be found.

'She left with Alice and Leslie to book a table at a nearby restaurant.'

Alice. I realize that while I told myself I was looking for blonde braids, I'd also been looking for uneven strands of black/brown hair. Then the rest of what Mother said registers. 'A restaurant.' I cut my eyes to her. 'Why?'

Giving me the innocent eye flutter that she'd passed on to her second son, Mother smooths down her dampened silk blouse. 'To continue the bachelorette party, of course.'

I blink. Or try to. It's feels more like a spastic twitch. 'You're going to *continue*?'

'Of course.' She waves down a hotel staff member circulating through the crowd with a tray full of whipped cream shots. 'We can't let the party end on such a sad note.'

'Sad?' I fight to remain calm. Or, at least, *appear* calm, because since stepping into the TSA security line at LaGuardia, I've felt everything *but* calm. 'You call the perverted combination of strippers, penis candles, Blow Job shots and a demonic cat setting fire to a hotel suite *sad*?'

She plucks a shot off the tray with two fingers, pinky up. 'What would you call it, dear?'

'A sign. A sign that this whole destination wedding was a huge mistake. That Vegas was a huge mistake.'

The staff member's practiced smile melts in the face of my

spastic eye twitching and he shuffles off, not bothering to offer me a glass.

Mother raises her hand yet again and waves to George, a few hotel-guest clusters over. 'I really don't understand what you have against a city that you've never been to.'

George says something to his stripper friend and hastens over, weaving through the crowd.

'Las Vegas is a city where inhibitions fall away.' My lips barely move as I mutter. 'It's what you and the rest of the bridal party seem to find charming about this hellish place.'

She licks the whipped cream off the shot. 'I take it you do not?'

Averting my gaze, as no one should see their mother take a Blow Job shot, my one good eye burns as I stare into the neon forest. 'Inhibitions are there for a reason. They keep one properly restrained. Hinder unsavory frivolity.'

She coughs. But not from the whipped cream. There's a twinkle in her eye which makes me suspect she's holding back a laugh. 'Unsavory frivolity?'

I find nothing amusing about the day's situations, piling up like bricks being used to build a den of iniquity. 'If you'd prefer laymen's terms – inhibitions keep one from making an ass of oneself.' My nose flares as I catch sight of Chase trying to stuff his cat up his shirt. 'Something our family could do less of.'

I gesture to the crowd of drunk hotel guests, the menage of Las Vegas strip walkers and performers lining the sidewalk. 'Las Vegas is apparently the Moore family's inferno.' I stab myself in the chest. 'And *I'm* left playing Dante, trying to figure a way out of this hellhole while the rest of you dance in the flames.'

'I never knew you could be so dramatic, dear.' She assesses me as if seeing me for the first time. 'Why are you so concerned with all this?'

A level of frustration I never knew I could reach burns inside me. Frustration from a complete lack of control that, before my reconciliation with my family, before this trip, was unfathomable.

I shift, fully facing my mother. 'I don't know, maybe because if my father had been less uninhibited our family wouldn't have imploded the way it did.'

Our mouths drop in tandem, both of us equally surprised at what I just said. My admission to feelings on a matter that I have thus far refused to talk about.

It's coming up on a year since I facilitated the incarceration of Stanley Winston Moore. It was completely justified and very much overdue, but that doesn't mean I like to talk about it. Talk about him. The man I spent my entire life compared to. A philanderer, narcissist and swindler. My father.

George reaches us. I notice he's carrying a Chanel quilted handbag.

'Yes, Emily?'

Snapping my mouth shut, I glare at my administrative assistant. 'Since when do you call my mother Emily?'

His eyebrows surge above the top of his glasses. I don't think I've ever taken such a harsh tone with him before. With anyone, really. My loss of control is a fast-spreading infection.

I don't like it. No. I *loathe* it.

Without a word, Mother takes the purse from George and rummages inside, coming up with a gold-hinged millefiori pill case. 'Here.' She clicks it open and shakes two white pills onto her hand. 'For your eye.'

She thrusts them at me and I stare, unmoving. I don't like medication. If I wanted to play psychologist, I might admit that dislike probably stems from my displeasure of not being in control.

I look around me at the drag queens, Blow Job shots, and general merriment in the face of fire evacuation. Control? What a laugh.

George blinks, looking shocked. And I realize I actually laughed.

My mother doesn't budge, her hand outstretched, pills on her open palm. It's like we're having a duel, but instead of dawn it's dusk. Instead of a dirt road, it's a paved sidewalk filled with people of ill repute. And instead of instrumental spaghetti western music, it's a baritone of Bette Midler's greatest hits.

The shrill whistle of a man in a hotel uniform breaks the tension. 'You are clear to head back into the hotel!'

Cheers erupt around us.

'And as an apology for the inconvenience, the hotel bar will serve free drinks for the next four hours, compliments of Thomas Moore.'

Louder cheers.

My eyes cut back to Mother, whose own are wide with surprise. 'Chase,' we both say.

Ignoring the way my eye pulses as I grind my teeth, I grab the pills from my mother's hand and toss them in my mouth before stalking toward the groom.

Like the Red Sea before Moses, the crowd parts, as if knowing on some subconscious level the menace that awaits them if they impede my path. Even with such a short, easy walk, when I reach my brother, still hugging his ugly sack of bones to his chest while his fiancée coos at its head poking out the neck of Chase's shirt, my temper fades almost as quickly as it sparked. Because it isn't my brother that I'm mad at. It isn't my sister for running away. It isn't my mother for her way of handling her divorce. It isn't even my father, currently locked up in a minimum-security prison.

It's me.

Mikey tries to dart out from beneath Chase's shirt, but Chase does some sort of ninja squat, grabbing him before his paws hit pavement. Still crouched low, I catch sight of my bottle of Old Pappy that Chase somehow kept hold of during the evacuation and shoved in his back pocket. The seam of his jeans threatens to pop from the strain of his recent movement.

Chase catches sight of me and smiles. 'Don't worry T-money, I...' He trails off, as does his smile, while he looks at me. 'Thomas?'

He flinches as I reach out, yanking the whiskey bottle out of his back pocket.

Then, continuing my way toward the hotel without so much as a backward glance, I flag down a concierge who needs to jog to keep up with me.

'I need a new room. And I need it now.'

* * *

Alice

Tell everyone to fuck off.

I giggle at Leslie's earlier advice while I rest my forehead against the mirrored wall of the elevator. I can totally envision Leslie saying something like that to anyone, but me? Even ten sheets to the wind, the thought of me even attempting to tell anyone to fuck off is absurd.

My breath fogs the mirror and I write 'fuck off' in the condensation.

But maybe its absurdity is why I *should* do it. I close my eyes and imagine responding to Kayla's next incoherent text with 'fuck off'.

I giggle again.

The couple in the elevator behind me whisper. I probably look highly suspicious leaning against the wall, shoes in hand, hair back to its stick-straight chaotic nature, writing profanity I can't bring myself to utter.

Another giggle.

I should've stayed out with the other girls instead of volunteering to escort Bell back to her room so she could get a good night's sleep before the wedding.

Although honestly, it was more like *she* escorted *me* back. I offered her my arm when we left the club, but as the shots I'd downed after Liz procured a private dining room at the hard-to-get-into Partage restaurant with the help of her brother's black Amex card were racing through my veins, I'm pretty sure Bell only took my offered arm in an effort to keep me steady during our short trip back to the Bellagio.

I'm not much of a drinker. But after the plane ride, all the effort I put into the party, Kayla's phone call, finally letting go and having fun only for it all to literally vanish in a puff of smoke, I decided to give it a shot. Or four.

My giggling continues.

And after the last one something magical happened.

I had fun. Real, uninhibited fun.

As sad as it is, in my twenty-nine years I've never been out with a group of girlfriends like tonight. Girls who genuinely like me for me. And I know they like me because even with as shy as I am in our normal daily encounters, and as much as I like to be the observer and let them have the stage whenever we're together, they noticed something was wrong with me – even in the midst of all our Vegas shenanigans.

Hopefully none of them saw me wipe a tear or two away at the table when they got me to admit who Kayla was and what she'd said earlier. They'd all offered comforting words (Bell), a hug (Liz) and advice (Leslie).

Fuck off, Kayla.

Another giggle, this one cut short by the ding of the elevator.

'Miss?' One of the gentlemen behind me taps my shoulder. 'Isn't this your floor?'

Using two hands, I push off the wall and glance at the number on the screen. 'Yessss.' I step carefully over the threshold. But my careful step is too slow, and the doors nearly squeeze me between them. With a hastened hop, I turn to thank the couple, but see the doors close on them in a hot embrace.

Maybe they weren't whispering about how odd I was acting. Maybe they were complaining that I was in the way of their elevator tryst.

Luckies.

Maybe if I stayed out, I could've found someone to tryst with.

My next giggle turns into a snort-cough at the imagined sight of *me* trying to land a one-night stand. I don't even know how to find one sober. Thanks to my adolescent fear of the opposite sex and teenage pregnancies, I never even learned how to flirt. Any dates or relationships I've had were initiated by happenstance and dumb luck.

Though I did take mental notes on flirting tonight while watching Leslie.

The tall, leggy, forty-something-year-old lawyer drew men around us like a siren. Yet she turned them all away. 'Girls' night,' she'd said. Very impressive.

Almost as incredible as Liz's impression of her older brother when I admitted to being the culprit behind the elder Moore's black eye.

'*Indeed*,' she'd said, shoulders back, eyebrows raised, looking down her nose with a serious expression.

Bell assured me that Thomas wouldn't fire me. That he couldn't due to the promise he made when Bell thought she was leaving New York for good. Bell got Thomas's word that I'd always have a job at Moore's if I wanted it.

Liz laughed and said she would've paid serious money to see her brother get dick whacked.

Leslie, as Leslie's prone to do, simply laughed and said, 'Fuck him.'

My mind, helped along with the shots and drinks I've had, suddenly imagines taking Leslie's advice literally. The images flashing in my mind have me bracing one hand on the wall of the long hallway, my other hand fanning my overly heated face.

The small wafts of tepid air don't help.

He's your boss. He's a grump. You assaulted him. You have to work with him.

The problem is, aside from the steamy hot scenes my over-worked and over-romance-novel-filled imagination is conjuring, even in the sober light of day I've started to think of the dreaded Thomas Moore as a kindred spirit. And Mrs Moore, Emily as she insisted I call her tonight, made sure to keep bringing him up whenever she and I talked.

I continue down the hallway, hand sliding along the wall as I go, until I reach what I *think* is my hotel room door. It takes a minute of squinting at the numbers until I confirm it's the two-bedroom suite I'm sharing with Liz, who is still out on the town with Leslie.

Pulling out my key card, I continue thinking about the privileged enigma known as Thomas. Not Tom or Tommy. Not even to his family – although Bell and Chase do like to try.

Besides myself, I don't think anyone else needed Vegas as much as Thomas Moore, on that Emily and I agreed. It would do him good to relax. Have a little fun.

Emily stressed that she thought it was high time Thomas find a woman to settle down with.

Another image, this one PG, but one I find more disturbing, flits through my brain.

Thomas, sitting in a club as Leslie had, drawing in all the women around him while he and Chase laugh.

My plastic key card cuts into my palm, the pain drawing me out of that disconcerting, wide-awake nightmare.

I laugh it off. The only time since the shots started that my laugh sounds forced.

With a beep, I unlock the door, attempt to pull down the heavy handle and push. It's a combination move that takes me more than one try and a lot more beeps until I've finally opened the door.

I'm sweating by the time I stumble inside, nearly landing in a heap in front of Thomas Moore.

Talk about your buzz kill.

9

THOMAS

I swirl the half-inch of amber liquid in the crystal glass, my good eye focused on the apparition that just heaved herself into my sister's hotel suite.

I *thought* I was already as far down the rabbit hole as I could get. But as Vegas has proven time and time again during this short trip, there always seems to be another tunnel to tumble down. Or maybe Alice has tumbled into mine.

Whatever it is – whiskey, pills, Vegas voodoo – I'm pretty sure it's the reason why I'm dreaming about my dildo-wielding marketing employee. Although why my subconscious decided to include innate details like her opening the hotel room's door with a grunt, then throwing herself inside, very ungracefully I might add, to land on the suite's foyer floor, I don't know.

Dream Alice giggles.

That solidifies it. This must be a dream. Alice doesn't laugh in front of me. In fact, she rarely smiles.

But she's doing both after stumbling into Liz's suite where I've been sitting for hours while drinking Old Pappy since, *apparently*, there were no more available suites for the night.

Something that would never have happened in New York, and also something I find highly suspect. However, after my last suite caught fire, I decided not to argue with the hotel staff. Instead, I have been lying in wait for my sister. If I can just get some answers as to where she's been since father was arrested, maybe I won't feel so... adrift.

I down the remaining whiskey in my highball glass before lowering my forearm on the armrest, my glass dangling from my fingertips.

One of those rare smiles curls up the sides of Alice's face. 'Hi, Thomas.'

'Hi, dream Alice.'

She tilts her head, her once wavy, but now poker-straight dark hair sliding off her shoulder. 'Is this a dream?'

'Must be.' The shorter pieces of her ill-advised bangs cling to the perspiration on her heart-shaped face.

'Why?'

I blink my blurred vision back into focus. Are dreams usually this inquisitive? 'Because I thought of you and you appeared.' I *had* been thinking of her. Even if those thoughts were centered around how *not* to think of her. Isn't that what they call a catch-22?

'Oh.' Alice nods slowly, multiple times. 'Same.'

'You thought of me?' This is *definitely* a dream then.

'Yes.' Alice pushes her shoes to the side, bracing herself on all fours as if readying to stand. 'But I didn't like it.'

My brow pulls down so low my good eye nearly closes.

'You were with other women.' She looks so accusatory that I can't help but turn my head one way and then the other, looking for these alleged women in the empty hotel suite.

'What women?'

'The ones in my imagination.' She crawls toward me on all fours and suddenly my vision is laser focused.

On her heavy-lidded eyes, her full and pouting lips, on her ass swaying one way and then the other as she crawls closer and closer.

She's only a few feet away but it feels like years until she reaches me.

And when she does, it becomes exceedingly clear that this is *not* a dream.

If it was, I wouldn't feel her hands wrap around my ankles. Wouldn't feel them slide up my legs until she's pressing into my thighs as she rises on her knees – every inch closer is another hard inch gained under the fly of my jeans.

'Alice?' I damn near choke on her name, my mind still fighting what my body knows is my fantasy come to life.

'Hmm?' Her thumbs come within a hair's breadth of my dick before skimming past and out, grabbing on to the chair arms to hoist herself up off the floor.

'What are you doing?'

Sinking a knee on either side of me, she settles her small ass on my lap. 'I thought I'd try doing what the women in my books do.'

I need to stop this. Stop her. Instead, my hips shift, remembering the snippet of text I read from one of her books on the plane. 'And what is that?'

With a sly, seductive smile, Alice is transformed. 'Anything I want.'

It's hard to swallow. Despite the large amount of whiskey I've consumed, I'm parched.

Her delicate hands skim down her body, grabbing onto the hem of her shirt and lift – revealing a perfectly simple, but nonetheless enchanting, white bralette.

With a thunk, the glass still dangling from my fingertips drops to the floor, and with it, my last thread of control.

* * *

Alice

'*Alice.*' Thomas's eyes darken and his arms, a moment ago resting languidly on the chair, wrap around me and slide roughly against my exposed skin.

The heat of his body that warmed my heart as I climbed on top of him becomes a memory as passion ignites.

I'm well aware of how attractive Thomas Moore is. His note-worthy scent, the way his stoic gaze cuts through you like a knife revealing insecurities you'd rather remain hidden, the annoying, yet inevitably panty-tingling way he speaks – rife with condescension and confidence all add up to Thomas Moore being one sexy beast of a man.

Though, while I may have noted these things, I also locked them away. In a box labeled 'Not for me'.

Right now, with Leslie's take-charge, do-what-you-want atti-tude fresh in my mind, I'm Pandora.

I run my nose up the column of his throat, inhaling deeply before flicking my tongue out, curling it around the shell of his ear.

His breath hitches. Trailing his fingertips down my back, around my ribcage, he pinches the peaks under the soft cotton of my bralette.

All my fantasies that I've also locked away over the years come rushing through my mind. The various pages of intimate scenes that I've read and wished I could recreate. All my late-night imagining. Wanting.

I release them too.

'Say my name.' My breath is hot against his skin.

'Alice.' Thomas's voice, still confident but now laced with passion rather than derision, sends goosebumps down my spine. 'Alice.'

The thought of this man wanting me as much as I want him has me grinding on top of him, desperate to get closer. Threads pull and split as I rip his thin cashmere sweater over his head before attacking his button-down shirt. Only Thomas would wear a sweater and button-down shirt in Las Vegas.

The small ivory discs ping against the marble floor, as I rip his shirt open, the sound, along with Thomas's groans, create a hypnotic soundtrack to my erotic fantasy.

He twists, helping me push the fabric off his shoulders, then shrugging it the rest of the way off.

What's revealed makes me pause.

Freckles. Thomas Moore has freckles on his chest.

An image of this stiff and proper man shirtless in the sun has me licking my lips, as if tasting the salty tang of his sweat. His chest flexes under my gaze. Smiling, I lean forward, biting around a group of freckles above his heart. His hiss blows over my ear, sending goosebumps across my body as I continue to nibble. All while riding the hard ridge of his lap.

His hand fists my hair, pulling my mouth up to his. Tongues swirl, teeth graze and the heat intensifies as our bodies press closer. So close that my knees strain against the arms of the chair.

Bracing my hands on his bare shoulders, I rise.

Things gets blurry, my movements suddenly heavy and slow, but when it refocuses, I'm naked. Thomas's eyes bore into me, all over me, from his seat in the chair. His expression declaring that I'm something worth salivating over. As if I'm Aphrodite rather than a scrawny girl-woman with limited experience.

I've never wanted something more. To feel wanted. And not only wanted but wanted by Thomas Moore. A man so discerning, so intriguing, so completely out of my league it's laughable.

And I do, the giggle erupting from my chest in one short but powerful exhale.

The corner of his non-bruised eye crinkles as he smiles in return.

Wow. If Thomas Moore is attractive while being sour and aloof, he is downright orgasm-inducing when he smiles. As proof, my whole body shivers, set off by tiny pre-orgasmic sparks of pleasure.

He speaks, low and soft. 'What next?'

I almost falter, overwhelmed with feelings and choices – my mind clearing enough to want to debate the right and wrong of the situation.

Swallowing back my indecision, I think What Would Leslie Do. And Leslie would continue doing whatever the fuck she wanted.

'Here.' I point to the spot in front of me.

My luck holds as, still smiling, he pushes off on the armrests to stand before me. The brow over his good eye arches.

I reach out, tugging on his belt. 'Off.'

Time slows down. The tinkle of metal on metal, the swoosh of leather sliding across denim, the cascade of fabric as it falls to the floor. Until only his grey boxer briefs remain.

For a moment I'm dumbfounded. Not only by the very large and very hard bulge straining behind the silky, athletic fabric, but because I was so sure that a man of his reserved nature would coordinate his uptightness with tighty-whities.

Maybe it's Vegas. Maybe Lady Luck is smiling upon me. Because I'm pretty sure I just hit the jackpot.

Stepping closer, I glide my hands down his chest and over his abs, which tighten under my touch. On a deep inhale, one of expensive cologne, whiskey and desire, I move closer still, my hands dipping into the elastic waistband at the back, fingertips digging into the firm flesh underneath.

It's delicious – the scent, the heat, his ass.

Thankful to have solid muscles to help steady me as I tug his briefs down, I drop to my knees and proceed to smack myself in the face with his dick. I laugh, blinking while wondering if this is considered karma, but my laughter fades as I refocus on the XXX before me.

I blink a few times, wondering if it's the alcohol or my day's penis overload that makes me disbelieve my eyes.

I've been surrounded by cocks all day. Girthy ones, vibrating ones, neon-colored ones. But on my knees, facing the very real, very *hard* penis less than an inch away from my mouth, I take a moment to thank everyone involved, including Mike Hunt, for orchestrating such an outlandish wedding weekend that led me to this moment. To this perfect penis.

'Alice.'

Gazing up past the cock before me, over the length of muscle and sporadic freckles and into Thomas's brown eyes, I'm recaptured. His hand cups the side of my face, his thumb pressing on my lower lip. The dream-like magic swirling around me once more.

Keeping my eyes on his, I lick. Up and down, getting a feel for the hot skin, soft on top, ridged underneath. Like a backwards Blow Pop.

I've always loved Blow Pops.

Wondering if that's where blow jobs get their name, I suck on the tip, swirling my tongue around and around.

Thomas's knees buckle and he staggers back, the sound of him leaving my mouth reinforcing my theory connecting the job to the 'pop'.

'*Alice.*' His expression, one of wonder from where I'm kneeling before him, blurs. Colors swirl and shapes move, segueing as dreams tend to do. I panic, worried Thomas may have been correct at the start, that this is a dream.

Thankfully, when everything stops moving, I'm still with Thomas.

On a bed.

* * *

Thomas

I let go.

Of control, rules, reasoning, and feast on the woman before me. Like a man starved for life.

Her lips, her ears, her neck. My tongue finds every spot that makes Alice moan, makes her *writhe*. It's as if my subconscious is taking this opportunity to exact revenge on the woman who makes me feel everything I've tried so hard not to feel. Everything I shouldn't.

I continue kissing and tasting her body, moving down until I've sucked the peaks of her small breasts into my mouth, nibbled and flicked their tips until Alice's increasingly jerky movements threaten to buck me off.

Alice is greedy.

I like that.

Holding myself up on my forearm, my other hand delves into the heat between her legs until my fingers are coated with her desire. Until her writhing suddenly stops, her body tightens like a bow and her voice keens loudly in the empty hotel suite.

'More, Thomas. *More*.' My name has never sounded more like a prayer, like the secret to someone's salvation. Settling on my knees between hers, I lift her legs off the bed, pulling her body toward me until her ass slides across the tops of my thighs and I can I finally thrust my cock inside her.

My grunt goes unheard over her scream of pleasure.

'Yes. Oh my God. Yes.' Even with only her upper back on the bed, Alice manages to find leverage to circle her hips, teasing the tip of my cock inside of her.

My teeth dig into my bottom lip, the pain just enough to keep from coming. I don't want to come, to end this too soon. Though the sight of my dick sliding in and out of her, my wet cock glistening under the neon lights streaming in through the bedroom window is making it hard not to chase my release.

Alice's eyes are half closed, her slender fingers wrapping around her small breasts, pinching her nipples.

Pausing in my thrust, I grab one of her hands and lower it to her damp curls, touching her fingers to her clit.

'Press.' My word must penetrate the haze of lust, because she does. And as soon as she does, I begin to punish her. Punish her for affecting me so deeply, so entirely that I'm without escape.

My thrusts are fast and deep. Out of control and yet setting the most satisfying rhythm I've ever heard. *Felt*.

With every surge inside her, her fingers jerk over her clit. Rubbing it. Teasing it.

I continue to pound into her until her feet flex, her back contorts and her eyes fly wide open, unseeing. 'Oh my God. Fuck. Yes. *Thomas.*'

Alice's cursing would be amusing if I had even an ounce of energy left to spare. But I don't. Because while her inner walls clamp down on my dick and her hoarse voice shouts my name, an intense spike of pleasure hits me. Rising to my knees, I thrust one final time, burrowing myself as deep inside her as possible. Roaring like the animal she's made me.

Things blur, time shifts and then I'm on my back with Alice spread out over the bed and my body.

Consciousness begins to wane.

Reasoning still gone with my climax, I act on pure instinct and pull her against me as everything goes dark.

10

ALICE

If shots are the devil and Las Vegas is hell, then I need to get my act together and start behaving if I want any chance of surviving the afterlife.

Every time my brain pounds against my skull, my eyes threaten to pop from their sockets.

Which is every other second.

On a happy note, this has to be the most comfortable bed I've ever slept in. One point for Las Vegas.

I nearly choke on my tongue when I swallow, cotton mouth having left me no moisture. One point hangover.

I try and go back to sleep, focusing on the cool sheets and soft pillows surrounding me. I'm not 100 percent certain, but I have the feeling I was enjoying a nice dream. Traces of a bright pink light, laughter and euphoria resound upon my pounding brain, like flashes of an impressionist painting. A really, really beautiful impressionist painting. One that also kind of makes you horny.

Yes. I cuddle deeper into the mattress and pillows, accepting my weird, perverted subconscious analogies like a large dose of ibuprofen. *If I can just go back to sleep, everything will feel better.*

But the moment the pain eases and my consciousness drifts, one of my pillows move.

Because it's not a pillow.

An ear-piercing internal scream erupts in my head, while my physical body stiffens like a possum playing dead. I'm fully awake, survival instinct has my blood, a second ago sluggish from sleep, racing through my veins. As do images, more concrete ones this time, through my brain.

Penises. Shots. Strippers. Fire Alarm. The girls. More drinks. Thomas.

Oh dear God –*Thomas.*

My eyes flash open, the harsh morning light coming through the bedroom window.

Instant blindness.

Squeezing them shut, I flare my nostrils and inhale slow and deep, forcing the nausea down while trying to make sense of the new, and more coherent flashes of my dream. Or really, my *memories.*

After walking Bell back to her hotel room, I found Thomas in mine. And then... oh God – I *crawled* to him. Then I *climbed* on him. Heat from both embarrassment and something else, something far more pervy, has me pressing my face further into the cool satin cotton pillowcase.

I straddled him. I kissed him. *I* did those things. *Me.* The girl who may read about adventurous, panty-melting sex but who only follows the leads of others fully focused on making sure *they* enjoy themselves. Always being left... unfulfilled.

The sound of seams ripping echoes inside my pounding head, forcing my memory recall back to last night. Where I literally tore Thomas's clothes off. The deep grunt he made as he thrust inside of me.

I was *definitely* filled last night.

The non-pillow stirs again.

I angle my face away from the light blazing in the window and toward the non-pillow next to me where I infinitesimally lift my lashes.

A wall of skin and muscle meet my eyes, nearly as blinding as the sun had been. A smattering of freckles crosses his back like a Pollock painting, making me wonder how often he had to be outside with his shirt off to develop them. I remember marveling at those freckles as I whipped his shirt off while straddling him.

More memories float to the top of my subconscious and any embarrassment ebbs as something else takes over, pulling me under its current until my breath is labored and my thighs press together.

Thomas shifts on the bed, his arm sliding across my midriff. I play possum again as the large, masculine hand skims up my abdomen and rests below my right breast, its thumb tickling the underside – igniting sensations in my panties that are not at all helpful to my mental cognition.

I MacGyver my left arm out from under the covers, using the back of it to wipe dried drool off my cheek. At the cool touch of metal on my chin, I pause, lifting my hand above me.

A band of gold with gaming dice engraved around it rests on my left ring finger.

As I stare uncomprehending, Thomas shifts his body closer, his fingers sliding around my side, something grazing over a rib. Something that also feels like metal. The cool touch stalling my lust-addled brain.

Unable to process the implications of our newly acquired matching accessories, I return to study Thomas, my eyes moving up his chest, the strong column of throat to his face, usually devoid of all facial hair, shadowed by dark pinpoints of whiskers. Stubble should make him look older, and yet the stoic tyrant appears young and boyish as he sleeps. He's adorable. Even with the mottled, swollen dildo-shaped bruise deforming his left eye.

With a shaky hand, weighed down by tacky jewelry, I raise the sheets. The first thing I notice is my lack of proper bikini line maintenance. Because of *course*.

The second thing is a very hard and very hot cock poking against my thigh. My brain stutters at the realization that *that* was inside me.

Once more it's hard to swallow. I touch my thumb to my new ring to help focus my thoughts without getting sidetracked by my new-found and surprisingly strong libido.

Very studiously not looking at the length of my boss lying next to me, I stare at the third and final thing of note happening under the covers. Thomas's left hand resting along the curve of my ribcage and the band of gold – a masculine match to mine – residing on it.

Knock. Knock.

'Alice, you up?' Liz, my suite mate for the trip, calls from the other side of my closed bedroom door.

Thomas stirs and I slap my hand over his mouth. 'Yes!'

He groans and I realize I missed most of his mouth, my palm colliding with his cheek – the one below his black eye.

'Shoot,' I whisper, grimacing at his death stare. 'Sorry.'

'Do you need help?' Liz's voice is layered with concern.

'No, no.' Though he hasn't spoken, I slide my hand off his cheek and over his mouth. 'I'm good.'

There's a beat of silence that I can't appreciate due to the sound of my heart trying to explode from my chest.

'You sure?' It must be the adrenaline rushing through my system, but I swear Liz sounds amused.

'Yes, yes.' I shake my head as if she can see me, which my dehydrated, pounding skull does not appreciate. 'All hunky-dory here.' *Hunky-dory?*

I hold my breath.

'Well, if you're sure you're okay.'

'Yes.' My lungs deflate in a rush. 'One hundred percent. Totally okay.'

'Then I'm going to head down and charge my brother's room for brunch before picking up my bridesmaid dress from the concierge.'

'Sounds good.'

'You want me to wait for you?'

'Uh, no, that's okay.' Though I'm suddenly starving and would very much like to retreat from this situation, there's no way I can leave. Especially without Liz seeing Thomas. 'I, uh, think I'll just sleep in a bit more.'

I think she laughs, but I can't be sure. But it wouldn't be surprising as I *am* acting like a nutjob.

'If that's the case, I'll grab your dress when I grab mine so you can sleep in.'

'Great, thanks. Awesome.'

'No prob.' She's definitely laughing now. 'I'll see you later.'

My hand stays flat against Thomas's mouth until I hear the door to the suite open and close.

As soon as I lift it, Thomas slides his body up under the sheets.

'Sorry, I, uh, panicked.'

He clears sleep from one eye. 'Yes, you did.'

'You are oddly calm.'

His fingertips brush over his bruise. 'Do you think so?' The sheets dip below his waist.

When I manage to look up, his dark eyes bore into mine – one of which is nearly swollen shut and ringed with purple. I might not remember locking the door, but I suddenly remember grabbing his shirt front and pulling him to me for a hot and heavy kiss before tearing said shirt off. And I realize that though his stoic expression is firmly in place and his tone level, his eyes burn.

He is *not* calm.

'Um... I think we're married.' I hold up my hand.

If this was happening to anyone else I'd find supreme satisfaction in the look of shock that comes over Thomas Moore's perpetually austere countenance. It's only for a moment, gone as soon as he lifts his own hand, frowning at the ring, but I saw it.

He pulls himself up to a seated position, the movement drawing my attention to his arms, his chest and then to the defined peaks and valleys of his six-pack that would give my romance novel cover models a run for their money.

I remember how hot and hard his body felt last night but I didn't stop to think what all those flexing muscles meant – Thomas Moore works out.

Like, a *lot*.

Who would've thought that behind those expertly cut suits and cool demeanor lived a gym rat. It shouldn't surprise me given that bespoke suits are cut close for a perfect fit, but this? You'd need to pump some serious iron to get the definition he's sporting in his shoulders, arms, abs and that delicious V at the top of his waist—

'I remember last night.' He stares so hard at his ring I expect it to melt off his finger. 'But not this.'

I run a hand through my hair, wiping away the beads of sweat as I do. Sweat that I'm telling myself is from my hangover and not the heat pouring off the extremely cut, half-naked man next to me, or my reaction to him.

My phone rings. I turn behind me to the nightstand. Bell's photo lights up the phone screen.

During my hesitation to answer it, Thomas's phone rings.

I blame fatigue for how hard I stare at his ass when he turns and bends over the side of the bed to retrieve his phone off the floor, totally forgetting to answer mine.

He pulls back and I feign interest in the ceiling.

'Yes?'

I could practice my whole life and never sound as commanding as Thomas does on the phone even after being up all night drinking and waking up married.

'Calm down.'

I bite my lip. It seems at forty-something years old Thomas hasn't learned the universal lesson that *telling* someone to calm down doesn't magically make the other person comply. In fact, in my experience – with Kayla – it does the opposite.

As predicted, the voice on the other end gets louder.

Thomas frowns harder, his black eye watering. 'Are you done?'

In the silence that follows his stern, whip-cracking question, goosebumps spread down my arms.

Thomas flicks a tear off his cheek, hissing when his finger makes contact with his cheek. 'I'll be right there.' When he lowers his phone, he sighs, the first sign of discontent he's shown since waking.

Well, besides when I slapped him.

Giving me his attention once more, he levels me with one of his superior gazes, which looks ridiculous with his hair mussed, his morning beard and his naked stature. 'What happened last night?'

I feel a nervous giggle rising in my chest and I fight it back down, drowning it under what's left of the shots and drinks from last night. 'I don't know.'

The look he gives me makes me feel like a toddler caught telling tales and all my amusement dies. 'I really don't.'

'Hmmm.' He turns, lowering his feet to the floor and grabbing his clothes off the floor.

Even irritated I can't help but ogle his backside as he stands and pulls on his boxer briefs.

'I can't rationalize my actions last night.' He pulls the ring from his finger and holds it before him like it's something Mike Hunt coughed up. 'For me, of all people, to act so recklessly with...' He takes a long slow breath through his nose as if so overcome by disgust he feels sick.

I do the same with my ring. Once off, I squeeze the ring in my fist while fighting the urge to junk punch my previously favorite appendage of his.

* * *

Thomas

I'm going to vomit.

I eye the bathroom door for a brief moment before deciding I'd rather not add to my chagrin by being sick in front of an employee. My *wife*?

So while my mind tries to make sense of fragmented memories of last night, I take long, slow, deep breaths in through my nose to quell the urge to regurgitate the bottle of poor choices I drank last night.

'I ask that you simply consider that my assets are not solely my own.' In through the nose. 'Any damage to me or Moore's is damage to my mother, sister and brother, and therefore, in turn, Bell.' Out through the mouth.

Alice frowns, the muscles in her jaw flexing and I wonder if she's fighting nausea, same as me.

Giving her time to process and calm her stomach, I pull on my shirt one sleeve at a time. The buttons are missing and it smells of alcohol, sweat and irreparable damage.

I make a note to have it burned.

So though I'm overheated from alcohol poisoning and feelings of withdrawal from whatever opioids my mother thrust at me last night, I grab my sweater, noting its outstretched shape and pull it on over the top to cover the gap of skin between my shirt's two sides.

The soft cashmere grazes my injured eye, which has a heartbeat of its own this morning, and I pause, needing a second to swallow back bile.

I deserve to be sick. I deserve this pain, I think to myself as the roiling in my stomach levels out. I'm as much sick over my actions as I am from over-imbibing.

This is something my father would've done.

Self-loathing crests the wave of unhelpful emotions as I grab my jeans. 'I've put Moore Inc. at risk. If anyone were to get wind that the heir to Moore fortune got black-out drunk and married an employee...' I pause, Alice's sharp intake of breath making me realize I'd been voicing my self-recriminations out loud. 'If you keep quiet about this, I'll see to it that you are well compensated.'

As if waking from a stupor, she rears back, clutching the covers to her chest as if I tried to snatch them away instead of remaining as far away from the bed as possible as I dressed. 'I am not stupid enough to not know the differences of our stations, but just because I'm a mere *employee* and beneath an heir to a fortune doesn't make me some whore out to steal your millions.' Her long lashes flutter rapidly. 'You don't have to worry about me, I'm not going to tell anyone.' She clears her throat and I have an odd feeling she's trying not to cry.

This is one of the many reasons I don't have relationships. The fears I unknowingly voiced were practical business concerns and yet she's made them personal.

Unsure of how to respond to her, I pull on my jeans.

Alice straightens in the bed, the sheet falling down the sides of her body, revealing the curve of her hips. 'An annulment.' She exclaims this as if she thinks she's found a winning lottery ticket, the excitement in her voice pulling my eyes up to hers. 'With you being a man with such assets, I'm sure you have a dozen or so lawyers at your beck and call.'

I ignore her sarcasm, mulling over her idea. 'Yes, I do.'

She rolls her eyes with a huff. I shouldn't think this, especially after last night, but childish Alice, with her lips pursed, her arms crossed and her naked silhouette visible is adorable.

My body, which should be solely focused on not vomiting and extracting myself from this potentially detrimental professional situation, reacts.

'I'll call my lawyer.' I turn my body, hiding the reaction by slipping on my shoes. 'Until then, not a word to anyone about this.' Not waiting for a response, or allowing myself one last look at Alice, I exit the bedroom.

I'm not trying to be dramatic, it's just that I've reached my limit and I know there's a trashcan in the other room. Grabbing it on my way out of the suite, I manage to make it down the hall and inside the elevator where I'm alone, before heaving the contents of my stomach into my makeshift bucket.

My luck runs out when the elevator doors open before I reach the lobby and an unsuspecting family is met with a waft of puke. Thankfully they decide to wait for the next available lift.

Fucking Vegas.

I was right to hate this place before ever stepping foot in it. It's the ruin of all good men. Not that I was very good to begin with, but at least I had rules. Boundaries I never crossed. Like having sex with employees. Let alone marrying them.

A stab of unease that has nothing to do with last night's consumption hits me. After all my hard work and sacrifices to oust my father from ruining the company, it would be an epic typhoon of irony that in one night my degenerate choices would be the thing to sink Moore's.

Married. To an employee. A veritable stranger. With no pre-nup.

It's my worst nightmare come to life.

The doors open on the lobby floor and I stagger out.

I puke two more times before finally getting a room.

11

THOMAS

'Not good enough.' Wedding over, I adjust my stance to make it seem as if I'm a part of the reception's activities while I listen to my lawyer give me rational and logical reasons why my annulment will not be instantaneous despite the large retainer I pay him. 'I'll be home tomorrow morning. We'll talk then.' A flash of blue catches my good eye, moving across the white marble floor of the Bellagio's Michelin-starred restaurant, Lago.

When he reminds me that tomorrow is Sunday, I hang up. If he wants to keep said retainer, he will damn well meet me on a Sunday.

'What did I tell you?' Chase claps me on the back, making me nearly drop my phone. 'The wedding was great, wasn't it? Not tacky in the slightest.'

I make a non-committal sound and slide my phone into my pants' front pocket. A tux that neither I, nor Susan, approved. It seems my brother was more aware of the wedding details than we thought.

Chase's hand moves to my shoulder, giving it a squeeze

before dropping. 'Even you have to admit that the chapel room was beautiful.'

'Indeed.' The Little Vegas Wedding Chapel was beautiful – *after* I paid the owner to allow Susan and me to nearly gut the place before Bell and Chase's afternoon's ceremony. Due to the tasteful renovations, it looked less drive-thru nuptials and more like an actual house of God than any other chapel in a twenty-mile radius of the Strip. But I keep that to myself. No need to burst Chase's Vegas bubble.

And yet, even with my expensive and careful planning, things still managed to escape my control. Things more glaring than this tux.

Like my black eye, which is more technicolor and grotesque today than it had been last night and rivaled the new stain glass window I'd had installed as the most colorful object in the chapel. And how the Elvis officiant, whom I vetted via an image attached to his résumé, was ten years and one chin past the picture he'd sent. Or, most unnerving – the bridesmaid dress Alice is wearing.

As my eyes follow the cool, white neon lights that run along the angles of the lacquered walls and various architectural reliefs, I pause on Alice cradling the ring bearer in her arms as she talks to my new sister-in-law and the maid of honor across the room.

I point to my brother's demonic cat, nuzzling the far too revealing neckline of Alice's dress. '*That* isn't tacky?' The feline had changed out of his ceremonial silk bow tie and into a teddy bear onesie.

'That's not tacky, it's meaningful.' Chase smiles as only a man in love can. 'That was the outfit Mikey wore when I—'

'Begged Bell for forgiveness when you acted like an ass – yeah, I know.' I remember all too well how unmanned and destroyed my carefree brother had become when Bell ended things with him. Rightfully so, but still. It was just another reminder on top of the pile of reminders my parents have given me over the years, that love is the catalyst for chaos.

Chase shrugs, unrepentant, and eyes the hotel staff I had stationed near the food with fire extinguishers in hand. 'At least no strippers were harmed in the creation of this reception.'

'Hmmm.'

Bell laughs at something Leslie says while Alice's bare shoulders shake.

I've seen Alice smile before, and even in my drunken haze last night I observed her giggling, but I've never seen her laugh without reserve.

Checking to make sure Chase is occupied with ogling his bride, I tug my Leica out from my interior jacket pocket to capture the moment.

Right after I snap the picture, my brother's cat has had enough of being shaken and jumps out of Alice's arms, making the most of his freedom by weaving around the base of the bar as if trying to decide how best to conquer his Everest – a cocktail shrimp tower.

Alice, hands on hips, shakes her head at the beast. In fact, everyone seems amused.

Except me. I almost drop my prized Leica on the high-polished marble when my brain registers what I'm seeing. Or rather, what I'm *not* seeing. And therefore, what everyone else is not seeing.

I had *thought*, based on Susan's written notes, that Alice would be wearing a custom Vera Wang cerulean silk slip dress – same as the other bridesmaids. But now, without the bouquet in front of her like it was during the ceremony, or the feline dressed in bear drag in her arms, it appears she's wearing two scraps of fabric, barely sewn together, rather than a completed dress.

'Aren't the bridesmaid dresses Susan chose for the girls just stunning?' Mother steps between Chase and I, encircling her arms around us.

A waiter offers Alice a glass of champagne and she shakes her head, revealing a beauty mark on the inside of her left breast as it plays peek-a-boo with each twist of her body.

'Stunning.' I repeat the word, testing it out. I would've gone with revealing, unchaste, obvious... but stunning seems to work just as well.

My fingers itch to reach for my phone again, but I refrain, conscious of my mother's gaze. In her navy satin and sequined cocktail gown Emily Moore looks less like a mother of the groom and more like a prom date.

'Hey, speaking of bridesmaids.' In my peripheral, Chase squares up to our mother, frowning. 'Did you know Liz was coming?'

I should pay attention. I should help my brother investigate why Mother left us out of the loop about Liz's whereabouts these past few months. Demand answers that somehow both she and our sister have managed to avoid this whole trip.

But I can't stop looking at Alice, whose dress may be the same cerulean blue as Liz and Leslie's but not the same cut. Leslie's halter straps are thick and secured by a pearl clasp at the nape of her neck while Liz's dress may be strapless, but the sweetheart neckline is high cut and demur. My wife is the only one missing half of her bodice – the dress's straps are no more useful than strips of blue angel hair pasta, and the deep V neckline stops an inch below her breasts.

Also ignoring Chase's comment, Mother leans closer to me, inspecting my face. 'How's your eye, dear?'

Chase snorts, dropping the interrogation before it begins. 'The wedding pictures are going to be epic.'

The same waiter from before hovers around Alice. I catch his eyes dropping to her chest.

My jaw clenches, causing my eye's pulse to double-time. 'It's fine.'

'Are you sure you don't need another painkiller, Thomas?'

Thankfully, the waiter moves on and I'm able to force my eyes from Alice and take in my mother, who's effectively given her youngest son the cold shoulder.

She glances toward the other side of the room and back.

'You look as if someone just kicked your puppy.'

Somehow, I know she's frowning, even if her forehead doesn't crease.

'No, thank you.' My tone causes Mother's eyes to widen. 'Being under the influence of your opioids once was enough.'

My own Vegas sundae: whiskey, a possible concussion and the pills as the cherry on top. It's the only plausible reason for how out of character I acted last night. For the reason I woke up with a wife. A wife whose dress should illicit an indecent exposure charge.

I should *not* have left the bridesmaid details to Susan. Needing to look anywhere other than at Alice, I glare at my blue suede shoes – a groomsmen gift from my brother and a reminder of another mistake I failed to see coming.

I should've double-checked the tuxes before having them and the dresses shipped out ahead of time.

'Opioids?' Mother gives me, and the garish paisley-embossed suit my brother swapped my custom Tom Ford tuxedo out with, a once-over. 'What on *earth* are you talking about?'

Her incredulity recaptures my attention. 'The pills you gave me last night.'

Mother erupts in laughter. 'That wasn't an *opioid* for heaven's sake. Who do you think I am? A Real Housewife of the Upper West Side?' She continues laughing, patting my shoulder. 'That was extra-strength Tylenol.'

The words don't compute. 'Impossible. There's no way I'd act like that on whiskey alone.'

Apparently, Mother and Chase find this amusing.

'Wait.' Chase's grin widens on one side. 'The stiff and proper Thomas actually took a pill without knowing what it was?' He snorts. 'And you drank on top of that?' His nostrils flare in and out as he tries to stifle his laughter. 'Is this because Alice whacked you in the face with—'

'It was an accident.' I force the words through clenched teeth and glare at my brother. Who, for once, shows good sense by looking anywhere but at me. A few choice words surface, but with my mother present, I swallow them back down and remind myself that this is Chase's wedding.

Instead, I draw his attention to the kitchen's rotating door across the way. 'Your cat is escaping.'

Smile gone, Chase whips his head around in time to catch his feline costumed companion poised in pounce position, waiting for his moment to jump the next time the door opens. 'Fuck.'

Alice

I'm sorry but the person you are trying to reach is unavailable.

Typical. Kayla called me when I was busy with the wedding, but when I try and call her back – no answer. And not only no answer, but it's obvious that her voicemail is full from that automated message. I don't even get the courtesy of a beep and a few seconds to vent my displeasure at her avoiding my calls. Or do what Leslie suggested and tell her to fuck off.

Which is exactly what I should've told Thomas this morning.

Fuck off, Thomas. Go fuck yourself with your stuck-up, holier-than-thou, blue-blooded, one-percenter fortune that I want no part of.

But since I can't say that to Thomas without fear of being fired, it would've been nice to at least check off 'stand up to Kayla' from my new to-do list that Leslie inspired me to start. A to-do list that will hopefully whittle down the problems piling up around me.

Like my bridesmaid dress that borders on pornographic. I tug my thin dress straps up for what feels like the bazillionth time, the cooling desert air on the balcony sending a chill down my deep-V neckline.

I should've asked to see the dress beforehand instead of opening the garment bag an hour before the wedding. Along with the sliver of hanging fabric was a note from Susan saying the dress will go perfectly with the sandals I chose. And if she meant they both have thin straps and show a lot of skin, then yes, they go together.

'Alice.'

If it weren't for the previously mentioned thin straps on both my shoes and dress, I would've jumped out of both of them at Thomas's sudden appearance behind me.

'Dear Lord.' I press my hand over my exposed chest bone,

my heart pounding just to the left of it. 'Does that ridiculous tuxedo give you ninja stealth?'

Thomas glances down at his black tuxedo. Black, with a subtle blue sheen that when the light hits reveals the paisley pattern on the custom-cut silk. A blue sheen also set off by the blue suede shoes on his feet.

He should look like Liberace in mourning. Instead, he looks good enough to climb. Again.

My face catches fire remembering last night. Unhelpful.

When he looks back up, his uninjured brow is raised.

I tug my straps up. 'What do you want?'

A weight settles in my stomach, remembering how he asked me the same thing just hours ago. I spent the hours before the wedding trying not to be sick whilst getting dolled up for the ceremony, and the two hours since it ended hiding from the deplorable Thomas Moore.

'We can't get an annulment.'

'What?' I think of all the romance novels I've read and movies I've seen. It all seemed so simple. Wake up married, get an annulment before lunch. 'Is it because we slept together?' I think I remember something about consummation being a sticking point. 'Because I am fully prepared to lie under oath if needed. It's not like I remember much anyway.' See? I'm lying right now. Because I remember *everything* about the consummation.

But Thomas doesn't need to know that. No one needs to know that. Not even the United States judicial system.

'Let me clarify the previous statement.' He peers down at me as he talks, back to his patronizing self. 'We cannot get a *quick* annulment. According to my lawyer, these things take time. Paperwork.' His lips purse slightly. 'And a working knowledge of when and where the ceremony took place.'

'Only in Vegas would they make it so easy to get drunk and married and so hard to get sober and divorced,' I mutter, the rose-colored glasses I wore on my flight over here fully broken. Vegas, it would seem, is not my happy place.

'Yes. That's why I moved up my flight to tonight.' His good eye narrows, his tone turning arctic. 'I'm meeting with my lawyer tomorrow.'

My gut clenches. I would *not* want to be his lawyer.

Good, though. He's leaving. I look over the balustrade at the crowd below swarming along the Strip. Maybe then I'll be able to enjoy the small time left on my all-expenses paid vacation.

But the longer I look, the more the details blur. It grates on me, him moving up his flight during his brother's wedding weekend. It highlights just how eager he is to dissolve our marriage. To get rid of me.

I turn back, glancing over his shoulders at the Lago's balcony doors. 'What about the reception?'

He follows my gaze. Once sectioned off to a private area of the restaurant, the wedding reception has now overtaken the entire establishment. Random hotel guests are now dancing with the wedding party – Bell and Chase quite happy to share their joy with strangers.

'No one will miss me.' He says it with his usual detached timbre, but I swear there's something in his expression that belies his tone. But when I lean in, it's gone with one painful-looking blink.

Must've been the neon light cast against his injured eye.

My phone buzzes in my hand.

Kayla:

Talk when u home

The protective case creaks under my tight grip.

Leslie's loud laugh draws my gaze back to the reception. She's standing with Mrs Moore and Liz, looking more at ease and confident talking to a matriarchal billionaire in a tight blue silk gown than I ever have in my normal everyday life.

And I ask myself – What Would Leslie Do?

She'd kick ass and take names, is what she'd do. Starting with the man who thinks I want a piece of his fortune so badly that I somehow masterminded a quickie wedding on the off chance that we not only both got incomprehensibly drunk but that he'd also miraculously be waiting for me in *my* hotel room when I got back from said drinking.

I spare a brief thought to my savings account, then remind myself that it's my money. That I saved it. And the whole point of saving it is so I can use it if I ever need it.

Besides, the sooner I get home the sooner I can 'talk' to Kayla.

And in true WWLD fashion, by talk, I mean tell her to fuck off.

Swiping the screen clear of Kayla's messages, I open my internet browser. 'What flight number is it? I'll see if there are any seats available.' Maybe he'll give me a ride to the airport since we're going the same way. I can save money there.

'You want to leave?' His incredulity, while uncommon, is annoying.

'Listen, *Mr Moore*.' When his eyebrow jumps, I take satisfaction that it isn't due to a sense of superiority. 'No matter what you might think, I do *not* want to be married to you. Never did. So if flying home early to meet with your lawyer can expedite an annulment, then I'm all in.' I shake off the twinge of guilt I feel over leaving early, but I know once I get to explain things to Bell, Leslie and the others, they'll understand.

'I see.' His injured eye bores into me for an uncomfortably long time. It isn't until another gust of breeze hits me, and I shiver, that I can look away.

'No need to purchase a ticket.' He jerks his shoulders up and back, shrugging out of his tux jacket.

I glare at him. 'And why's that?' If he gives me some condescending line about a person of my station being in the way while he and his highfalutin lawyer decide my future without me, so help me I'll give him a matching set of black eyes.

'I bought the seat next to me.' Once off, he shakes out the fabric, managing to look pretentious even with a black eye and blue suede shoes, before settling his jacket around my shoulders. 'I'll have the airline transfer it to your name.'

I want to ask why he bought the seat next to him, but instead I'm focused on the heat from his jacket, his scent surrounding me like an embrace. A hot, silken embrace.

My questions evaporate. My nipples pucker.

I glance down to make sure I'm not high beaming my boss between the lapels of his tux jacket.

Nothing but smooth silk.

'Thank God for pasties,' I mutter.

* * *

Thomas

'What was that?' I can't tell in the dim light of the balcony, but I have the feeling she's flushed. Her cheeks and her mostly exposed chest.

'Um, I just wanted to know the price.' Alice doesn't look me in the eye.

'The plane fare is free.'

That jerks her eyes up to mine. 'What do you mean? I can—'

'I have miles that will expire if I don't use them.' Which is true. I always have miles that expire. But I hadn't used them this time. I'd used Chase's credit card. Payback for charging last night's open bar to my hotel room.

Juvenile, yes. But not as juvenile as also purchasing the seat next to me on the plane to ensure I wouldn't have to suffer through inane small talk with some chatty stranger.

But Alice doesn't need to know that.

She's worrying her lower lip with her front teeth. Lips that were around my cock last night. I grit my teeth at the physical reaction to that memory, this blasted paisley tuxedo not leaving much to the imagination. The patterned jacket was bad enough, but Chase had the pants made to match. And do not even get me started on the shoes.

I should've chartered a private plane with my brother's card.

'I *have* had enough of Vegas for a lifetime.' She cuts her eyes over my shoulder to the reception happening behind me while I wonder if she's including our night together in her assessment of Sin City. 'And there aren't anymore bridesmaid duties...'

She pulls her lip back under her teeth after trailing off and I fail to control my lower half's reaction.

I turn my back on her, pretending to assess the party. 'If you want to come then go pack.' My words snap military orders. Once more I'm frustrated, angry – with myself.

Because no matter how much distance I put between myself and this godforsaken place I know I won't have complete control again unless I also distance myself from Alice Truman.

And still, I want her to say yes. Spend five more hours with me even if it is thirty thousand feet in the sky, breathing recoiled air and eating painfully reheated food.

Putting personal desires before responsibilities like this is something my father would do. As is sleeping with and having less than professional thoughts about an employee.

And yet.

'Plane leaves in three hours. Red-eye.'

'Oh.' A rustle of silk and she quick steps past me. 'I better hurry then.' She continues toward the doors – the ones on the left, nearest the dance floor, *not* the ones by the exit.

'Don't.'

She freezes, pivoting on one slim-strapped heeled sandal, facing me with a frown.

I know she wants to say goodbye to Bell and Chase and everyone else. Apologize for leaving, make excuses. I know that because she's a good person. A polite person.

I'm neither.

'If you tell them you're leaving they'll want to know why, and/or try and convince you to stay. And knowing them, they won't stop until you do and I'm not waiting around for that.'

She sucks her lip back in and I wonder if this new tic developed because her hands, the ones that usually twist and fidget when she's unsure or thinking, are busy clutching her purse. 'I—'

Whatever she was going to say gets cut off when the newly enlarged wedding party erupts in loud cheers as an R & B mashed-up Elvis song starts blasting from the speakers.

I wonder if the King would be pleased his music is still relevant or disgusted at the gross liberties taken in reproducing his song for modern listeners.

I'm not sure if it's my logical explanation, or the chaos she'd have to fight in order to be a good person and say goodbye, but Alice's shoulders slump. 'You're right.'

'Of course.'

Her eyebrows jump and for some reason she looks like she's trying to hold back laughter.

I smooth a hand down my dress shirt, concerned it might be overly creased from the tight-fitting jacket and today's shit-show of a wedding. 'Meet me in the lobby in thirty minutes.'

'Yes, sir.' She salutes me with a smile before fast-walking through the doors on the right, my jacket billowing out behind her like a cape as she sneaks along the edge of the reception area and out the door to the elevators.

I stand there, against my own advice to get moving, until I have control of my body once more.

It takes much longer than I'd like.

I make a mental note to have HR send Alice a memo instructing her to *never* call me 'sir' again.

12

ALICE

Most of the past hour is a blur. All that really sticks out is that despite my hangover and the Saturday night Vegas traffic, I've managed not to be sick while Thomas's driver got us to the airport in less than thirty minutes after our record-breaking packing.

Despite George's earlier disgust at my essentials-only packing, my minimalism paid off when I had just minutes to get everything together and get out the hotel room door. And any worry or regret from leaving Vegas early evaporated into relief once I sank into the oversized leather seat holding my first-class bag of slippers, blanket and pillow to help me sleep through the red-eye flight.

Well, relief and one more less helpful feeling.

I shift in my seat, trying to get comfortable, wondering how I'm going to make it through the next five hours with my new, immediate and physically distressing situation.

Thomas eyes me as my shoulders hunch under the blanket draped over me, trying to subtly lift my shirt away from my chest. 'What's wrong?'

'Nothing.' I really wish he hadn't insisted on giving me the aisle seat. Just as with the tux jacket earlier, he continues to confuse me by vacillating between asshole and gentleman. And besides confusing, his gentleman tendencies tend to make things more awkward than necessary. Because if I could turn toward the window, this would be a lot easier.

Actually, if the stupid drink cart wasn't in the way, I could go to the bathroom and take care of it myself.

'Tell me.'

Not looking at him, like a child who doesn't think others can see them if they can't see others, I slide my hand under my shirt. 'It's nothing, really.' And maybe he would've believed my lie if I didn't follow it with a sharp intake of breath from trying to peel the adhesive off my nipple.

Through the tears welling in my eyes, I see Thomas lift a hand toward the call button overhead.

'No!' I jerk my arm out and grab for his arm, but the sudden movement only makes the chafing worse and I let out a rare curse.

His good eye narrows to the size of his injured one. 'Tell me.' His tone as harsh as it sounded when he told me to go pack for the flight.

I glare at the seat back in front of me, hating that one of our last memories as husband and wife, no matter how unwanted, will be with this 100-percent-kill-me-now embarrassing situation I've gotten myself into. I close my eyes against the overhead fluorescent lights. 'It's the pasties,' I whisper through the side of my mouth.

'Pasties?' He doesn't bother to lower his voice.

'Shhh!' My eyes fly open, darting to the older woman across the aisle reading. Her hand pauses in turning the page of her novel.

Sighing, I lean closer to Thomas and continue my futile attempt at keeping my booby pain on the downlow. 'I was in a rush when I changed out of the dress and I didn't take them off. But now they hurt and I don't know what to do.'

You could light a match on my face right now.

'Come.' And just like at the wedding, he grabs hold of my elbow under the blanket and lifts me to my feet, ushering me down the aisle.

The stewardess manning the drink cart opens her mouth, probably to ask us to return to our seats until drink service is over, but I look over my shoulder in time to see Thomas give her one of his well-known hoity-toity looks and her mouth snaps shut. It's one of the looks I judge him for but now makes me want to hug him when, following his expression with 'She's ill.'

He's not wrong. Between the alcohol last night, the nerves during the wedding, the rush to get to the airport, and the pasties, my queasiness is at new heights.

Literally.

Between my expression and Thomas's, the stewardess nods and rushes to unlock the cart brakes.

A second later and our path to the bathroom is clear.

Thomas hustles me to the bathroom's narrow accordion door and pushes me inside.

Then follows me in.

'Wait. What are you—'

'Let me see.' Turning me in place so I face him, he gives me *the look*.

Not as troubled by his glare as I was before Vegas, or as appreciative as I was seconds ago when he gave that look to the flight attendant, I hesitate to comply.

I'm very sober right now. And sober Alice knows with

complete clarity that showing your nipples to your boss is a no-no. But then, so is getting married to him.

The war in me has me hesitating long enough that his expression changes. However, much to my surprise, it doesn't harden, it softens.

As does his voice. 'Let me help.'

Though his plea makes me feel more at ease, what really helps me comply is the cramped space. First class bathroom or not, it's still smaller than a New York City apartment closet in here. There's not an inch to spare between us, and with our height distance making my chest level with his stomach, I'm thinking he won't see much anyway.

Something Thomas discovers and rectifies when, while I have the hem of my shirt raised slightly over my breasts, his hands encircle my waist and lifts me up until my slippered feet rest on the closed toilet lid.

Surprised at the sudden move, I freeze, hands still holding up my shirt, pasties now bared under the harsh fluorescents no more than an inch from his face. The only thing more shocking to me than my current circumstance is that I haven't melted into a puddle from embarrassment.

Thomas's nose flares at what he sees and I contemplate kicking the flush button and hoping for a Harry Potter Ministry of Magic escape.

I settle for averting my eyes, where, in the tiny mirror above the even tinier sink, I watch Thomas's hand move toward my breasts – small red splotched mounds topped with flesh-colored, flower-shaped pasties.

Just before his index finger makes contact, I close my eyes. Whether it's to brace for pain or pleasure, I'm not sure.

Either way, it doesn't work.

His other hand joins the first, one keeping the tender skin

of my right breast taut while the other, using the very tip of his finger, lightly rolls the edge of the adhesive back.

It doesn't hurt as much as I thought it would, although that could be because I feel like I'm having an out-of-body experience.

With slow, methodical touches, the adhesive lifts and rolls away and the pain is replaced by goosebumps, Thomas's cool touch on my irritated skin doing things to me I never thought Thomas Moore could do.

But no, that's wrong. He *has* done such things. Just last night. But I'd assumed the alcohol had intensified my memories. That what I recalled as I cursed and avoided him today was intoxicatingly exaggerated.

Thomas's fingertips pluck the rolled pastie off my breast and I have to bite my lip to hold back a moan.

Apparently not.

'There we go.' Through slitted eyes I watch him throw the first pastie away, before beginning the same process with my left breast.

My lungs scream for more air, but I refuse to oblige, not wanting my chest, on full display, to give away my newly wanton libido with my sudden rapid breathing. My legs stiffen, wanting to shift, but I suppress that too by pressing my thighs together.

By the time the second petal falls, I'm seconds away from passing out, dots of light swimming underneath my eyelids.

Hoping he thinks it's because I'm relieved to be free of the pasties, I allow myself to suck in a deep breath, slump forward, bracing myself on his shoulders.

My shirt should've lowered back in place, covering my exposed skin. Except it doesn't. Instead it has fallen over the backside of Thomas's brown hair, trapping him millimeters from my nipples.

Shoot me now.

But instead of a gun to put me out of my misery, Thomas uses his lips, kissing my nipples like one might kiss away a boo-boo.

A whimper escapes with my next breath.

His lips trail across my chest, moving from one nipple to the other, giving it the same service.

Wet heat soothes my skin when he adds his tongue to the touch.

My whimper evolves into a full-fledged groan, my hands fisting his shirt at his shoulders, pulling myself closer to his mouth. His hands slide under my shirt from the back, pressing me closer still.

But it isn't close enough.

If anything, the alcohol last night only served to dampen the intensity. That would scare me if I wasn't so turned on right now.

When the tips of his lips pull at one nipple, sucking it, I raise one leg, hooking it under his arm, anchoring it across his back.

This time, *he* groans.

The pulse between my legs beats harder. Hotter.

'Thomas...' It's a plea, but I'm not sure what I'm asking for. I told myself that last night was a blip. A fantasy. An aberration from my normal, daily boring life.

And yet this not only feels very real but insanely wonderful.

In answer to my plea Thomas nibbles, the tiny bite of pain making the pleasure that much more intense.

'Ahh—'

Knock, knock.

I jump, causing Thomas's seal around my nipple to break with a painful pull and my head to bang into the bulkhead while the stewardess lectures through the door about turbulence and the fasten seat belt sign.

Seeing stars, my leg around Thomas's waist drops as I slump forward, my other slippered foot sliding off the seat.

With my vision blinking in and out I'm only aware of the sounds – a loud woosh from the toilet flushing, a crash followed by various voices shouting, nausea, held successfully at bay all day, surfacing.

When my vision clears, I'm sprawled out on top of Thomas in the small landing in between the cockpit and first class, his head still under my shirt and my knee wedged hard between his legs.

I blink up into the sour-faced expression of the stewardess. 'Feeling better?'

'No.' And then I throw up.

*　*　*

There is something wrong with you.

My reflection in JFK's baggage claim bathroom doesn't argue. My hair, once perfectly quaffed in an elegant chignon, is now half porcupine, half dreadlocked. In addition, I have wet splotches on my jeans from my attempt to clean them of vomit splatter.

Fortunately, I was able to change my shirt. Unfortunately, George's belief that I hadn't packed enough was proven correct when Thomas had to offer me an extra T-shirt of his to change into, seeing as I had nothing clean in my small duffle.

Thomas. My nipples, bare and overly sensitive under the white cotton fabric, perk up. After vomiting, I'd changed and pretended to sleep the rest of the flight. As soon as we landed, I moved as if in a sleep-deprived trance, when really, I was immobilized by acute embarrassment and confusion.

With an exasperated huff, I push one of the still-crunchy-from-hairspray tendrils out of my face and front tuck Thomas's T-shirt into my jeans' waistband. A woman next to me on her phone reminds me that I haven't turned mine back on since landing.

I may have told Thomas I'd drive directly with him to the lawyer's office, but if I can call Kayla and arrange to meet her afterwards, I can cross two things off my WWLD checklist in one day.

Except as soon as I turn on my phone, it lights up like the Fourth of July. Text messages, missed calls and voicemail.

The texts are from Kayla.

need u

M is hurt

call

@ hospital

My hand is shaking by the time I bring up voicemail. But it isn't from Kayla.

'This is child advocate Lorain Hendrix calling from Allenton Hospital. I'm calling to inform you that earlier today a Ms Kayla Rogers admitted her daughter, Mary Rogers, for a laceration to her temple. Since Mary's admission late last night, we've been unable to locate or contact Ms. Rogers. As you are listed as Mary's emergency contact, if you would call us back...'

Mary.

Grabbing my duffle, I sling it over my shoulders and race out the door. Frantic, I swivel one way, then the other, panic keeping me from remembering which way I need to run to get a taxi.

'Alice?' Thomas calls out from across the way, standing next to his roller bag.

I wonder if he's been there the whole time, instead of in baggage claim where he said his driver would meet us, but I don't have time to ask.

'I'm sorry, I need to go.'

He closes the distance between us and rests his hands on my shoulders, as if knowing I'm about to bolt. 'Where?'

'The hospital. I need to get there *now*.'

13

THOMAS

'Mary Rogers' room?' a very frazzled and flushed Alice asks the nurse sitting at the reception desk.

The nurse's eyes flick to me and my black eye before checking her computer.

'Room four twenty-one.' The nurse points down the hall. 'Take the elevators to the fourth floor. The pediatric department will be on the right.'

I was neither required nor even asked to enter the hospital when my driver slowed in front of the main entrance and Alice jumped out before the car came to a complete stop. And yet here I am, keeping pace with her as she speed-walks toward the elevators. Just as I inserted myself into her pasties situation.

I'm still reeling from my actions on the plane.

After cleaning myself free of vomit, I spent the remainder of the flight researching altitude impairment while Alice feigned sleep under her blanket. Apparently, altitude sickness only affects people breathing oxygen-deprived air, *not* the recycled, fully oxygenated air inside the plane.

And seeing as I was not in Vegas, or under the influence of

alcohol or extra-strength Tylenol, I'm left with only one reason for my continued perplexing actions –*Alice*.

Though silent on the elevator ride up, her hands twist together in front of her, speaking volumes about her state of mind.

As soon as the doors open, she strides down the hallway toward pediatrics and room four twenty-one's open door.

'Mary!' Alice rushes toward a small, dark-haired child with a large bandage on her head who's sitting quietly in bed, coloring with a woman in scrubs.

The little girl has a second to smile brightly at Alice before being engulfed in a full-body hug.

'Sweetie, are you okay?' Alice pulls back as fast as she came in, doing a full body scan before tsking and fretting over the obvious injury near the little's girl hairline.

'I'm fine.' The girl's smile is still in place, but when her eyes shift to the side at the woman next to her, it turns stiff.

Alice kisses her right cheek hard, then her left forehead gently. 'I was so worried.' After one more hug, she calms down, like a balloon deflating, sinking onto the edge of the bed next to the little girl.

Scrub woman does a double take when she sees me follow Alice in.

I turn so my injured eye is out of her line of sight.

Recovering, the woman stands from her chair on the opposite side of the bed. 'Hello. I'm Rachel Clatch.' She holds out the hand. 'I'm a child advocacy team member here at Allenton.'

Alice shakes the offered hand but doesn't respond, nor does she release Mary from her other arm's hold.

Miss Clatch nods, as if expecting such a wary reaction. 'A few hours ago Ms Kayla Rogers came in and admitted Mary—' she nods at the child '—and then left.'

Alice's fingers twitch in her hold around Mary.

Looking down at the little girl, Miss Clatch's serious expression morphs into a smile. 'But Mary here has been such a brave little girl.' Her words are bright and cheerful, and if you ask me, very fake.

From Mary's raised eyebrows, I can tell she thinks the same. Smart girl.

'She didn't cry once, not even when the doctor stitched her up,' Miss Clatch continues, her voice remaining upbeat and yet a wealth of meaning lay behind her words.

Memories of standing straight and appearing unaffected in the face of my father's caustic attitude toward my broken arm in fourth grade surface.

I push them back down.

As if drinking from the child advocate's Kool-Aid, Alice's voice mimics her faux happiness. 'Is that so?' She brushes a stray hair from Mary's face. 'That's my girl.'

Mary doesn't react to the praise, just turns her face up to Alice. 'I can go home with you, right, *Aunt* Alice?' Her eyes widen as if she's trying to replay an unspoken message, but her expression is too overtly obvious to be close to secretive.

I make note of the *Aunt*. Alice has no beneficiaries. At least none listed in her personnel file that I just happened to have read earlier this year. Another completely out-of-character decision that's happened since becoming aware of Alice's existence.

Alice briefly closes her eyes before squeezing Mary close to her once more. 'Of course.'

Miss Clatch grimaces, her cheerleader-like facade gone. 'I'll just go get the doctor.'

I can tell by Alice's expression that she doesn't like that response. But she stays quiet until the advocate leaves.

'What happened, sweetie?' Alice turns Mary to face her. 'How did you get hurt?'

'I slipped and hit my head.'

'At home?'

'In the shelter.'

There's a long pause, and although I can't see Alice's expression, I can almost hear her mind working overtime to process that. Mary uses the moment to go back to her coloring.

'Shelter?' Alice's voice is a pitch higher than before.

'Uh-huh.' Mary fills in a heart with the blue color. 'We went there yesterday.'

I fight the urge to point at the red crayon lying just beside the coloring book.

'I see.' Alice takes a breath, oblivious to the wayward coloring job. '*How* did you slip?'

'Mom knocked over her cup.' Her narrow shoulders rise and fall. 'I slipped in the water when I got up to go to the bathroom.'

'Oh, well.' Alice kisses the top of her head. 'Accidents happen. I'm just glad you're okay.'

Mary peeks over Alice's embrace. 'Who are you?'

If all children enunciated as well as this child, they'd be a lot easier to deal with. 'Thomas Moore.' I hold out my hand.

Both females frown at my outstretched hand, and I'm reminded that good enunciation or not, my brother was correct when he said I wasn't good with kids.

However, just as I'm about to lower my hand, Mary leans forward and takes it. 'Mary Rogers.'

'Nice to meet you.' I pump her small hand once, thankful it's her head that's injured and not her arm when her whole upper torso shakes with it.

She giggles.

Alice's head moves back and forth between us, frowning.

'Wanna color?' Mary holds up her crayon to me.

Before I can respond or take back my earlier thought on the girl's elocution, the child advocate re-enters the room with a woman in a white lab coat holding a clipboard. 'This is Dr Frost. She was the doctor on-call when Mary came in early this morning.'

'Hello.' The doctor addresses Alice and me before looking at Mary. 'How's your head?'

Despite the doctor's friendly demeanor, Mary shrinks into Alice's side. 'Fine.'

'That's good then.' She looks between Alice and me. 'Mind if I have a word in the hall?'

'Of course.' Alice hops up from the bed. 'Be right back.' She gives Mary another quick kiss on top of her head before walking out with the doctor.

I nod at the little girl before following, closing the door behind me.

I have no business talking to a doctor about a girl I don't know. But I'd rather listen to a random kid's diagnosis than color with said kid. Especially when they play so capriciously with color.

Dr Frost crosses her arms around her clipboard. 'As you may have been told, earlier this morning Mary came in with her mother with a laceration on her left temple.'

Alice glances behind her at the closed door. 'She told me she slipped and hit her head.'

'Yes, that's what it looks like – a small gash brought on by striking the corner of a piece of furniture.' The doctor checks the chart in her hands. 'We numbed the area with a small shot of lidocaine, then cleaned and stitched the wound. It probably only needed five to eight stitches, as it wasn't a large laceration

—' she shrugs '—but I did twelve as the injury is in such a visible area. It shouldn't scar too badly.'

Alice bites her lip, probably only just realizing that Mary will be marked by this permanently. 'Thank you.'

The doctor shifts on her feet, as if debating the best way to say something.

Picking up on the doctor's change, Alice's hands twist together.

'It was noted that the socks Mary was wearing when she arrived smelled of alcohol.' Dr. Frost clears her throat. 'As did the mother.'

Alice's hands drop to her side.

So much for the spilled water story.

'Because of this,' the doctor continues, 'and Miss Rogers' disappearance, the police have been notified.'

Alice sways. I rest my hands on her shoulders to keep her steady.

'I'm sure they'll be in contact with you soon, seeing as you're her sister.'

Alice makes a strangled noise.

'But the good news is that Mary seems fine.' The doctor's voice turns soothing. 'Though, since she hit her head and we don't know the exact circumstances, I'd like to order a CAT scan.' She holds up her hands as if to ward off any concerns. 'Just to be safe. And then she'll be good to go.'

Alice nods a few times as if lost in thought.

'I'm on call until noon.' Dr Frost slips the clipboard under her arm. 'I'll make sure to come back with the CT results before I go.'

When Alice doesn't respond, I speak up. 'Thank you, Doctor.' Then, hands still on her shoulders, I guide Alice back into the room where Mary's coloring pink clouds.

One look at her aunt and Mary averts her eyes to me. 'Can we color now?'

'Hmm?' The question jars Alice out of her thoughts, and she glances at me, as if just remembering I'm here. 'Oh, no.' She steps forward, my hands falling from her shoulders. 'We can't bother Mr Moore anymore than we already have.'

Mary's expression falls, her pout niggling at my conscience, her pink clouds and blue hearts making my good eye twitch.

Still, I don't refute Alice's words. Despite not wanting to subject myself to color anarchy, I *am* bothered. By my eye, the cheap gold ring in my pocket and my current life situation. All things that tie me to Alice. A woman who has done nothing but herald chaos into my precise and predictable world.

I nod once in farewell before stepping toward the door.

'Thank you.' Alice's voice gives me pause and I look back from just outside the hospital room door.

She's pale and appears so much smaller than usual in my white T-shirt that's nearly sliding off her shoulder. Her expression exudes exhaustion and a sadness tinged with hope matched by the dark-haired little girl beside her in a white and blue checked hospital gown.

I stop myself from offering to help. To take control of the situation. I need to draw a line.

I'm her boss. Alice is my employee. The girl, her relative, not mine.

Not only is there no need for me to be here, I *shouldn't* be here. Be anywhere near Alice Truman unless it's absolutely necessary and 100 percent work related. With that in mind, I nod and exit the room, pulling out my phone to warn my overly paid lawyer on my imminent arrival.

* * *

Alice

'Should we wake her?'

'I would, the police are here.'

My eyes snap open and I rise from the couch like a vampire from a coffin – with a straight back and what I'm sure are bloodshot eyes.

Mary, her soft cheek pressed into the pillow, is still asleep after getting the all-clear from her CAT scan earlier.

I squeeze my eyes shut, trying to draw moisture. I must've fallen asleep after talking on the phone with social services. I reopen them to focus on the two women in the doorway. One I recognize as the advocate from earlier, the other in a red blazer I do not.

A police officer comes up behind them.

My bladder decides at that moment to declare itself full and ready to explode. Deciding to take a moment to regroup before beginning my argument to take Mary home with me, I hightail it to the attached private bathroom with a whispered, 'One sec.'

It isn't until my bladder is empty, my face washed, and teeth brushed from the toiletries in my small duffle, that panic sets it.

I'm a single woman living in a studio efficiency apartment in a questionable part of the city. That was supposed to be strategic, help me save money to care for Kayla and Mary, but now it's a huge albatross keeping Mary out of foster care.

The irony kills me.

I can look for a better place, but I'm not sure what would happen to Mary in the meantime.

It's as if I've gone back in time when all I could do was wait, helpless and scared, for others to decide my fate. Child services, judges, social workers, police. And this time, even though I'm older, it's so much worse. Because it's Mary's life in limbo.

Moving quickly, I fight back tears of exhaustion and fear as I smooth out my hair as best I can and reapply my travel-size deodorant. It doesn't make me feel as confident as I'd hoped, but it's better than nothing.

As expected, the two women and the officer are still standing in the doorway when I emerge. Walking quietly past the bed, I wave them out the door. 'I want to let her sleep.'

Miss Clatch smiles another forced smile. 'Of course.'

I know I'm in trouble when I catch myself longing for Thomas. If he was here, standing behind me, looking his superior self, it would give a boost of courage.

The woman in the red blazer offers her hand. 'I'm Silvia al Abbas. I'm with child protective services.'

I shake it, wishing my hand didn't feel so limp in her hers. 'I'm Alice Truman, Mary's aunt.'

Though I'm sure she knows that isn't the full truth, she doesn't let on, instead stepping back for the police officer to speak.

'I'm Officer Doan. As the missing person's closest point of contact, I'm here to inform you that a warrant for Miss Kayla Roger's arrest has been issued. If you've seen her or can think of anyone who might know where she is, please tell me.'

I expected it. But expecting it and actually hearing out loud that your one-time sister is a fugitive are two different things.

Officer Doan continues to stare at me as I process what he's said. It isn't until he shifts impatiently on his black-soled boots that I realize he's waiting for me to give him that information *now*.

My breathing quickens. 'Um, let me see.' I rattle off her last place of employment and her ex-boyfriend's name, though I don't have either of their contact information. 'The last time I heard from Kayla was Friday night.' I frown at the memory, now knowing since my earlier call to her landlord that it was the night before Mary and her eviction.

'I see.' He hands me a card. 'If she contacts you again, or if someone mentions seeing her, call this number.'

There's no sense of relief when he leaves, just more trepidation when Ms al Abbas clears her throat. 'Miss Truman.'

I can help but stiffen. 'Yes?'

It's the heavy sigh that does it. Her eyes drifting to the right, her hands coming together. I've seen this stance a hundred times over from social workers. Telling me the couple who interviewed me decided not to go through with the adoption. Letting me know that the foster family I had just gotten comfortable with was just temporary and that I needed to move – *again*. Handing me my temporary Medicaid card on my eighteenth birthday and wishing me the best but not expecting much from me.

She's going to tell me that she looked into my place of residence. That CPS determined it unsuitable for fostering. That I'll have to watch, helpless, as Mary is taken to an emergency foster placement.

The tears of frustration that I've worked so hard to keep back surface and I turn my head to blink them away.

If only I had a better place to live. More money. A respectable background. Those are things that matter in these situations. Not how much I love Mary, not how staying with me is infinitely better than shuffling her to a house full of strangers, as well meaning as they might be. I'm her family. *I'm* who she needs.

After a deep breath, I manage to quell the tears again.

And for some unknown reason, when my vision clears, Thomas Moore is walking toward me.

He's showered, clean shaven and wearing a three-piece suit, looking every inch a *GQ* cover model – minus the black eye. Though even with the black eye the sense of money and power he exudes is still evident.

Money. Power.

A horrible, selfish idea percolates, mixing with my growing panic. But before I can take a breath, think things through, Ms al Abbas begins her let-down speech.

'You see, Miss Truman, it's the belief of—'

'It's Moore, actually.' The crack in my voice echoes in the hallway. Out of the corner of my eye I see Thomas pause midstride.

Ms al Abbas frowns. 'I'm sorry?'

I try for a light laugh but grimace at how brittle it sounds. 'It was such a crazy morning that I forgot to inform you of my recent marriage.'

Thomas begins walking again. Faster.

The social worker's forlorn look morphs to surprise. 'You did?'

When Thomas is within reach, I grab the sleeve of his jacket, tugging him closer. 'Yes, this weekend.'

Her eyes widen further at Thomas, then drop to my death grip on his suit.

'My, uh, husband, and I were actually flying home from our elopement when the hospital called.' I turn enough to hide my expression from the women, squaring up to Thomas. 'Isn't that right, dear?' I stare intently at him, hoping my wide eyes convey what I need them to – *please, please go along with me, I'll do* anything.

His expression, handsome as it is, gives nothing away. As usual.

'*You.*'

Startled at the vehement tone, I look back at Miss Clatch.

She gives me a good once-over, disbelief written all over her face. Her first genuine expression since I've met her. '*You,* married *Thomas Moore?*'

14

THOMAS

'Do you know me?' I stare down the woman, regretting that I'm not as much of an asshole as people take me for.

Because if I was, I wouldn't be here. Instead, I would've given my lawyer Alice's contact information and let him call her for whatever else he needs to begin the annulment – even if she's currently dealing with family issues.

I watch the overly familiar woman in front of me turn as red as the blazer worn by the woman next to her. 'We met earlier.' She sticks out her hand. 'I'm Rachel.'

I remember the fake smile, but I also remember not giving her my name. 'Indeed.' I continue to stare at her until her cloying attitude melts away.

'And I, ah—' she retracts her hand, using it to smooth her hair '—just remembered seeing your picture in the paper recently.'

The woman in the blazer snaps to attention. 'You're Thomas Moore, one of *the* New York Moores?'

I fight the urge to react. I may hold power and sway in New York, but that doesn't mean I'm normally recognized in public.

I'm not a celebrity. I'm not my brother with his many Page Six exploits. But I *am* a part of a family that does considerable charity work, and a lot of those charities are youth focused. Which is probably why Red Blazer knows my name.

Rachel, on the other hand, seems more a gossip rag enthusiast. Meaning the picture she mentioned is probably from one of the many articles about the recent Moore family drama involving my father.

Which also means, Alice boldly claiming to be my wife in front of either of them cannot be allowed to happen.

Ignoring both their acute interest and questions, I lift the arm Alice has a hold of. 'If you'll excuse us.'

I don't wait for them to answer before stepping back into the hospital room behind us and closing the door on their slacked-jawed expressions.

As soon as the door clicks, I turn on Alice. 'What in the—'

'Shhh!' Alice raises her hand, two fingers resting over my lips. Though this time she misses my bruised eye, I still flinch at the contact – memories from our night together always close to the surface of my mind.

Oblivious to my thoughts, Alice studies the little girl lying in the bed. 'Let me check and make sure she's still asleep.' She tiptoes to the other side of the bed.

My lips tingle as I watch Alice peer down at the little girl who's laying on her side facing away from me. Over her dark brown hair, I watch Alice's eyes soften, her face transition from anxiousness to a mixture of concern and love.

It makes me... envious?

I brush the back of my hand across my lips.

'She's asleep.' Alice's words are whispered as she tiptoes back.

Shaking off whatever wayward emotions are trying to cling to me, I refocus on the task at hand. 'What the hell?'

She flinches at the harshly whispered question.

'You said, *multiple times*, that you would not tell anyone about our marriage.'

'I'm *sorry*.' Hands up, she looks as apologetic as she sounds. 'They were going to put Mary in foster care.'

'Why? You're her aunt.'

'I'm not her *real* aunt.' She glares at the door behind me. 'Not by blood, anyway.'

I continue to stare until she shifts on her feet.

'And since I'm not her relative I had to volunteer to foster her, but when you foster children, you need to meet certain requirements and—'

'A requirement is marriage?' My incredulity echoes in the room.

'Shhh!' She watches Mary for signs she's awake. 'No, the requirement is a large enough place of residency.'

My eye pinches as I frown. 'What's wrong with your apartment?'

'It's a small studio in High Bridge.' She rubs a shaky hand down her face. 'And fostering requires designated bedrooms.'

'Why do you live in High Bridge?' While not the worst, it definitely isn't the safest place to live. Not for a single woman.

Ignoring my question, she continues. 'If I use *my* address, Mary goes into emergency foster care. Even if I can find a suitable apartment, I'm not sure they'll revert her care back to me if they've already settled her somewhere else. But—' Alice grimaces '—if I use *your* address, my *husband's* address, there's no way they'd turn down my foster request.'

It wasn't what I had in mind when I thought she'd use me for my money and name, but I was right none the less.

'Please, Thomas. Just until Kayla comes back and can take care of Mary.'

I lack the confidence she seems to have on Mary's mother returning. But that isn't my problem. My problem is something my lawyer told me a little over an hour ago. 'The basis of the annulment is that we were not in our right minds when the marriage occurred.'

She raises her fingers toward my mouth again, this time looking furtively over *my* shoulder where the police officer and social workers wait.

Reluctantly, I lower my voice but keep my distance. 'If our marriage is recorded on legal documents and you register my address as yours, our reason for annulment won't look as reasonable. It will probably mean we'd need a divorce.'

'That's fine.' She shoots more glances at the door. 'Doesn't matter.'

I will my shoulders to relax. 'It might not matter to you, but it matters to me.'

Her teeth press into her lower lip, like a last-ditch effort to keep herself in control. 'If you want me to sign the post-nuptial agreement, then this is what I require.'

Ice seeps into my veins. 'Is that so?' Even to my own ears, I sound menacing.

Swallowing, Alice holds her ground. 'Yes.'

'Do you honestly think you could win against me in a court of law?'

She shrugs, trying to play it off, but I catch her hands shaking.

Although I recognize she's desperate, I don't like being cornered, especially not by someone who promised me they wouldn't.

Her bravado doesn't last long. 'Please.' She reaches out and grabs my hand. 'I'll do anything.'

Maybe I *am* as much of an asshole as others think I am. Because only an asshole would have such a cruel idea and then let it take root in their mind. Only an asshole would make a woman in duress pay such an unfair price.

If I were to say no to her little scheme right now and follow through with the annulment as planned, we would cease to be legally tied – whether she signed a post-nuptial agreement or not. With my legal resources and the fact that both of us were too drunk to even remember getting married, there is no way I wouldn't be awarded an annulment. The Moore family assets would be safe, and I could minimize any publicity hit the family may take from my actions with the help of my lawyer and a public relations team.

However, due to my promise to Bell about ensuring Alice's job, I can't fire her. Annulled, I'd still have to see her at work.

'If I do this, you owe me. Whatever I say goes in addition to the NDA and post-nuptial agreement my lawyer will draw up.'

She nods so fast I wonder if she even hears me.

'Fine then.' I consign myself to being an asshole. To using her moment of weakness to regain control. 'I'll have my lawyer draw up the paperwork.'

Alice hugs me, causing me to stumble back into the door with a bang, my arms instinctively wrapping around her, holding her to me.

Just so she doesn't fall. No other reason.

A second later the door hits me in the back.

'Everything okay in here?' The social worker smiles wide as she pushes herself into the room. 'I have paperwork for you both to sign.'

* * *

Alice

'We should be there in a few minutes, Mr Moore, sir.'

Thomas's chauffeur seems to have gotten over his shock of meeting his boss at the hospital entrance with two women and an six-year-old girl in tow.

I have not. Gotten over my shock, that is. Over Thomas, Kayla, my job.

I angle my head toward Mary who's leaning against the window while hugging the stuffed cat I bought her at the hospital gift shop before we left. It was a lame attempt to make her feel better about her mother not returning, but she seems to like it.

After making the deal with Thomas, we signed paperwork that would release Mary into our care.

Contrary to what I would've guessed, Mary hadn't shown much reaction to being told about my marriage. She took it a lot better than I had.

Instead, and maybe this was because of her recent stay at a shelter, her eyes *had* lit up when Thomas mentioned she'd have her own room. Now those eyes are at half-mast, the nap she took in the hospital not having done much to make up for the loss of sleep from the night before.

I feel her pain. My eyes feel dry and itchy, but the hum of anxiety keeps them wide and alert.

As soon as the ink was dry, Ms al Abbas insisted on accompanying us to Thomas's house 'to get the pesky home check out of the way'. So now I'm wedged between Mary and Thomas –

my right leg flush alongside his left while the social worker rides shotgun.

Minutes feel like hours as New York crawls past us in Sunday traffic.

'I promise—' I barely breathe as I talk to Thomas out the side of my mouth '—as soon as Kayla returns and Mary is safely cared for, we'll leave.'

Eyes forward, I see the bruised skin around his eye stretch as his brow arches. '*If* she returns.'

'What do you mean, "if"?' The usual defensiveness I get about Kayla or Mary fails to reach its normal vehement peaks, but I still can't help the sharpening of my tone.

Ms al Abbas's head jerks to the left at my voice, apparently now discernible from the front seat.

I feign interest in the passing traffic, pulling Mary toward me in a hug.

After a few minutes of silence, Mary's eyes close completely and Ms al Abbas continues her conversation with Brian, the driver, about pesky New York traffic.

'This is temporary.' I whisper once more, smoothing the hair off Mary's face. 'Kayla sometimes acts rashly, but she'll come to her senses soon.'

I'm not sure if I'm trying to convince him or myself at this point.

'Here we are, sir.' Brian pulls alongside the sidewalk in front of a massive, whitewashed brick house. I've taken walks in Central Park many times – a free form of entertainment in an expensive city – and I always wondered who would be lucky enough to have such an expansive amount of green in their backyard smack in the middle of Manhattan.

No surprise that the lucky person is Thomas.

Except it's his front yard, the park and house separated by a well-kept, tree-lined sidewalk and a two-lane road.

'Thank you, Brian.' Thomas opens the door, holding it open for me as Brian strides around the vehicle to do the same for Ms. al Abbas.

Unable to carry her, I shake Mary awake. Once out of the car she raises her head and rubs her eyes with the hand not holding her stuffed animal. 'Which window is yours?'

Thomas and I follow her gaze at his multi-level and five window wide house. Everything about the classic architecture screams old money – with the contrasting royal blue door and brass door knocker is a little unexpected.

A house to match its owner.

'All of them.' Thomas's tone as brisk as ever.

Mary's already large eyes widen. 'Which is *my* window then?'

'Your window faces the backyard.'

'There's a *yard*?' She stares at him, excitement driving all traces of sleepiness from her eyes. 'How big?'

Thomas gestures to Brian to open the trunk. 'Not big.'

'Is there a swing?'

'No.'

Her small chest heaves in disappointment, then she pats his arm as if consoling him. 'That's okay.'

His impassive expression falls, as if affronted someone found fault with his home.

I step between him and Mary, not wanting his conde-scending attitude to hurt her feelings.

Ms al Abbas smiles back, ending my amusement with a new flood of anxiety and guilt.

Thomas clears his throat, pointing over the roof of the car, directing Mary's attention across the street. 'There's probably a swing in that park.'

Mary tugs on the end of his suit sleeve. 'Will you take me?'

Thomas stares at her, a frown making his eye look more menacing than usual. 'Where?'

Mary seemingly unaffected, points to the park as Thomas had.

Thomas's eyes flick across the street and back again, frown still in place. 'To the park?'

She nods, staring at him expectantly.

Thankfully, Brian steps up beside us with my duffle and I move forward to take it, saving Thomas from having to let Mary down in front of an audience. 'Here, Brian.' I hold my arm out. 'I'll take that.'

Brian keeps it at his side, but he smiles as if thanking me for the gesture. 'That's alright, Mrs Moore. I'll take it in for you.'

It takes me a minute to realize he's talking to me, and when I do, I choke on my next breath.

'Isn't this *beautiful*.' Ms al Abbas, as if forgetting her true purpose – the child – seems oblivious to everything except the house in front of her. 'I bet the inside is even *more* impressive.'

Thomas's eye ticks. I'd like to think it's from his injury, but I'm betting it's a rare tell indicating that he's reached his limit.

Then again, maybe I'm wrong, because he inclines his head at the social worker's compliment and gestures her ahead before following behind as she crosses the sidewalk and fairly hops up the front steps.

I wrap the arm outstretched for my bag around Mary and walk behind them.

'Wow.' Ms al Abbas voice echoes as Mary and I enter the foyer.

Mary, also awestruck at the twenty-eight-foot-high ceilings, the three-tiered swoop-arm brass chandelier and original inlaid parquet flooring, blinks around the room. 'It's even better than the library.'

My eyes freeze on a mirror above a small table.

My hair, once smoothed down with hairspray for the wedding sticks out at odd places, even after I tried brushing it at the hospital. Dark under-eye circles stand out under the chandeliers, stark against my pale skin. And even though it's probably more expensive than anything else I've ever worn, Thomas's T-shirt is wrinkled and damp from all my nervous sweating and fidgeting, the large size making me look malnourished and unfortunate.

I'm reminded of the childhood game – what doesn't belong. If we were to play it now, the answer would be, without a doubt, me.

Story of my life.

'You have a pet?' For the first time since the name Moore was mentioned, the social worker sounds less than pleased.

All eyes move to Mary sitting in the middle of the foyer's Persian rug, squeals in delight as her cheek is licked by none other than Mike Hunt.

* * *

Thomas

'That is not a pet. It's Satan's sidekick.'

Four sets of eyes turn to me, the feline's the most judgmental.

I stare down the hall in search of its owner. Because if the beast is here, that means my brother must be too. Which will complicate my life even more than the stupid feline Eskimo kissing a giggling child on my floor.

Ms al Abbas, her previous look of awe having vanished at the sight of the animated sack of bones, steps back from Mike as if he were a rattle snake. 'I was not informed of any animals living in the residence.'

While everyone stares at the obscene creature, I move to the side. 'I can assure you, that thing does not live here.' If I can just reach Chase before he sees Mary and the social worker, I can blackmail him into silence. I have *years'* worth of material at my disposal that I'm sure Chase would rather Bell not—

'Why, hello.'

I freeze mid-step at the polished, lyrical voice reverberating from the top of the stairs.

Fuck.

Resigning myself as a man on the other end of a firing squad, I pivot on my heel and watch my mother descend the staircase like a Regency grand dame.

'Whoa.' Mary's mouth drops open as she catches sight of my mother dressed in head-to-toe cashmere and diamonds.

Only Emily Elizabeth Moore would be brave enough to wear a cream cashmere suit in New York City.

I pinch my brow between thumb and pointer finger. It fucking hurts, but I welcome the pain. 'What are you doing here, Mother?' Taking a breath, I look up into her innocently blinking eyes. 'I thought you were leaving for a cruise after Vegas?'

Unperturbed by my blatant irritation, Mother ignores me and rests her hands on Alice's shoulders, kissing the air on either side of her. 'Alice, dear. How *wonderful* to see you again so soon.'

My mind races, trying to come up with some excuse, some logical reason to manhandle my mother out the door before what I considered a decently thought-out plan to evict Alice from my life implodes into further chaos.

Mother's eyes fall upon Mary, then move to the social worker whose expression is back to worship-mode.

'Mrs Moore.' Ms al Abbas cuts in front of me, near sprinting from across the foyer, hand outstretched. 'I am *honored* to meet you.'

Mother glances at it for a beat, her eyes meeting mine. Then a slow smile pulls at her pale pink lips and I know two things – one, this is where Chase gets his mischievous side, and two, I'm fucked.

'Pleasure.' Mother accepts the offered hand only to have her slim fingers flashing diamonds that have nothing to do with matrimony and everything to do with old money heirlooms, encased in both of the social worker's.

Most people think I learned the business from my father. But watching my mother enjoy my discomfort as Chase would and hearing her invoke a million dollars' worth of meaning into that one word with a single eyebrow arched makes me think we've given my father far too much credit for who Chase and I have become.

Alice's wide eyes meet my own and I draw an infinitesimal amount of comfort in knowing she feels as ill equipped for this turn of events as I do.

But mostly I resent the hell out of this slip of a woman for putting me in this situation to begin with. The Moore most feared in all business dealings. The Moore they call an iceberg and a plethora of other cold-hearted names. All of them true.

Somehow Alice, with her innocent eyes, her unbecoming

haircut and her scheming machinations, has managed to do what the *Titanic* could not. She's sinking me.

'I heard you speak once at a charity event for New York's education project,' the social worker continues. 'Your donations and commitment to the children of New York is truly commendable.'

Mary and Mike blink at Mother and her diamonds sparkling under the crystal chandelier, ignorant to the many undertones surrounding them. 'Are you a princess?' Mary asks.

Mother's eyes widen and she laughs, stopping suddenly as if her amusement surprised even herself. She tugs her hand free from Ms al Abbas's cloying clutches and glides over to Mary.

Mike eyes Mother's many-faceted necklace.

'Oh no, sweetie.' The woman who graduated from not one but two debutante schools, squats before Mary. 'I'm not a princess.'

Only my mother can squat in ladylike fashion.

Bereft of my mother's touch, Ms al Abbas claps her hands together looking like Santa bestowing gifts to the masses. 'This is your new grandmother!'

The last word echoes in the twenty-plus-foot ceilinged foyer.

The only visible reaction from my mother is a slight pause when reaching out to tuck a strand of Mary's hair behind her ear.

It's probably only due to such stringent, well-mannered education that my mother refrains from incinerating the woman on the spot.

'You don't *look* like a grandmother.' Mary frowns while studying my mother's unlined face, perfectly upswept blonde hair and trim figure while absent-mindedly petting the damn cat.

And by petting, I mean shifting his wrinkled skin one way then another over his bones.

Mother nods, her imperial expression softening at the little girl's genuine compliment. 'Thank you.'

Silence follows.

This is good. People usually dislike silence in social situations.

I can use the silence to motivate the social worker to get on with whatever inspection she needs while I urge my mother out the door and—

'Mary's my niece.' Alice step toward the group on the floor, easing the awkward moment.

My mother turns an interested eye to Alice and the social worker smiles again.

'I'm watching her until her mother, uh—' she cuts her eyes to the social worker '—comes back.'

'And that's my Aunt Alice's husband.' Mary points to me. 'I saw them hugging in my hospital room.'

I pinch the bridge of my nose again. *Hard.*

Mother rolls her lips, as if redistributing her pale pink lipstick, then she stands with nary a knee pop or strain. Brushing non-existent lint off her cashmere trousers, the New York society queen smiles. 'Yes, of course, dear. That's why I'm here.' She turns to me, smile slightly more mischievous. 'To welcome you—'she points to demon bag of bones in Mary's lap '—and to bring you your *other* charge you promised to look after.'

As if on cue, Mike licks himself.

Fuck me.

15

THOMAS

Alice peeks around the corner into my den as I read the newspaper.

'Thomas?' Stepping fully into the room her hair wet drips onto the shoulders of yet *another* of my T-shirts.

'Can we talk?'

Since getting off the phone with my lawyer I've been sitting here contemplating my life. I've never really done so before. Never needed to.

A few months ago I admitted to myself that I had been complacent in my father's poor choices for too long and went about to correct it, but that's about all the self-reflection I've done. Everything else in my life has been as it was supposed to be. How I chose it to be.

Until Alice.

I lower the paper I had been trying and failing to read. 'Yes.'

There are things that cannot wait until the morning. The call with my lawyer did not go well – for him or for me.

After I informed him that I'd need to postpone said annulment or possibly change it to divorce proceedings I used his shocked silence to further explain that Alice and I were fostering a child in my home, or *our* home, as it will be listed on legal documents submitted to the state by child services.

In the resulting silence, I thought he might quit.

And when he did find his voice, I thought I might fire him.

We just finished securing Moores' assets from your father and now you *let in another threat?*

The only thing that saved his job was my acknowledgment that even if it was unasked for, his opinion mirrored my own.

I am at fault. For my father. For Alice. For everything. It took me far too long to take action and remove my father. I won't make the same mistake again. The sooner I remove Alice by fulfilling my end of our bargain, the better.

'Oh good.' Alice sighs in relief and steps into the room. 'I hadn't known what to—'

'What—' my eyes home in on the hem of my cotton T-shirt sliding across her bare thighs '—are you wearing?'

She freezes, her cheeks flushing. 'Oh, I, uh, after dinner your mother suggested Mary and I use your T-shirts to wear for pajamas.' She tugs the hem down, which is completely ineffective, before crossing one arm over her chest and hugging the other to her side. 'She must've taken the rest of my clothes to be washed because when I got out of the shower they were gone. Even those in my duffle bag.'

'Hmmm.' I shake out the paper in front of me, needing a moment to internally curse my mother and rein in the violate emotions simmering to the surface.

I spent far too long this afternoon watching Ms al Abbas fawn over my mother whilst my mother fawned over her 'granddaughter'. And while my mother's presence did ease the awkward moments when the social worker noticed the complete lack of Alice's clothing and toiletries in my bedroom –

'Well of course *her things aren't here. You didn't think she'd spend the night before they were married, did you?*' – to which the Emily Moore Fan Club of One took as gospel, I would've rather not have my mother intertwined in the complicated web I'm weaving.

More jarring was that she kept close to Mary, even at the dinner she had her personal chef bring, so I couldn't probe as to why she wasn't upset, or even surprised about my marriage.

'Wow.' Alice surveys the room as if just seeing the original marble mantel and half-wall of original twenties African Umbila millwork.

The designer I hired when I purchased the home wanted to paint it Pigeon Gray. I'd informed him that if he so much as neared the exotic wood with a paintbrush, he'd find himself with plenty of time to feed the real pigeons as he'd be without a job.

Alice drops her head from the inlaid coffered ceiling and assesses me in my wingback chair as if I were a part of a painting. 'If it weren't for your clothes, you'd look like something out of a Jane Austen film sitting in here.' She huffs a laugh, the awkward joke doing nothing to ease my turbulent emotions.

My eyes flick to her thighs. 'Edith Wharton.'

'Who?'

I force my gaze to her freshly cleaned face. Alice must not wear much, if any, make-up. Her lashes are just as long and dark fresh out of the shower as they are under Moore's overhead lights during working hours.

Something I hate myself for noticing.

Swallowing, I study the dentil molding trim along the wainscoting. 'It would be more accurate to say I look right out of an Edith Wharton novel as this house was built in the Gilded Age, the end of the nineteenth century, at the time she wrote *Age of Innocence*.'

'Oh.' Alice slides one bare foot over the other and I'm back looking at her legs. 'I haven't read that one.'

Remembering what she *does* read has me folding the paper in half, then half again before resting it on my lap. 'Indeed.'

Goosebumps spread down her arms, two hard points poking out from behind the soft cotton of my Mack Weldon undershirt. Why did my mother have to steal a *white* T-shirt?

In the silence, Alice's forced smile fades. 'Your mother...' The firm points beneath the white cotton rise and fall as she sighs. 'I was hoping we could tell her what was really going on once Mary was in bed, but she left before I had a chance.' In apparent exasperation she funnels her hands through her hair, the hem of my T-shirt riding dangerously high as she tugs at the dark strands.

I rise quickly, stepping over my newspaper shield to get to her. 'It's fine.' My hands encircle her wrists, forcing them down and therefore the shirt as well. 'I don't plan on telling my mother anything she doesn't need to know.'

Her bewildered gaze moves from my hands around her wrists to me. 'You want to keep lying to your *mother*?'

There's an emphasis on 'mother' that I don't understand but makes me think she believes matriarchal subterfuge is on a par with murder and theft.

'We haven't lied. We are married.'

'Yes, but not for the reason she thinks.'

I shrug. 'It's unfortunate that my mother knows at all, but after how well she took the news—' as suspicious as it is '—it's probably best to let it play out.'

She bites her lip. 'Won't she be upset when she finds out the truth?'

I release her wrists and step back from the temptation of holding her. 'Won't Mary?' Gaze averted from her tears and her legs, I reach into my back pocket and procure the handkerchief I always carry with me and hand it to her.

Alice's shaky fingers brush mine as she pulls the fine linen from my grasp. 'Yes. But it's just that I hadn't wanted her to have to lie in front of or to the social worker.' She bites her lip, as if second guessing that decision. 'I didn't want her to feel pressure or anxious about saying something that might jeopardize her staying with me.'

I feel somewhat small for being so concerned over how my actions made me look rather than how my lies would make my mother feel. But not small enough to think I'm wrong. Sometimes you need to make hard decisions.

I'm good at that.

'It's better this way.' For me or my mother, I'm not sure, but Alice, tears wiped clean, nods. I appease myself by remembering my mother is off on a singles' cruise that departs tomorrow. Even with her over-the-top enthusiasm and ready acceptance of my new bride and child, Mother won't have time to become overly attached.

And if I get my way, neither will Alice and Mary.

Tomorrow my lawyer will have the paperwork drawn up. Alice will sign it. The errant mother will return and all of this will be taken care of by the time any members of my family get back from their respective trips.

'Don't worry, Kayla will be back soon.' Alice, as if reading my mind, finishes dabbing under her eyes. 'And when she is, Mary will be so happy to have her mother back that she'll forget all about this.' She rests a hand on my chest, her eyes locking me in place. 'And if your mother does get upset, I'll take full responsibility. I'll tell her how it was all my doing and that you were just nice enough to help me out.'

The heat of her skin sears away my common sense and I wipe away a tear with my fingertip that the handkerchief missed.

I need to tell her that I'm not as nice as she thinks. That she won't be the one telling my mother anything as she'll be long gone from Moore's when this is all over. But the traces of tears on her face convince me to wait until tomorrow. That it will be kinder to allow her a night of worry-free rest before revealing the price of making me her accomplice.

She must read my silence as something more than kindness because she raises her arms once more, but this time to hug me.

I'm more startled than when she bashed in my eye with a purple cock.

* * *

Alice

This is the most awkward hug in the history of hugs.

And considering I grew up bouncing between various, well-meaning foster parents, that's saying something.

Thomas is holding so still, so stiff, I can't even tell if he's breathing.

It's endearing. Sort of.

It's clear Thomas Moore is not a hugger.

Or he was never given enough opportunities to know how to hug. Either option tugs at my already taut heartstrings and my hold on him tightens. A moment later, I'm about to pull away when his shoulders ease and his arms slide around me, drawing me close enough that I can rest my cheek against his chest.

My body rises and falls as he inhales deeply.

Contrary to today's roller coaster of emotions, I'm not usually a crier. I might choke up during a sad movie or sigh deeply at a particular poignant section of a romance novel, but I grew up knowing that crying never solved anything, so I never really did.

But today got to me. A few times. All of them in front of this man. A man who I may have blackmailed but whom we both know could've rejected my plea and walked away relatively unscathed.

When I'm finally confident I can speak without crying again, I tilt my head up to thank him once more. Though when my eyes meet his, I falter.

His expression remains as stoic and reserved as before, but there's a warm intensity that wasn't there a moment ago.

His head slowly descends toward mine, his eyes darkening, as if under a shadow – the brown iris black, the bruised skin around his left eye a mottled array of midnight hues.

Or were his eyes always that dark and I just forgot?

Just as I'm about to close my eyes and welcome what will hopefully be another round of the best sex of my life that will erase today's drama from my mind for a few blissful moments, he retreats.

I blink at him. 'Thomas?'

Clearing his throat, he drops his arms and steps back. It's like watching a curtain fall the way his demeanor shifts, as if he's entering a business meeting.

'This can't happen.' Hands now clasped behind his back, he

retreats even further, the distance between us growing a lot more than just the two feet of Persian rug between us as he collects his paper on the floor by the chair.

'Aunt Alice?'

My niece's small voice startles me and I swipe under my eyes before turning toward her. 'Mary, why are you out of bed?'

She tightens her hold on the stuffed cat in her arms. 'Can you sleep with me?'

My heart squeezes once more and I wonder just how much more I can take tonight. 'Yes, sweetie. Of course. It'll be just like it used to.'

Mary's face lights up and I wonder how it's possible to love someone so much.

I take two steps before Mary tugs her hand free, then pads barefoot to Thomas who's sitting behind his newspaper again. 'Goodnight, Mr Thomas.' She sticks one hand out.

There's a pause and my heart lurches, wondering how or if he'll respond. But then he folds his newspaper horizontally and peers over at my niece.

'Goodnight, Mary.' When he takes her hand in his and shakes it, very carefully, I release a breath I hadn't known I'd been holding.

Smiling, Mary walks back to me.

It isn't until we're in the hallway that I *think* I hear him wish me goodnight as well.

16

THOMAS

'Morning!' Mary's gap-toothed grin smiles at me over a massive pancake-batter explosion that covers my entire island countertop.

I lower the water bottle from my mouth and double-check the time on my watch. Six thirty.

I was up at my usual four thirty this morning, even after my erratic sleep schedule these past few nights.

Between my internal alarm clock being back in working order and a strange restless energy circulating inside my body, I took it as a sign I was well past due for a punishing workout.

I've been using exercise to exorcise since I was old enough to run. Family. Work. Failures. Emotions. All the problems that have plagued me throughout my life I've sweated out like toxins, until my body is exhausted and my mind is clear.

This morning I attempted to exorcise my biggest demon yet –Alice Truman.

It apparently didn't work, considering the harbinger of chaos herself steps out of my pantry holding a massive bag of chocolate chips that I didn't even know I owned, and the expression on her face when she sees me cuts me.

'Oh. You're up.' Her eyes look me over from my sweaty scalp to my lacrosse shorts. Shorts I've had since my prep-school playing days which I like to wear because, one, they're comfortable, and two, it gives me a sense of pride that my forty-year-old body measures the same waistline as my twenty-two-year-old body did.

'You've *been* up.' For a second, interest lights up her eyes, but it's gone in a blink.

Which is a problem because even though she's found pants to wear, my interest does not abate so easily, and I wonder how on earth I found the willpower to step back from her last night.

Her hair is in a messy topknot that lists sideways on her head, her oversized shirt and leggings, that were probably once black but now a faded charcoal, somehow combine with the smear of batter on her cheek to make one very seductive picture. And *despite* two long hours of weights, cardio and plyometrics, the two thin layers of clingy mesh fabric don't do anything to hide my reaction.

I step closer to the countertop. 'I worked out.'

Alice steps out of the pantry, her eyes focusing on my arms, exposed from the sleeveless shirt I'm wearing. 'Yeah, I can see that.'

Then, as if she hadn't meant to say that out loud, Alice turns bright red and pulls at the sides of the bag to open it.

'I hope you don't mind.' When she pulls too hard, a few chips spill out on the counter next to an open carton of eggs, a bowl of batter, and an empty butter wrapper – butter residue side down. 'I thought I'd make pancakes for breakfast.'

Mary, more color in her cheeks than yesterday, goes on high alert from her seat on one of the island counter stools.

'That's fine. If you need anything write it on the notepad by the refrigerator and my housekeeper will get it.'

Not meeting my eyes, Alice pours out batter in a large frying pan. 'Would you like some?'

'No.' Stepping alongside her, I procure my blender from the cabinet next to her. 'No, thank you.'

While Alice uses a measuring cup I've never seen before but that goes perfectly with my kitchen decor, I use my blender to make my usual morning protein shake.

Mary's bare feet kick a tap-tapping pattern on the lower cabinets of the island where she sits. 'Sit here.' She pats the stool next to her, her invitation troublesome as I'd planned to retreat to my den.

'Hmmm.' I remain still, wondering if I can ignore her invitation as I would if an adult had made it.

The little girl looks over her shoulder at Alice busy flipping the pancakes, then slides a chocolate chip in my direction.

It smears across the white marble.

'Psst.' Her little finger taps the countertop near the chip in case I didn't see it.

Feeling no choice in the matter, I pick up the chip.

When she pats the seat next to her again, I sit.

Mary's smile is conspiratorial as she watches me chew said pilfered chocolate beside her.

A few minutes later, and five more smears across my counter, Alice lowers two plates of pancakes on the island. 'Here you go.' One plate in front of Mary, the other in front of the stool on Mary's other side.

'Yesss.' Mary pumps her fist. 'Aunt Alice's pancakes are the best.'

I stare at the three, one-inch-high pancakes that are more chocolate chips than batter.

'Syrup?' Alice offers the little girl, holding a jug of imported pure Canadian maple syrup that some Canadian client gifted me and that my housekeeper must have stored on the rare chance I'd have her make me pancakes.

Mary takes the jug, drizzling syrup over her pancakes in a perfect spiral. With much more control than I thought she'd be capable of. Except just as she completes the last rotation her hand slips, pouring a Canadian tsunami of sugar over her three-tiered cake.

'Oops.' Mary sets the jug down, looking the opposite of surprised. 'That's what you call a happy accident, isn't it, Aunt Alice?'

Alice's mouth, having dropped open at the start of the tidal wave, closes with a twist. 'Uh...' Alice bites her lip as if holding back a laugh. 'Yes.' She pours a glass of orange juice and slides it in Mary's reach.

As if *more* sugar is the answer to this diabetes-inducing breakfast.

Mary pauses, a fork full of dripping pancakes halfway to her mouth, frowning at me. 'You're not having any?'

Alice responds before I can. 'He has his breakfast.'

Mary looks at the green liquid in my glass and shakes her head at me as if *I'm* the child making poor dietary choices first thing in the morning. 'That's not right.'

Mary moves her fork closer to her mouth, then pauses again. 'Here.' She holds it up to me. 'You can have some of mine.'

Three drops of syrup fall on the counter between us before I react. 'No thank you.'

Undeterred, she leans closer, touching the fork to my lips. 'It's good. I promise.'

Over Mary's head I see Alice's eyes widen in tandem with her mouth.

'I—' A mouthful of sugar and carbs is force-fed to me and it takes all my concentration not to choke.

'See?' Looking quite satisfied with herself, Mary stabs a bite off her plate for herself. 'Told ya.'

Alice's face is near purple from containing laughter.

With a drink from my water bottle, I manage to swallow the mouthful down. 'Thank you.'

Mary flashes me a pancake-stuffed grin.

I stand. 'Now, if you'll excuse me.'

Alice's amusement wanes to a frown and I take it as my overdue cue to retreat down the hall with my protein shake in hand.

A few minutes later, settled in my den chair, I can still hear them. Chattering about their day, pancakes and Mary's lament that Disney has yet to create an astronaut princess, because 'princesses can be astronauts too'.

And... I don't hate it.

My usual quiet morning of solitude has exploded with an abundance of noise and confectionary and yet I find myself nodding along when I should be reading the newspaper or checking my email before heading into work on a day I already marked off for vacation, thinking, they really *should* make an astronaut princess.

It's quiet.

Brian picked me up minutes ago and I noticed the absence of sound as soon as I slid into the back seat and he closed the door.

My knee bounces. Probably a reaction from my insulin levels spiking after just one mouthful of syrup with a side of pancake.

I replay the conversation between Mary and Alice that I couldn't help but overhear. Besides astronaut princesses, they had discussed taking the subway to retrieve Alice's belongings from her apartment.

It'll take three subway changes to get to High Bridge. Alice may have a few clothes with her from the Vegas trip, but even cleaned, Mary's pajamas have blood stains and the only footwear she had at the hospital were worn slippers.

It bothers me. Probably because, at least on paper, Alice is my wife and Mary my niece. Or ward. Or foster child. Well, whatever she is, I'm in charge of her. Responsible for her well-being. How would it look if a child under Moore supervision was sent outside in stained pajamas and threadbare slippers?

'Brian?'

My long-standing chauffeur flicks his eyes to mine in the rear-view mirror. 'Sir?'

'When you drop me off, circle back to the house.'

'The house?'

'Yes, I believe Al—uh...' I turn my gaze out the window '...my *wife*, will be in need of a car today.' Brian is one of the few people who know, and hopefully it stays that way as he's signed an iron-clad NDA upon his hiring. Something I need Alice to sign – stat.

There's a pause as he makes a turn onto Fifth. 'Yes, sir.'

Out the window I see a lot of men and women in business suits, each holding an insulated cup of coffee. Alice would always make use of George's high-maintenance espresso machine every morning. She hadn't mentioned my lack of coffee machine in the house, but she's probably just like all these workers, addicted to caffeine.

'And Brian?'

'Yes, sir?' He pulls in front of Moore's, the usual busy drop-off lane near-empty due to the early hour.

I grab my briefcase from the seat beside me. 'Wait in the valet section. I'll have the café bring you out a latte to-go.'

'Sir?' He glances at his thermos resting in the cup holder beside him.

'For Alice.'

The skin around his eyes crinkle.

I close the car door a little harder than necessary.

Brian lowers his window. 'And perhaps a hot chocolate?'

I remember the chocolate smears Alice was cleaning off the counter when I left for work. 'Yes, alright.' She should really try and limit how much sugar Mary consumes, but as the little girl is already sugared-up, a little more couldn't hurt. 'A *small* hot chocolate.'

It isn't until I catch my reflection on Moore's brass-trimmed, double front doors that I realize the skin around *my* eyes is crinkled as well.

'Good morn—' Raymond, holding the door open chokes on his words. I'm not sure if it's the black eye or the smile.

Either way I do not like how my stalwart, constant floor manager is suddenly tongue-tied over two things that are, yet again, entirely Alice Truman's fault.

Letting my expression fall, I make do with the slight pinch of pain and raise my usual eyebrow. 'Raymond.'

The older gentleman snaps out of his shock. 'Yes, Mr Moore?'

'Have a medium, non-fat latte with one pump vanilla and a

small hot chocolate...' I pause, remembering the demon cat '...
sans whipped cream, brought out to my driver please.'

Recovering quickly, there isn't a trace of inquisitiveness in
his expression or tone as he inclines his head. 'Yes, sir.'

Pulling out my phone on my way upstairs to my office, I call
a number I should've called before.

'Mason Investigations, Mason speaking.'

'Mr Mason, Thomas Moore here.'

'Ah, Mr Moore. Have you decided to find where your sister
is living?'

I pause, mouth open.

I should investigate Liz. Obviously giving her time is not
working. She may have shown up for the wedding, but she still
eluded my efforts to talk to her. 'Yes.' I nod to myself. 'Yes on my
sister but at the moment I have a more pressing matter to
discuss.' Ignoring the stares and double takes from my
employees at their various counters, I head toward the elevators. 'I need you to find one Kayla Rogers.' I pass a mirrored
pillar, as a light casts a shadow over the uninjured side of my
face, leaving me looking disorderly and unrecognizable to my
own eyes. 'And I need you to find her *now*.'

* * *

Alice

Mike Hunt is playing dress-up like a champ.

'Why, sir, you look so handsome.' Mary's voice carries from
the cat room downstairs, where she's been dressing and re-

dressing Chase's cat in all his various outfits, to my spot on the third floor in Thomas's closet.

I stare at my clothes hanging next to Thomas's tens of thousands of dollars' worth of suits, shoes and watches. Though probably unnecessary, I hung the few items I had with me from Vegas that I found in the laundry room this morning, on the off chance there's a surprise visit from Ms al Abbas. It was all I could think to do after I spent an hour calling every place and person I could think of that had even the smallest connection to Kayla.

Sprawled back on the chaise longue set up under the window of Thomas's closet –because of course he has both – I try to drum up enough energy to start the long trip to my apartment. It isn't that far away, but the subway changes required will tack on a lot of time. And I lack coffee.

What kind of man doesn't have a coffee maker in their house? He has fifteen different watches – I counted them under the glass-covered center console of this closet – but no coffee maker? I almost said something to Thomas this morning, but then I thought the less I engage him, the better.

One, because the man goes hot and cold faster than the Arizona desert at night, and two, after last night my new plan is to be as small and unobtrusive as possible.

I just wish my newly awakened libido would get with the program.

From what I remember – all sex, no marriage – my night in Vegas was life changing. Or, at least, sex life changing.

The morning after... not so much. Add in a confusing, yet passionate mile-high club introduction, and now I also know our chemistry isn't alcohol induced.

Which is irrelevant.

He is my boss. I am his employee. I am living here on his

charity/my blackmail in order to protect my niece. Any sexual involvement, although guaranteed delicious and mind-melting, would be unwise.

But the other parts of me – everything from the neck down – wants to junk punch logic in its dangerously thin and clingy workout shorts.

Why did he have to look so adorable sitting next to my niece this morning at breakfast?

'Purple really is your color.' Mary continues to play, seemingly fully recovered from yesterday's traumatic events. 'Purple is the color of royalty.' She giggles, probably from something Mike did.

Who would've thought a hairless cat would be such a good therapy animal?

'Wake up little rosebuds, wake up!' A posh, lyrical voice reverberates from somewhere farther away in the house.

I spring off the chaise.

The voice sounds eerily like Mrs Moore. But that's impossible. Because Thomas's mother is on a cruise, sipping cocktails and doing things billionaires do far, far away.

'I'm up!' Mary shouts, followed by the sound of her racing footsteps.

I'm up and running to the stairs myself, cursing tall mansions for having so many levels. I'm out of breath by the time I've sped down two flights of stairs.

I really should do more cardio. The word cardio makes me think of Thomas in his workout apparel this morning and, well, it's best not to think about that.

When I reach the foyer, I can barely see the inlaid parquet floor, it's covered with so many bags.

'A princess dress!' Mary jumps up and down in front of Mrs Moore who's holding up a lavender child-size ball gown.

Mike slithers between the bags, rubbing up against them. Black glossy bags with Moore's gold and green logo on the side.

'Mrs Moore?'

'Emily, dear.' She hands the dress to Mary who hugs it to her chest. 'Call me Emily.' She bends over and pulls a matching set of purple shoes out of another bag and Mary squeals. 'Didn't I tell you to call me Emily?'

'Oh.' I'd just thought it a one-time deal for the wedding. 'Uh, yes. Sorry, Emily.' I stop on the second to last step, too tired to navigate my way through all the bags. 'I thought you were leaving today for your cruise?'

Mrs Moore pauses while rifling through another bag. 'Leaving?' She laughs. 'Why would I leave when I have a princess to spoil?' Mrs Moore, *Emily*, unveils a tiara with a flourish.

Mary, staring at the sparkling silver half-crown, looks fit to burst with happiness.

Those better be rhinestones.

'And a new daughter-in-law.' Emily reaches over the empty bags to hand me a large full one.

Frowning, I grasp the bag from the bottom and peer inside. 'For me?' There's too much tissue to be sure, but I *think* there's a Chanel blazer inside.

'Of course, dear.' Emily claps her hands together. 'Now where did Brian go?'

'Here, ma'am.' Brian pushes open the front door.

My eyes pause on the two paper insulated cups in his hand and, despite my sudden flush, I fight the urge to bowl everything over in my sight and chug whatever they contain.

Emily starts grouping the bags. 'I gave my driver this week off as I thought I was going to be away, so it was lucky you arrived when you did, Brian. I don't think the taxi driver was in any mood to play valet.'

'Pleasure, ma'am.' Brian shuffles around the retail mayhem and hands me the larger of the two cups in his hands. 'For you.'

'Thank you.' I grab it as if I was offered a drink from the fountain of youth and take a long gulp. When the taste registers, I frown. 'How did you know my usual order?'

'Mr Moore had it ordered, ma'am.'

'Mr Moore.' I repeat the name slowly. 'Thomas?'

'Yes.' Brian smiles. 'And he told me to take you and Miss Mary wherever you need to go today.'

'Well, at least that's something.' Emily frowns and picks up another bag. 'I wasn't at all pleased when Brian told me Thomas went to work today when he was already scheduled to take it off.'

'Look, Alice, I'm a princess.' Mary, who pulled the dress on over her pajamas, throws her arms out and twirls, the skirts of her princess dress flaring out.

Mike Hunt paws the air in front of him like he's miming clawing at the glittery fabric.

Still feeling as if I'd been slapped upside the head by a two-by-four, I try to smile. 'You look so pretty.' And she does, the lavender striking against her dark hair.

'And now your turn.' Emily waves me upstairs.

'I'm sorry?' Thinking my brain needs more fuel to function I chug the latte uncaring of the burn that makes my eyes water.

'To change, dear.' The Moore matriarch raises one eyebrow, reminding me again of her eldest son, as she assesses my faded black leggings and oversized T-shirt. 'You can't go out looking like that.'

17

THOMAS

'There is no way that you and Alice leaving together was a coincidence.' Chase's exasperated sigh creates a buzz of static through my office phone.

So much for screening Chase's calls.

I've had his ringtone silenced since I left his wedding reception for the airport in Vegas. However, the temp filling in for George at the office today must not want to do anything out of her contractual 'answer phones, take messages,' seeing as she put his call through despite being told expressly not to.

Cradling the receiver between my ear and shoulder, I grab the mouse and open my email, scanning my inbox. 'Coincidences happen all the time.' Nothing from my lawyer. Or the private detective.

Chase snorts. 'Bullshit.'

Shifting in my chair, I try and ease the ache in the muscles I strained this morning. It's only a few hours into the working day, but still, ever since I ordered Brian to be of service to Alice and Mary, I've been on edge. It's probably remnants of my earlier sugar rush.

'Are you really not going to tell me?' Chase's voice takes on a hurt quality.

I can just imagine the toddler-like mutinous set of his jaw. 'You sound more and more adolescent with each whine and complaint.'

'I bet Liz knows,' he mutters. 'She was the only one not surprised when we all realized you two were gone. And then she left soon after before I could question her about it or ask her where *she's* been.'

Considering the poor acting job Alice performed in the hotel suite for Liz the morning after our drunken nuptials, I can't even refute his claims about Liz suspecting something. It's a good thing I had the private eye look for her as well. Best to know where all my ducks are so I can keep them in their rows.

Chase continues. 'And then you forgot Mike.'

'Hmm.' Forget? Left? Same thing really.

'Good thing Mom decided to fly home before her singles cruise or I'd have to kill you.'

'Tell Alice I said hi!' Bell's voice carries through the phone, as clear as my brother's.

I stop perusing the shipment schedule of the lights for the store's new display on my computer. 'Do you have me on speaker?' I *hate* being on speaker. Something my brother is very well aware of.

Chase pauses before answering. 'Maybe.'

'How's my baby doing?' Bell asks.

'Hey.' My brother sounds as insulted as he was for my reticence. '*I'm* supposed to be your baby, not Mike Hunt.'

'Aw, are you jealous?' Bell's baby-voice is followed by kissing noises.

For someone as accomplished and smart as Bell, I don't know how she finds my brother's petulance attractive.

I pinch the skin between my eyes. The pain isn't as sharp as it was yesterday, but it's enough to distract me from their obnoxious display of affection. 'Do I need to be here for this conversation?'

'Sorry, sorry.' Bell's voice is back to normal. 'But really, how is Mikey?'

I remember the beast's beady little eyes, so full of judgment from his perch on the stairs as I left for work this morning. 'Alive.'

Chase laughs, his earlier ill humor apparently forgotten. 'No need to sound like that vexes you, Tommy-kins.'

'Is he eating okay?' Bell asks, ignoring my brother's amusement. 'How about his bowel movements? We all know he doesn't travel well.'

My silence speaks volumes.

Chase, knowing full well how capable I am of dropping her 'baby' off at a boarding facility, jumps in. 'Babe, I don't think—'

'Did Emily explain about the litter box?' Bell continues. 'I wrote it down in the informational binder I had delivered along with his toys and bedding, but sphynxes have extremely potent bowel movements so it's best to...'

I'm about to hang up when another voice enters the phone call.

'What. The. Hell.' This time it isn't Chase exasperated, but George.

I sigh, equally as piqued. 'Just how many people are—'

'Why was your mother buying children's clothes this morning?' George nearly screeches. 'Are you guys pregnant?'

'Wait, what?' Chase sounds as shocked as I feel. 'No, of course not.' There's a beat of silence. 'Or are we?'

'I'm not pregnant.' Bell's voice is firm. 'At least not right now.'

A bad feeling grows in my stomach where the pancakes are probably still lodged, glued together with a copious amount of syrup. 'How do you know our mother was shopping for children's clothes?'

'It's all over the employee Facebook group.' George's voice is back at a normal pitch now that Bell's imminent birth has been disproved. 'There are pictures of your mother in the children's department buying princess dresses.'

'That can't be.' I pinch the bridge of my nose harder, but the pain doesn't dispel my growing sense of doom.

'I thought Mom was on a cruise?' Chase asks.

'She's back!' George's voice rises again. 'Someone just posted they saw Mrs Moore in the women's section with a woman and young girl.' George pauses. 'Ooo, there's a picture.'

My computer mouse nearly breaks in my grip.

'Who is it?' Chase's voice fades and I can imagine him facing away from his phone to look over George's shoulder.

'Huh. I swear I've seen that dark-haired woman next to Emily before,' George muses. 'Isn't that—'

I lower the phone onto its receiver with a soft click. Pressing the intercom I direct the temp, in a clear, direct and somewhat menacing tone, not to let any calls through except those from my lawyer and the private detective.

Then I drag my creaking mouse over to the internet browser and do something I never thought I'd do in a million years – join Facebook.

* * *

Alice

I've never been to the ocean before. But if I ever went and was then unfortunate enough to be caught in the undertow, I think the feeling would be comparable to spending the day with Emily Elizabeth Moore.

'I only got a few things when I was here this morning.' Emily speaks to me as she holds up yet another item of clothing worth more than my smartphone while I sink lower behind a rack of leather coats. 'Some fun stuff for Mary. You know, dress up things.' Finding some flaw in the clothes, Emily shakes her head and hangs it back up. 'So it's great you mentioned needing your laptop. Now we can get a few more things.'

While Brian drove us to my apartment, I made the mistake of checking my email on my phone and mumbling about wishing I had my laptop. Not only are the new marketing department hires starting tomorrow, but I got a confirmation email that the lights Thomas approved are being delivered as well.

Seeing as I'm not sure if I can go to work tomorrow since I have Mary, I thought getting some work done today would be helpful. What is not helpful is Emily's insistence that she and Mary accompany me to the store since we were 'already out'.

I check my phone for the millionth time – still no response from Thomas to my many texts and calls to both give him a heads up and ask him if he has any ideas on how to contain Emily once we arrive.

Mary skips over, her princess heels clacking. She's come to Moore's in full royal regalia. After putting on the 'fun stuff' that Emily brought to Thomas's this morning, she hasn't taken it off. 'Is there a bookstore in here? I wanted to read Prince a story.'

And by Prince, she means His Royal Highness Michael Hunt, who is being led around on a lavender velvet ribbon leash while dressed in his finest purple cashmere hoodie sweater, the hood folded back in such a way that it looks like a cape.

Mary and Mike are living their best lives this morning.

'Of course, dear!' Emily brightens as if the thought of spending more money is an excellent idea. 'Why don't we head there after your aunt finally agrees to let me purchase a few things.'

Mary smiles. 'Thanks, Queenie!'

And by Queenie, Mary means Mrs Moore. After Brian drove us over to my apartment so I could pack some more things to take to Thomas's, Mary and Emily had a discussion in the town car about the differences between princesses and queens. Most of which I didn't pay attention to as I was busy trying and failing to come up with a reason for both of them to wait in the car while I grabbed my computer.

Despite my recently caffeinated brain power, the discussion between my niece and my boss's mother concluded with Mary calling Mrs Moore Queenie and Mrs Moore exclaiming how much she loved her new nickname all while directing Brian to Moore's main entrance while I open and closed my mouth like a fish caught in the proverbial undertow.

'Mrs M—I mean *Emily*, you don't need to buy Mary any books.' I'd only conceded on the items Emily brought with her to Thomas's house this morning because Mary does need clothes. I only have an extra nightgown at my apartment and as we don't know which shelter Kayla has moved them into, I can't get any of Mary's things.

True, she doesn't need *designer* clothes, but I'm focusing on battles I might have a small chance of winning. Obviously the battle of returning to Thomas's instead of going to Moore's was not one of them.

'You can't honestly argue about books, can you?' Mrs Moore weaves through the racks of clothes toward the dressing rooms, following in Mary and Mike's wake. 'You should always encourage reading in children.'

'Yes, of course.' I follow, nearly knocking over a mannequin in the process. 'But Mary has a library card. I can take her there this weekend.' Shifting sideways, I turn my back on the sales counter as I pass a saleswoman on her phone.

She's been hovering around and asking if she can be of assistance since we ascended the escalator. Her name is Brynn. And while she and I have had multiple conversations over the past few months about the various displays in the women's department, she has failed to recognize me. I hadn't thought I was so forgettable.

I'm both hurt and grateful.

Earlier, I'd been right – it *had* been a Chanel blazer in the bag Mrs Moore gifted me.

And against my better judgment, I'm wearing it. My acceptance of Emily's morning gifts was the price for her silence on her eldest son's marriage.

I had to make up reasons like 'I didn't want to be treated differently by my co-workers' and 'Thomas and I want to tell everyone ourselves.' I felt like the worst kind of temporary daughter-in-law, lying to her while standing in my new designer outfit. In the end, though, she agreed. So I guess the pretense was worth it?

Worth. Just thinking of the monetary and emotional cost makes my blazer feel as if it's made from acrylic instead of delicate, hand-cut strands of white, blue, lavender and peach tweed, bouclé and silk woven together in an iconic fashion statement I never, not in a million-ca-trillion years, ever thought I'd wear.

Added to the blazer were rag & bone straight-legged jeans, Tori Burch flats, a Laguna Smith long-sleeve cashmere under-wire bodysuit and last-minute hairstyling and make-up appli-cation by one Ms Emily Moore.

Emily stops and turns, her emerald studs flashing under the recessed lights – an unusual and yet perfect complement to the silk turquoise blouse she's wearing with wide-leg cream wool trousers. 'Why can't we do both?'

'Both?' Lost in my thoughts, it takes me a minute to remember what she's talking about. 'Oh, the books.'

'Yes. I'll buy her a few books now to tide her over until the weekend. It's only Monday, after all.' Emily waves Brynn over.

Brynn speed-walks toward us in her Moore's black blazer and pencil skirt uniform. 'Yes, Mrs Moore?'

Emily gestures to me. 'She's ready to try things on.'

'Certainly.' Brynn turns her megawatt-I'm-helping-the-boss's-mother sales smile on me.

'Whoa.' I back up a step. 'Mrs Moore, I am not trying things on.'

The Moore matriarch pouts at me – a feminine version of her youngest son.

'*Emily*.' I take a deep breath, doing my best to ignore the interest on Brynn's expression. 'Thank you for this morning's gifts.' I rub one hand down the sleeve of my jacket. 'But no more, okay? We just came here so I could get my laptop.'

Emily sighs and brings one hand up to cup my cheek. It's gentle and endearing and so maternal I find my eyes starting to sting. 'Oh Alice, live a little.'

Out of the corner of my eye, I see the moment Brynn puts three and five together and comes up with the surreal answer to this morning's random equation. Her smile freezes, her eyes widen as she finally sees through my voluminous blown-out hair, red lipstick and brown smudged eyeliner that Emily insisted would look 'chic with Chanel'.

Then, like this morning's melted butter on Mary's triple stack of pancakes, her smile slides off her face. '*Alice?*'

I raise my hand and wiggle a few fingers. 'Hi, Brynn.'

18

THOMAS

I'm seeing red.

Yes, I'm agitated. Not unlike a bull being teased by a matador's cape, as Alice's unpredictable actions continue to make me lose all common sense.

But it's the literal red I'm seeing that blanks my mind.

'I love it.' My mother opera claps as Alice twists back and forth, assessing her reflection in the three full-length mirrors in front of her, sliding her hands down the silhouette of her body, the clinging red fabric so tight it doesn't shift under the caress.

I'm stock-still behind the sales counter some fifty feet away trying to remember how to breathe.

Ten minutes after joining my first social media platform, I pinpointed the exact location of my mother and Alice's shopping rendezvous thanks to my employees using their phones during working hours.

I'd make a mental note to send out a company-wide email about personal phone use during business hours – except my lungs finally kick into gear and now I'm panting like a dog in heat, my brain incapable of rational thought. A vexing, yet common occurrence when Alice is near.

My eyes rake over the scarlet virgin wool blend.

It isn't just the dress. It's the hair, the make-up, the reveal of the soft angles and curves of Alice's lithe body. Before this moment I hadn't realized that I cared about being the only one to see those curves.

Alice, oblivious to my presence, frowns at my mother in the mirror. 'I don't think this is appropriate for work.'

'What are you talking about?' Mother rises from her spot on the couch and circles Alice. 'This is a classic Victoria Beckham.' She gestures toward the painted-on fabric. 'A simple knit long-sleeve, T-shirt dress. It even hits below the knees. I can't imagine anyone having an issue with its appropriateness.'

The elevator across the way dings and a male customer emerges. It could be that the dressing platform is directly across from him, or the overhead lights make it impossible not to notice the eye-catching fabric clinging to Alice's body. But the man pauses. Much like I had. Dumbfounded and enthralled.

Moving to the left, I block the man's line of sight. '*I* have an issue with its appropriateness.'

Alice doesn't turn, but I watch her face pale in the mirror as I stride toward her, making sure to keep myself between her and the elevator.

'Thomas, dear.' Mother smiles at me, not looking the least bit surprised at my interruption. 'So glad you decided to bless us with your presence.' She turns back to Alice standing stock-still on the platform. 'Doesn't Alice look lovely in this dress?'

In the mirror I watch the man from the elevator move on to whatever his destination is, while his neck keeps swiveling back to Alice as he walks. 'No.'

Alice flinches.

The saleswoman clears her throat. 'It also comes in black and Kelly green.'

Her attempt at helpfulness is ignored as my mother rounds on me, hands on her hips. 'Excuse me?'

Now that my interference play has run its course, I feel the full weight of the three women's stares. Well, two, seeing as Alice hasn't fully looked at me.

Somehow that makes my anger feel petty. I hate feeling petty.

I straighten, smoothing down the line of my jacket with a hand as I try to regain control of myself and latch onto the word from their earlier conversation. 'It isn't appropriate.'

Mother closes her eyes and sighs. 'I don't know how I managed to give birth to both a notorious flirt *and* a self-right-eous prude.'

'It's fine, Emily.' Alice turns away from the mirror, her eyes cast down. 'I'll go get changed.' She moves to step off the plat-form but my mother stops her with a gesture.

As annoyed as I am at *everything* that's happened since finishing my workout this morning, it doesn't help that Alice is now on a first name basis with my mother. As if they're friends. As if this is real.

'How in the world is this dress inappropriate?' Mother reassesses Alice, whose arms are now wrapped around her middle. 'It covers her from her collarbone to her wrists to her knees.'

My eyes hit upon each part of Alice's body as she says it. By the time I'm able to look away from her, Mother's exasperation has melted to smugness.

'Ms King just purchased this dress a few weeks ago in green.' The saleswoman continues to be unhelpful. 'She's worn it to the store for work.'

Mother smiles at the woman as if she's handed her the winning argument.

I level my employee with a look that's made grown men quiver. 'That's different.'

Alice steps down. 'Really, it's fine. Please don't—'

Mother huffs. '*How* is that different?'

'Because I said so.'

'Who are you to say so?'

'Her boss.'

Alice and the saleswoman ping-pong between my mother and me.

Small lines form around my mother's eyes as they narrow. 'You don't go around telling other employees what they can and can't buy.'

'Um, Mrs Moore?' Alice backsteps toward the dressing room.

Her feet are bare. For some reason that annoys me further. 'Alice is different.'

If I was in my right mind I might question the sudden gleam in my mother's eyes, the mischievous bend to her smile. 'And just *how* is she different?'

'Hi, Mr Thomas.' Mary emerges from a clothing rack looking like a purple cupcake in a big poofy dress. A purple cupcake who seems to think the adults around her are a bit short on the uptake.

Never more grateful for a child's interruption, I incline my head. 'You may simply call me Thomas.'

Though, in true child form, instead of being grateful for the rare allowance, Mary frowns. 'What about Uncle Thomas? Since you're married to Aunt Alice.'

Grateful feelings evaporate like steam as my temper boils and silence rings out over the sales floor.

I swear I see the saleswoman's fingers twitch near her pocket, as if yearning for her phone so she can toss the first stone to start the inevitable avalanche of gossip that my statement will cause.

Oblivious to the bomb she just set off, Mary points to her feet. 'Look, Thomas. Mike Hunt is a prince!'

The saleswoman chokes.

The devil cat, emerges from under the ballgown, looking squinty-eyed and aggrieved in his purple hooded sweater, his collar attached to a lavender velvet ribbon tied around Mary's waist.

'Mary, sweetie.' Mother brushes an errant strand of hair back behind the little girl's tiara, looking every bit as maternal as she was never able to be with me due to my father's interference. 'Remember Mike's new title?'

'Oh yeah.' Mary squats down and picks up the purple monstrosity under his front legs with a grunt – his two back legs and male parts dangling in the air-conditioning. 'He's Prince Michael, now.'

Frustrated and angry, my voice comes out sharper than I intended. 'That's ridiculous.'

Mary's face falls. Mother's is etched in disappointment.

'You.' Alice, finally meeting my eyes, burns a hole through me with their ferocity. 'Come with me.'

Not waiting for me to acquiesce, Alice grabs my forearm and pulls me into the hall toward the dressing rooms. Finding the large one at the end, she pushes me inside, slamming the door and resting both hands on her hips.

Her very clearly defined hips.

'I get that you're mad.' Her eyes, rimmed with eyeliner, shimmer with rage. 'I knew it as soon as you walked over like you were on the warpath.'

Shifting my gaze to the mirror, I find my expression is as dark as the slash of bruising around my eye.

She jabs in me in the chest. 'But I don't care how mad you are, you do *not* talk to my niece like that.'

The stab of guilt about Mary forces me to counter-attack. 'What are you even doing here? And with Mary and my mother?'

Lips that match the red of her dress turn down.

'Listen, I did *not* want to come here. But seeing as *you*—' she jabs me again '—didn't want to tell your mother the truth, I couldn't figure out a way to say no.'

The bruising around my eye throbs as does the spot on my chest she keeps poking. 'If that's true you should've at least called and let me know.'

She grabs a Chanel jacket laid out on the dressing room's chair and rummages through its pockets. Rising, she thrusts her cell phone in my face. 'Oh, you mean the twelve calls and eights texts I sent that you never answered?'

Damn it. My teeth clack together, increasing the pain in my face. I'd put my phone screen down with the ringer off on my desk. A failed attempt to ignore Chase's onslaught attempt at communication.

Alice's nostrils flare and it hits me that I've never seen her so upset. 'Everything was fine until you showed up acting like a raging bull. If you had just ignored us we'd be gone by now.'

'So this is my fault?' I'm drawn back to Alice and her mascara-thickened eyelashes. Her make-up agitates me in a way her dress doesn't. I can't pinpoint it, which only agitates me further. 'It isn't enough that you promised an annulment then blackmailed me into staying married. *Now* you're breaking your word about not wanting my money by buying a whole new wardrobe.' I advance a step, bringing us an inch apart. 'You say one thing then do another.'

Instead of backing down, Alice rises on her bare tiptoes trying to get eye-to-eye with me. 'You're one to talk. First you act like sleeping with me was beneath you, then make out with my nipples on an airplane.' Her chest, clearly defined beneath the tight, thin fabric, rises and falls in rapid succession.

'Yes, well, around you I'm racking up a lot of regrets.'

There's a stunned silence as Alice's cheeks heat to the color of her dress. The expression on her face more painful than the throbbing around my eye.

'I...' Words fail me as I watch her wide eyes narrow and her hands curl around the lapels of my jacket.

'Regrets, huh?' She pulls herself against me, my body relishing her touch, absorbing her heat. 'Then what's one more?'

And just as the portent of personal disorder I believe her to be, Alice slams her lips to mine.

Even as surprised as I am by the near-violent kiss, it doesn't take me but a second to fall into the embrace. To remember the way small pants of breath escape her mouth as I tilt my head to deepen the kiss. The soft moan when I palm her ass with both hands and thrust my body against her.

No panty lines. She's either wearing a thong or nothing at all under this scrap of fabric labeled a dress. Either scenario is enough to have me backing her against the wall and tugging fabric until I can wedge my knee between her legs and press.

The steady undercurrent of anger in our embrace ignites into something else as her hands stop pulling my jacket toward her and start pushing it off me.

Once it's off, her body is that much closer to mine. But not close enough.

Still pressing my thigh against her core, I pull the dress up further until the sight of her bare ass in the mirror behind her and her pussy riding my wool trousers bring me to my knees.

Literally.

I hook one leg over my shoulders, her thatch of dark curls centimeters away.

'T-Thomas, I—ah!'

I taste her. Lick her. Devour her as she has my ability to think and behave rationally.

My tongue laves at her clit, tasting sweeter than any diabetic disaster pancakes ever could. *This* is what I crave. *This* is what I've been fighting against for so long.

Her fingers grip my hair, moving my face closer against her. The leg still standing shakes until it freezes, all her muscles tighten along with her fingers in my hair. Her moan the sexiest thing I've ever heard.

Before she can come down, before she can even open her eyes, I'm up, unbuckling my belt ready to thrust inside her. Pump her full of my agitation, all the chaos and mayhem she's imbued into my life. Become the unchecked man she makes me feel.

I shift, ready to lift her by her ass and—

'Mr Moore?'

I freeze, cock in hand, as Alice's eye flare open.

'I was just wondering if you wanted me to bring the other dresses that I mentioned?' The saleswoman prattles on as a bead of sweat trails down my temple.

Alice's gaze flicks from the closed dressing room door to my hand wrapped around my dick that's pointing right at the apex of her thighs.

Over her shoulder, my eyes are dilated, my hair wild, my lips swollen and glistening from her orgasm.

Closing my eyes from the evidence of my failure, I take a breath. Roll my shoulders back. Then slowly, methodically, I tuck myself back into my trousers, muffling the clinking of the belt with my hand.

'Mr Moore?' A soft knock. 'Alice?'

'No.' I clear the passion out of my throat. 'We're done here.'

Alice flinches as she did earlier on the platform. Now is the time I should tell her the price of my regrettable decision to help her. Solidify her hate for me. Finally make it easy to walk away when all of... *this* is over and done.

However, I'm very conscious of the eavesdropping saleswoman outside the dressing room door. So rather than finally put an end to whatever this is, I'm forced to grab my jacket from the floor while ignoring Alice's stunned expression and half-naked body and shrug it on.

Then, without a word, I unlock the door and leave. Ignoring the saleswoman on her phone and my mother whose smile vanishes as I stalk past her sitting on the couch with Mary and Mike Hunt.

On my way to the office, my lawyer calls.

19

THOMAS

'What do you mean we're not married?' I place my phone, full of texts from my brother on my desk. Texts that alternate between asking about my marriage to Alice, which is all over the Moore's Facebook Group page, and gifs – the last one of a cat with throbbing heart eyes.

'I mean exactly that.' Henry Farrier, a senior partner at Fielding & Church law firm, leans back in the chair opposite my desk, resting his ankle on his knee. He looks quite pleased with himself.

He could be pleased with the post-nuptial agreement he delivered for Alice to sign, or the announcement he just made, but my money is on his sly smile being due to his 'unavailability' to talk until after office hours were over.

But seeing as I was already working overtime on another issue, if his late appointment was a form of petty revenge for me having him work on Sunday, the joke's on him.

'You and Alice Truman are not married.' The light from my desk lamp makes his veneers glow.

As I let his words sink in, I can't help but study the older man. I'm pretty sure he's only about ten years older than me, but, ironically, with all the work he's had done, it seems more like twenty.

Hair plugs are never a good look.

Shaking off my judgments, I gesture for him to continue. 'Explain.'

He chuckles, the sparse, military-like rows of hair falling across his pate. 'It seems you haven't discovered how the marriage process works in Nevada since coming home on Sunday.'

Yes. It's definitely pettiness that has him smiling.

He's right, though. I should've looked into it. I should've been calling the hotel, checking with the concierge to see if I ordered a car at some point, and if not, asking for security footage to find out what seedy chapel we must've walked to.

However, my time has been spent at a hospital in the midst of an employee's soap opera family drama which led me to kowtowing to an effusive social worker and opening my home to an orphan and her aunt like I was Daddy Warbucks. And today I spent the working hours trying to manage little orphan Annie's slip-up.

At least Annie came with a loyal mutt. All I got was a hair-less demon cat.

Instead of admitting this, I stare at my lawyer until the smile falls from his face.

'Well, uh, what I mean is—' he uncrosses his legs and sits up straight '—it isn't as easy as people think.' He leans over and picks up his briefcase from the floor. 'See, you can't just show up at a chapel and get married these days. At least not legally.' Briefcase on his lap, he removes a manilla envelope from inside. 'You need a license.'

A vague memory of Chase and Bell running off to sign paperwork before the wedding surfaces.

'And marriage licenses are a matter of public record in Nevada.' Briefcase back on the floor, he slips a sheet of paper out from the folder and slides it across the desk.

It's a column of names starting with Molina and ending with Mount.

He taps on one he's highlighted in yellow. 'While I found Mr Chase Moore listed, there is no record of a marriage license with either your name—' he pulls out another sheet of paper, this one with names beginning with a T '—or one Ms Alice Truman's. Not in Clark County or in the whole state of Nevada.'

I frown at the paper, trying once more to remember details of my night with Alice. I don't remember leaving the room. Signing papers. But then again, I don't remember buying or exchanging rings and we woke with evidence of that happening. 'Could there be a delay in the filing?'

Henry shakes his head. 'Everything is electronic these days, and the marriage bureau in Clark County is open even on weekends.' He snorts. 'Man, I bet the night shift sees a lot of interesting people.'

His laugh cuts short and his complexion pales under my glare. 'Ah, sorry. I didn't—' He clears his throat and focuses on my fountain pen aligned perpendicular to my keyboard. 'Bottom line – in the eyes of the law, you aren't married, and you and your company's assets are safe.'

I stare at the yellow slash across the white paper until it's burned into my retinas. If my name isn't listed under my brother's, then what the hell happened that night?

'Good news, right?' He smiles, his expression frozen as if waiting for my approval.

'Yes... good news.' While I may want to second guess my

choice of lawyer based on his personal demeanor, he has given me exactly what I want. A way out of the mess I've made. A clear path back to my life pre-Vegas.

One without Alice.

So why am I not pleased?

For starters, even if he's correct, with what happened this morning, the entire store still thinks Alice and I are married. Which is why, at precisely eight tomorrow morning, when employees arrive and begin store opening procedures, an email will hit their inboxes. One with an updated employee handbook complete with a detailed section on social media professionalism and strict rules regarding personal phone use during work hours.

True, the new guidelines won't stop the gossip but the new handbook I spent most of today working on, and the email instructing George to shut down the employee Facebook group, should help mitigate it.

Henry slides out another stack of papers. 'The only sticking point is the paperwork you filed to foster Ms. Truman's niece.'

Ah, yes. Mary.

He lifts the top page of the stapled documents, scanning over the words and the signature I recognize as my own and grimaces. 'Because your signature is on a legal document where Mrs. Truman has listed your address as hers and then signed as Alice *Moore*, things might get a little... legally gray.' Spinning the documents toward me, he taps his knuckle on my desk.

My eye twitches.

'Since you allowed the paperwork to go through and are fostering one Miss Mary Rogers, you have legally acknowledged that you believe yourself to be married. At least, in the common-law definition.' He places both hands palm up as if delivering his final argument. 'Even though you're *not* married, each time you acknowledge the possibility or represent your-self as such, you continue to leave yourself, and therefore the company, at risk. Ms Truman *could* seek legal compensation.'

Alice would never do that. That's my first thought. But then I remember her dressed in Chanel and shopping with my mother this morning, so I keep that thought to myself.

'Are you saying that all the money I pay to have you on retainer would fail against a lawsuit that a woman with very little means *might* bring against me?'

'Ah, no. Of course not.' He leans back, as if completely unconcerned. 'I was just thinking of the optics, what with all that the company just went through legally with your father.'

'Indeed.' My fists clench under the desktop and my eyes drop to the drawer above them. Earlier, but well after making a bigger mess for myself with Alice in the women's department, I found a drawing in my briefcase. A drawing Mary must have snuck in my briefcase post-pancakes and before I made my escape to the office.

It was of the demon cat, sitting on the grass wearing a crown and surrounded by hearts and clouds. The hearts were blue, not pink or red and the clouds pink. I seriously question what kind of education Mary's had thus far to make her so capricious with her color choices.

Even so, her letters were neat and straight when she wrote 'To: Mr Thomas' at the top and 'From: Mary' at the bottom. And 'Prince Michael' under the damn yellow-colored cat.

Looking over the oddly colored drawing, my anger – aimed first at Alice and then myself – drained. And when I remem-bered Mary's earlier look of hurt when I so rashly called her nickname for the cat ridiculous... I can't remember ever feeling so callow.

I'd slipped the drawing into my desk drawer, unsure what

to do with it, and set about trying to make amends as best I could. Which meant working all day with Human Resources and making use of Moore's personal courier service seeing as Brian was busy driving the Moore women on their shopping spree.

Then I finished my workday by sending an email to my brother informing him of my marriage and that I would not be taking any questions about it at this time. I may have also vaguely threatened the well-being of his cat if he chose to ignore my wishes and try getting in touch. But that is neither here nor there.

Because if what Henry says is correct – Alice is *not* a Moore.

I find my usual mantle of detachment ill-fitting. 'If I choose to revoke the foster paperwork, as I believe you'd like me to do, what would happen to Mary?'

He shrugs, unconcerned over the fate of an abandoned six-year-old. 'Child services will figure that out.'

Henry Farrier is one of many exceptionally competent lawyers from his firm. Which, during the legal issues with my father, was what mattered when I hired them. And yet, right now, I'm thinking I need to refine my standards.

'That is not what I asked.'

He pauses at my tone, which isn't as impassive as it was a moment ago.

He adopts a look of pity, one that suits him less than his hair plugs. 'The child will probably remain with Ms Alice Truman as long as she can find a satisfactory place to live and retains her job.'

The deal was we'd remain married until Mary was safe from foster care. If I come forward now and say we *aren't* married, then besides the scandal and gossip, Alice and my deal is off. Whether she retains fostering Mary or not, there is no incentive for her to sign the contract, no hold I have over her to remove her from my life.

'Hmmm.' I turn my chair to face the floor-to-ceiling window behind me, needing a moment to think.

For once, Henry is smart enough to remain silent.

It's hard to see where the lights on the skyscrapers end and the stars begin. And the more I look, the more it blurs until my eyes refocus on my own reflection. So different than the one in the women's dressing room mirror just hours ago. My hair is perfectly styled, my tie still tight and straight. My suit, though worn all day, has barely a wrinkle. The only mar is the bruise on my eye, but even that is fading.

This reflection is the one I know. The one I'm used to. The one I could get back to if I just...

'Mr Farrier.'

In the window's reflection, he shifts in his seat behind me. 'Yes, Mr Moore?'

'I want you to draw up a new contract.'

* * *

Alice

'I'll hide!' Mary jumps off the kitchen counter stool and races down the hall as soon as the words 'hide-and-seek' leave Emily's lips.

I want to hug this woman. I want to thank her for being so amazing. For giving Mary much needed love and attention during such a traumatic time. For instructing Brynn to send everything to the house after I emerged from the dressing room some ten minutes after Thomas. For entertaining Mary while I tried to handle the deluge of calls from Bell, Leslie and George after news of the marriage circulated the Facebook Group, all of which I let go to voicemail and answered with, 'I'll explain later.' Which might actually be a lie because of the non-disclosure agreement I told Thomas I'd sign.

But seeing as I also want to cry on Emily's shoulder and ask her if her son suffers from multiple personality disorder, I settle for asking a question that hopefully won't give anything away.

'Emily?' I wait for her to catch my eye. 'Why are you being so nice to me? To Mary?'

She looks amused at my question. 'Should I not be?'

'No, I... What I mean is, I suddenly married your son and brought a child into his home. I'm just confused as to why you aren't upset.'

'Is it sudden though?' Emily shrugs, still smiling. 'I felt it was long overdue.'

I wonder if it's a Moore trait to be so irritatingly confusing.

Emily pats my hand resting on the countertop. 'While I may not have been allowed to be the mother I wanted to be to Thomas...' She pauses, frowning. 'No, I can't lay all the blame on my ex-husband. I should've never given up or backed down on being able to spend time with Thomas.' Shaking herself out of her memories, she squeezes my hand before releasing it to adjust the diamond bracelets on her wrist. 'But that doesn't mean I don't know my son. Know how stuck in his ways he is, and worse, how stubborn he can be when he thinks he's right.' She winks at me. 'He may get that last part from me.'

I chuckle thinking about all the 'necessary purchases' Emily made on Mary's and my behalf today.

'So where other mothers may worry when their child does something out of the ordinary, quite frankly I was tickled pink.

I thought there was something going on between you two. And, as I said, I do love being right.'

There's a beat of silence while I digest that. 'Um, why did you think something was going on between us?'

This time Emily laughs, as if the answer is obvious. 'I don't need George's Facebook group to know what goes on in the store.'

'But...' I frown, thinking back on all our past interactions. All of them clipped and full of tension.

'I'm ready!' Mary shouts from somewhere at the back of the house.

'Oh! I forgot I was supposed to count.' The Moore grande dame shoos me away from the island. 'You better hide well.' Emily covers her eyes with her jeweled hands. 'I'm pretty good at this game.'

Head swimming, I walk out of the kitchen barely noticing the empty bags and boxes in the foyer, trying to make sense of what Emily said. But between everything that's happened since Friday, I don't think I have the brain, or heart capacity to make sense of anything right now.

Arriving at the den, I look inside for a place to hide. Last night it contained a wingback chair where Thomas read his paper, and a side table. Though a stunning display of millwork, the rest of the room was bare. Not even a curtain to step behind.

Now, it's full of Mike Hunt's things. Apparently while we ate, Thomas's housekeeper removed all of Mike's things from the guest room to ready it for Emily to stay over. I shiver thinking of how Thomas is going to react.

'Ten, eleven, twelve...' Emily counts loudly from the kitchen.

Hurrying down the hall, I find a back staircase I didn't notice before now. Unlike the front staircase, this leads lower.

I circle a small landing on my way down. Being a New Yorker, I've rarely been in a basement. Besides my apartment building's laundry room, Moore's inventory room is the closest thing to one I've been in. In my mind, house basements are creepy, dusty and full of broken furniture and scary furnaces. (Thank you *Home Alone*.)

So when I reach the bottom of the stairs and find a state-of-the-art fitness center, I'm almost disappointed.

'Ready or not, here I come!' Emily's lyrical voice calls out from upstairs.

A giggle emerges from behind a large, grey exercise ball in the corner.

'Mary?'

Her tiara pokes out from behind the rubber sphere. 'Hurry. *Hide*.'

Hearing Emily's footsteps above, I hustle to nearest closet.

But it's not a closet.

Instead of opening when I push the door, it turns, spinning like a turnstile. The light from behind me vanishes and a split second later everything is red.

'Holy photos, Batman,' I murmur, my eyes squinting against the red bulb in the overhead light. The room is as large as the den above it but whereas the den is a study of millwork and sparse but expensive furniture, this room is cluttered with photographs hanging from wire strung wall to wall, with unfinished beat-up shelving units that look oddly like the ones in Moore's shoe room but cut down to counter height.

But while the dented and worn shelving may be jarring against everything else in this house, it's the photographs that capture my attention.

Photographs of skyscrapers, busy streets, pigeons, and street signs. I'm surrounded by New York City, but a New York

City I don't know. One that's clean and crisp and artfully composed.

Moving closer to the string of photographs nearest me, I bump into a stack of bins, like the ones from airport security, against the wall.

Steadying them with one hand, I keep my eyes on Mike Hunt. Or rather a photo of him with his head tilted back in exultation as Chase scratches under his chin. Only the forearm and hand are visible but the hand belongs to Chase. I recognize the couch Mike's on from his office. And honestly, what other man would pet Mike so affectionately?

I want to say it's probably the monochrome filter that makes Mike look genteel and suave. The black and white style harking back to a heyday of glamor and refinement. But really, only a truly gifted photographer could make Mike look that handsome.

Next to Mike is a photo of Bell, resplendent in her wedding gown, eyes glassy with emotion, clasping hands with Chase as they lean into each other and dance. In the foreground, Leslie's laughing. Though I remember standing next to Leslie during the bride and groom's first dance, I'm not visible in the photo as I'm blocked by Chase's shoulder. Which means the picture was taken on the opposite side of the reception venue from where I stood.

A light goes on inside my brain.

The pictures in Thomas's office, the pictures in the rest of his home. I always thought he wasn't in them because he didn't like getting his picture taken or wasn't present during the family events captured in them. But no.

Thomas *took* the pictures. My eyes travel left and right over the pennant-like banner of photos. There's one of Raymond standing tall and proud in the middle of Moore's main entrance. One of Liz, sitting in a window seat, reading.

One of... I suddenly can't breathe.

I hear more giggles from Mary in the gym, but I can't tear my eyes away from the photo smack in the middle of the row.

It's me.

I mean, it *is* me but... it isn't? The woman smiling in the full-color eight by twelve photo, with eyes twinkling as if she just finished laughing, is much too beautiful to be me.

I don't think it's low self-esteem, but rather healthy realism, when I say that beautiful is not a word I'd ever considered using regarding my own appearance. And yet, in this photograph, I am.

In it I'm wearing the baby blue bridesmaid dress, so there's a lot of skin showing. However, instead of looking how I felt – like a scrawny kid playing dress up, the woman looks like a model in a *Vogue* layout.

I vaguely register the door spinning open behind me.

'Wow.' Mary skips to my side. 'You look like a princess, Aunt Alice.'

It isn't until she threads her fingers in mine that I can look away. 'Thank you, Mary.'

'It might be a bit petty of me—' Emily moves around to my other side '—but I must say, I'm quite pleased that I'm not the last to know about Thomas's hobby.'

Mary frowns at Mrs Moore. 'Mr Thomas took the pictures?' She sounds as confused as I feel.

We haven't been back from Vegas very long and yet the pictures from that weekend and others are all freshly developed. Thomas isn't just working out when he wakes up before the sunrise.

Mary releases my hand to move around the room and study

each picture, stopping at a close-up of Mike in a Teddy Bear costume. 'But why does he take pictures of Prince Michael when he doesn't like him?'

'Good question,' I murmur, stepping forward to look at another row of photos.

Though not having believed Emily about Thomas having feelings for me, a small seed of doubt is sowed when I count how many photographs of his I'm in.

One of me at work, talking with co-workers in the shoe department. Setting up a display in the women's department. Even one of me focused on my work tablet while drinking coffee in Moore's in-store café.

I'm not dressed up, or even wearing make-up in the photos but somehow Thomas managed to make me appear radiant, even in the ones where I'm standing next to his vivacious sister-in-law or the always put-together Susan.

'Because—' Emily arches a brow '—despite what my son says, Thomas doesn't dislike Mike.'

For the first time since they met, Mary looks at Emily in disbelief. 'You think he *likes* Prince Michael?'

Emily laughs and pulls Mary toward her into a side hug, squeezing her tight before leading her back toward the door. 'Yes, believe it or not, Thomas only takes pictures of things he likes.' She gives me satisfied grin. 'Of people he likes.'

Finding it hard to swallow, I look back at the photographs. Besides the pictures of New York the people are all his family members. Liz, Chase, Mrs Moore, even Raymond, Susan and George – employees that have been with Thomas most, if not all, of his life. And me.

'Let's go upstairs.' Emily shields her face from the overhead bulb. 'This red light hurts my eyes. Besides, something just arrived for you both.'

Reluctantly, I follow Emily and Mary through the rotating door and up the basement stairs. It isn't until we reach the foyer that Emily finally stops and picks up one of the many bags on the floor – but this one full. 'Brian just dropped this off.' She hands it to Mary then looks at me. 'With a message that he won't be back until late tonight.'

'Ah.' I'm not sure if him working late is a normal occurrence or if he's avoiding me. And if he is avoiding me, is it because of what happened in the dressing room? Or something else?

Mary pulls out a rectangular package wrapped in Moore's signature green and gold wrapping paper. Tearing into it, Mary's palms slap her cheeks when the presents revealed. 'No way!'

I push aside the crumpled paper with my foot. 'What is it?'

'It's the Moon Landing set!' Mary holds up the box to show me. 'Look!'

Something slides out of the overturned bag.

Mary peers over the box in her hands. 'What's that?' She sets down her Lego set and plucks what looks like a purple belt off the floor. 'It's a collar.' She frowns at the gold, heart-shaped tag dangling from it, reading the inscription. 'Prince Michael'. Her face lights up. 'It's for Mike!'

She races off, presumably to find Mike and officially bestow on him his new royal moniker.

Emily looks after her and sighs, suddenly looking much older than usual. 'Due to the many faults of his father, and quite a few of my own, Thomas is not well versed when it comes to properly communicating his feelings.' She picks up another bag out of the pile. 'Even now, without his father breathing down his neck, or harassing him if he cares about anything that doesn't have to do with the store's bottom line, my son still struggles.'

I find it hard to believe Thomas Moore struggles with anything.

'He loves it!'

Emily and I glance up at Mary, who's leaning over the balustrade while Mike prances down the stairs in his new collar, acting like he's the King of Sheba himself.

On the last step he pauses, one foot out, as if striking a pose.

Smiling, Emily catches my eye. 'Pets are handled with love and affection. Things Thomas doesn't know much about.' Emily leans over, her French manicure scratching behind Mike's ears. 'But he pays attention to those who matter to him. To the people and things he cares about.'

I stare at the Lego set remembering Mary talking about astronauts and princesses this morning over pancakes. He must've been listening.

'So while he still grumbles and glares when he's unsure of how to act around those he cares about—' Emily hands me the bag in her hands, an amused smile making her youthful once more '—I have a feeling you'll help him figure it out.'

20

THOMAS

Most of the lights are off in the house by the time I get home. Just the ones on a timer remain lit, allowing me to get to my room without tripping in the dark.

Alice and Mary must be asleep by now.

A flare of disappointment hits me as I climb the stairs, making me pause at the landing. Shaking it off, I continue down the hallway, pausing outside Mary's door and chance a peek inside.

Just to make sure everyone is where they're supposed to be. Just to make sure there aren't anymore surprises like there were today.

Pushing the door open, the dim hallway light falls across the bedroom. Mary is right where she is supposed to be, in bed. She's on her side facing the door, the covers pulled up so high all I can is her nose and forehead. Curled up at her side is the demon cat, his eyes glowing yellow in the dark.

But who I don't see is Alice.

If Mike is here, then Alice must be in the other guest room. Creeping in my own home, I push open the next door. But instead of Alice and a bunch of useless cat toys, I find my mother. She's flat on her back, snoring with a silk sleep mask covering her eyes. If only the society ladies could see her now.

With the fourth bedroom made into my office, I'm left with my bedroom.

My steps quicken going up to the next floor. My heart beat a little faster. I refuse to think on why.

But when I enter my bedroom, the bed is empty.

More disappointment. No, annoyance. That's what it is. How can I regain control if I don't know where the people testing it are?

Tugging my tie loose, I head to the closet and flick on the light. Then just as quickly flick it off.

I give myself a few seconds to let my eyes adjust back to the dark before stepping further inside. The light from the window is just enough to outline Alice's sleeping form, curled up on the chaise longue. The one the interior designer said would lend an air of elegance to the wardrobe even though I thought it completely nonfunctional.

I remember thinking who needs a place to lay down in a closet? Now I have my answer – Alice.

She's wearing an old T-shirt. This one not mine if the small holes around the shoulder seams are any indication. New pajamas must not have been on the shopping list today. But glancing around, almost everything else was.

The formerly unused 'her' side of my bedroom's his-and-her closet is full of clothes. Even in the dark, the worn, older ones I recognize from Alice's own wardrobe, easily discernible against the new designer purchases. That and the dim light reflecting off all the dangling price tags.

Backtracking out, I grab something to change into before I close the door and do something I loathe doing – laying my bespoke Henry Poole suit over the side chair in the bedroom rather than hanging it back up in its designated spot between the gray houndstooth Huntsman and gunmetal gray Tom Ford – before crossing over to the bathroom.

Minutes later, standing in a steaming shower, I'm annoyed yet again. Because even the heat fails to alleviate the stress of my chaotic day. Not when my mind is focused on Alice, sound asleep in my closet with her bare shoulder peeking out from the neck of her T-shirt. Close enough to possess my every thought, but not close enough to do anything about my body's reaction to it.

Going to bed hard and hot is not conducive to a good night's sleep.

* * *

Someone is watching me.

I can feel them, their stare, as I lay on my side in bed, my consciousness slowly awakening.

And given my recent luck, it's probably a burglar about to bash my head in. Hopefully this time, instead of a dildo, it's something more substantial that will do the job properly and put me out of my misery.

I open the eye not obscured by the pillow.

Not a burglar, but something equally, no, even *more* frightening.

Mike Hunt. Hovering next to the bed.

'Mr Thomas?'

Worried my mind has finally broken under the collective stress of the past few days, causing me to see floating and talking cats, I open both eyes and raise my head from the pillow. The demon cat is still there, but now I see it's being held aloft by Alice's niece.

'Thomas.' My voice rumbles like tumbling river rocks.

Mary steps back and Mike hisses.

Unused to being awoken in the middle of the night, or have anyone to speak to if I was, I fight the urge to hiss back.

Instead, I clear my throat and try again. 'It's Thomas. You can call me Thomas.'

Mary nods, still wary. 'Where's Aunt Alice?' She rises on her tiptoes as if trying to look over me, searching for Alice on the other side of the bed.

I blank, unable to think of an excuse for Alice not being here. A glance at my phone charging on my nightstand explains why I'm so groggy. Two in the morning. The last time I looked at the clock, right after I last glanced at the closet door, it had been midnight.

'Is she in the bathroom?' Mary looks behind her at the door to the master en suite.

'Yes.' I grasp at the excuse. 'That's where she is.'

'Oh.' Hugging the grotesque beige gargoyle closer to her chest, she pivots, toward the bathroom door.

Worried she might go look for her aunt, I clear my throat again. 'Did you need something?'

'Um...' She ducks her head behind the cat's. 'I had a bad dream.'

Probably due to my exhaustion, a memory from my childhood that I thought I'd forgotten surfaces. I think I was seven at the time.

I'd watched *E.T.* on the television before going to bed. Hours later, I jolted awake, covered in sweat from a bad dream about flashing lights and one long, crooked finger getting closer and closer. I'd laid in my bed, my heart racing, while each of the shadows cast by the moonlight coming through my windows morphed into evil apparitions thanks to a distraught, overactive imagination.

I'd been so scared that, for once, I hadn't thought through what my father's reaction would be, I'd simply run down the hallway to my parents' room.

They were still sharing one at the time.

On instinct, I'd approached my mother's side of the bed. 'I had a bad dream.'

Without a word she'd thrown back the covers, letting me crawl under them and cuddle close.

I'd felt soothed and safe, my heart returning to its normal pace.

Until my father woke.

Don't be such a baby. Boys don't cry. Suck it up, be a man.

I could tell Mother was working up the courage to argue but I hadn't wanted to be the cause of another fight between them, so I feigned bravery and left.

Mary takes a step toward the bathroom, breaking me from my memories.

'Here.' I pull back the covers, thankful I grabbed my pajama pants and T-shirt before closing Alice behind the closet door. 'Would you like to sleep here?'

A smile lights up her face and it does something to my chest. Breaks it, maybe just cracks it, I'm not sure, but I glare determinedly at my brother's cat until the odd feeling is gone, replaced only by the aggrievance of having my bed invaded by a feline devil.

I contemplate throwing him out until Mary kisses the top of his head when he curls into her chest after she situates herself under the covers. I swear the cat smirks at me.

Mike's eyes shut after a second kiss and Mary yawns. 'Will Alice be back soon?'

My brain, finally working at one gear higher than neutral, realizes the situation. I'm a grown man with a little girl in his bed.

'Yes.' I slide out of bed, Mike opening one eye to glare at me when the bed jostles. 'You try and sleep, I'll go get her.'

'Okay.' Her eyes flutter shut.

I wait until her breathing evens out before stepping softly to the closet door, not the bathroom door, under the watchful, judging eyes of Mike Hunt.

* * *

Alice

Mmmmm. So comfy...

Soft sheets warmed by body heat, a massive pillow cradling my head that fits perfectly into the spot between my shoulder and neck.

This is the best.

I roll to my side, curling my knees to my chest, sinking back into slumber.

Something hard and heavy drapes over me.

It takes a second to register that it's an arm before my brain goes on full alert.

Earlier tonight when Mary declared that she was fully capable of sleeping by herself, and with Emily taking over the other guest room, I had no choice but to head to Thomas's room on the fourth floor. The room Emily expected me to share with her son – *my husband.*

Up I climbed to the fourth floor, telling myself I'd wait for Thomas so we could have a much-needed conversation about *all the things.*

When I'd opened the present Thomas sent me along with Mary's Legos and Mike's collar, I was significantly less annoyed with him than before hide-and-seek – but even more confused.

Thomas gave me *the* shoes. The Kate Spade heels I nearly dipped into my savings to buy. Just the sight of the asymmetrical, oversized bows almost brought me to tears.

Because whereas Thomas may have overheard Mary talking about astronauts, and she'd told him Mike's new moniker, I never once said anything about these shoes. I stared at them. I fantasized about them. But I never actually said I wanted them.

And yet, he even got the right color – red.

Cut to me sitting in his bedroom chair, getting exceedingly uncomfortable as time dragged on while I waited for him to get home.

The bed being the only other seat in the room – and that seemed like a dangerous choice – I took refuge in the closet on the chaise longue.

The only problem is that the chaise longue is more comfortable than the bed in my apartment and the book I chose to read to stay awake did not do the trick. Thomas may have said *Dangerous Liaisons* was a classic, but that doesn't mean it's exciting. I should've stuck with my new shifter romance series.

Because I somehow find myself *not* on the chaise longue and with no memory of how I got here. And this time I hadn't had a drop of alcohol.

Dropping my left shoulder back, I twist far enough to stare directly into Thomas Moore's chest. I'm in Thomas's bed.

Something shifts at my feet and I jerk my head up, my neck straining at the sudden movement.

Yellow eyes glow in the dim light. I blink until my vision adjusts enough to make out Mike's body, curled up the foot of the bed under Mary's feet, who's sleeping on my other side.

How in the world did I get here?

I wiggle closer to Mary, thinking the more distance I have between Thomas and myself the better. But his arms tighten in his sleep, dragging me back, closer than before. Until my bottom snuggles against his groin. When I attempt to move again, Mike raises his head long enough to threaten me with a beady-eyed glare before resettling.

I lay there, stiff and unsure, my heart beating at a quick, steady rhythm. Minutes track by, though I'm not sure how many. Thomas's heat sinks into me as I sink further into the plush bed, Mary's open-mouthed breathing and Mike's purring snores harmonizing into an interesting lullaby.

Eyelids heavy, I can't help but close them, wondering how I can be so anxious and so relaxed at the same time.

* * *

'Morning, Mrs Moore.' Raymond, the ever-present floor manager, bows in my direction.

I turn thinking I'll find Emily behind me even though I know she's at Thomas's house listening intently to Mary's instructions on how to fold the best paper airplanes.

When I don't see her, I realize Raymond is addressing *me*.

'Oh.' I laugh awkwardly. 'Right, uh, good morning.'

'Congratulations on your recent nuptials.' Raymond is the only man I know who's more stoic than Thomas.

A few employees enter behind me, glance my way and do a double take. It seems Raymond isn't the only one who knows about my new last name. Straightening my shoulders, I smile. 'Thank you, Raymond.'

Even though I might not have a real family, I've felt especially lucky these past ten years to have the best work family I could hope for. Even now, with everyone looking, he's giving me his stamp of approval before anyone else can make a comment. And most people know better than to go against Raymond.

He nods and I move on, my new shoes clicking across the marble. Not for the first time since I rushed around getting dressed this morning, I second-guess my decision to wear them.

Because while I went to bed last night devoid of anger, I was once again annoyed when I awoke. I pass the Louis Vuitton handbags and curve left down the path toward the shoe department, my feet moving a little quicker.

Thomas left for work without me.

No explanation. No note or text. Just got up and left leaving Mary to explain to me over French toast that she'd had a bad dream. Thomas must've moved me into to the bed then as that's the only thing that makes sense.

I'm annoyed for two reasons. One, because as the queen of avoidance, it's extremely aggravating to have the tables turned. And two, with everyone knowing about our marriage and with George and Susan returning to work today, it would've been nice to get our stories straight.

Susan and George will have gotten home yesterday from Vegas. Which means it's their first day back at work. Meaning

Thomas and I need to have a chat about what he wants to say and how he wants to act at work.

And then there was the phone call I made to the police station, asking about an update on finding Kayla. *'Nothing to report.'*

I slide between two racks, cutting the corner into the shoe department, nearly toppling over a rack of Dooney & Bourke's with my backpack – the only thing I'm wearing that's actually mine. My work tablet and camera are upstairs in my office, but my notes are still stuck on the shoe inventory room's shelves.

I'll grab them and head upstairs to Thomas's office. I glance at my phone, checking the time. There should be just enough to grab a coffee from the break room on the way to—

'No wonder Alice was promoted.'

My slick new soles slide to a stop behind a pillar.

'Sleeping with the boss?' the familiar voice continues. 'Who would've thought she had it in her?'

Peeking around the corner, I'm disappointed to find the familiar voice belongs to Clarissa, my old co-worker. A woman I shared countless lunch hours with.

I knew this was coming – the gossip. But hearing it first-hand from someone I thought was my friend reminds me of fifth grade, when I overheard the little boy from the family fostering me tell his friend I kept trash in my room, even though he knew full well that the black bag I hauled to each new home acted as my suitcase.

'I know, right?' The woman Clarissa's talking to, whom I don't recognize, scoffs. 'I always thought Alice was a nice girl, but I guess it was all an act.'

'And you know it can't be a coincidence that the Facebook Group got shut down after everyone started posting about their marriage.'

'And now a new employee handbook?' Clarissa scoffs.

I hadn't thought much of it, but now, with Clarissa's snide voice in my ear, the email from Human Resources I read on the car ride here takes on a whole new light.

That was Thomas?

My phone still in my hand chimes with an email notification. The women look over, finding me within hearing distance. Their expressions would be hilarious if I was in a mood to laugh.

Ignoring them, I open it, a flare of excitement hitting me. Then I glance at my watch. 'Dang it.'

There goes my coffee time.

21

THOMAS

'Everything I was able to gather is in your inbox, Mr Moore.'

I hold the phone away from my ear as Detective Mason's voice barks out of the receiver, echoing in my quiet office.

After I carried Alice to my bed last night, situating her between myself and a sleeping Mary, instead of a night spent staring at the ceiling whilst laying at the edge of the bed as I'd resigned myself to, I dropped into a deep, peaceful sleep. I might have even slept past my usual 5 a.m. workout hour if the demon cat hadn't woken me by pouncing on my dick.

But as he did, I was able to work out and leave for the office before either Alice or Mary woke.

Clicking open my email, I skim the documents, surprised at what I find.

'Alice was in foster care?'

'Yes. That's where she and Kayla Rogers met. Kayla's parents fostered Alice for six months before they died in a vehicle accident.'

Jesus.

'It seems the women lost touch for a while before Kayla

showed up pregnant and needing help.' Papers rustle in the background. 'No father is listed on Mary Ella Rogers' birth certificate.'

'And no leads on her mother?'

'No, but I have calls out to all the shelters in a twenty-mile radius of the hospital she took her daughter to. I figure if she was drunk when the child was hurt, she probably went to the closest facility.' He clears his throat. 'The real worry is the ex-boyfriend.'

I click to the next document. 'Drugs.' Everything I read adds to the sinking feeling in my stomach.

'Nothing hard,' he continues like a man used to living in the gray. 'Pot, pills. One arrest, but only for possession, not for intent to sell.'

I'm silent for a while, trying to piece together what this all means.

I study the blue horse drawing on my desk blotter. The newest morning art edition that Mary slipped into my briefcase.

If drugs are involved, Kayla isn't going to be able to care for Mary any time soon. If ever.

'Our best bet is to find her before the police.' Detective Mason says exactly what I'm thinking. 'And hope it's only the abandonment charge we have to deal with and not anything drug related.'

'Then let's do just that, Mr Mason. Let's find her first.'

* * *

Tap tap tap-tap. Tap tap tap-tap.

It's uncomfortably quiet in the conference room, save for my fingers drumming on the table. Ben and Chris, Bell's employees, look half asleep. I've always noted that neither are morning people, and yet, as far as I know, they've never been late. I respect that as I, myself, prefer to keep to a schedule.

Usually.

The long hand of the clock above the door shifts a millimeter to the right, the small tick drawing everyone's eye.

One minute to nine.

Besides Ben and Chris, the three new hires, Deborah, John and Amanda, sit opposite from me at the long conference table. Alice is the only person scheduled to be here who isn't.

I check my phone once more, making sure I hadn't missed a call or text.

Nothing.

Her lack of punctuality bothers me for multiple reasons. One is that Brian checked in twenty minutes earlier to let me know Alice arrived safely and it's only a five-minute trip from the front entrance to the administration level. Two is that the new employees are eyeing me like a feral tiger, and Alice's presence usually has a calming effect on everyone. And three is that after my early morning call with Detective Mason I'm filled with restless energy.

Tap tap tap-tap. Tap tap tap-tap.

Just as the second hand touches the twelve, the door swings open.

But instead of Alice, it's George.

He tosses a manilla folder on the table then steps back to stand beside the doorway like a tantrum-throwing sentinel.

He arrived this morning rabid for the who, when and how of my marriage only to receive a formal letter from Human Resources telling him to shut down his More Moore's Facebook group which they classified as 'facilitating a hostile work environment'.

To say George has been eerily non-verbal and full of open resentment since receiving said letter would be an understatement.

My chair creaks as I lean forward and open the folder to disperse the meeting's agenda.

Chris, seated a few chairs down the table, glances at his watch, frowning.

I grab my phone, about to text Alice when the door opens, hitting George in the backside.

'Sorry!' Alice peers around the door, looking wide-eyed at my disgruntled assistant. 'Are you okay, George?'

Tugging his lapels down with both hands, George deadpans, 'Fabulous.'

Ben tries to hide his laughter behind a cough.

Alice gives George one last apologetic look before facing everyone seated at the conference table. 'Sorry I'm late.'

When she meets my eyes, her smile does something to my heart rate that my morning workout failed to do.

She's wearing what she normally wears – a black blazer, white button-down and a black pencil skirt. The main difference is that instead of her old Moore sales uniform, these items are new, designer, and probably hand selected by my mother during yesterday's shopping spree.

'The butterfly lights were delivered just as I arrived. I wanted to make sure they weren't damaged before they were signed for.' Her smile actually widens. 'They weren't and I think they're going to look amazing.'

'Speaking of looking amazing...' Ben makes an exaggerated pretense of looking her over. 'Seems like Vegas agreed with you.'

Chris jabs him in the side. 'Hi Alice, good to have you back.'

Alice turns her smile on the rest of the room.

I don't like it.

'Hi, I'm Alice, I'm the lead visual merchandiser and social media coordinator.' She gives a little wave. 'I'm really happy you're joining the marketing team.'

The new employees take turns saying hello and shaking hands before she moves to sit. And seeing as the only available seat is the one next to me, she rounds the table in my direction.

My eyes fall to the red bows on her shoes.

* * *

'Here's your Americano, Mr Moore.' The Moore's Café barista, the one who, just a little under a week ago, shrank at my presence, smiles warmly as she hands me my to-go cup.

Today requires a rare, but much needed, hit of caffeine.

Even for an accused workaholic, the past few days and nights are catching up with me.

'Thank you.' Unused to such an effusive greeting, I drop a twenty in the tip jar.

Her smile widens and she holds out a second cup. 'And congratulations.'

Instead of acknowledging the well-wishes, I stare at the offered drink. 'I didn't order anything else.'

Her smile falters. 'Um, no, it's for Alice.' She glances at the cashier who looks equally flustered. 'Alice hasn't stopped by yet, so we, uh, thought you might want to take her coffee to her.'

It's only now, nearing midday, that I've ventured out of the administrative level. I would've been content to work in my office all day if I hadn't felt it unwise to ask George to make me something from his Italian monstrosity of an espresso machine in the break room.

I'd expected glares, disgust and just-like-his-fathers from

my employees after the news of my marriage to an employee spread. Instead, I've been met with smiles, congratulations and free coffee.

'Thank you.'

The barista's smile brightens again. 'Have a nice day, Mr Moore.'

The odd interactions continue as I walk through the store. All but a saleswoman in the shoe department have no trouble meeting my eyes and smiling, some even venturing to call out 'congratulations' as I pass.

I've had more friendly interactions with my employees in the past ten minutes than I've had in the past year.

I pause at the elevator, vacillating between taking the extra coffee back up to my office and delegating its delivery to George, or simply taking the service elevator down to the inventory where Alice took Deborah after the morning meeting concluded and deliver it myself.

Seeing as George is still annoyed with me, I nix the idea of asking him for a favor.

I glance at the brass trashcan in the corner but decide against throwing out the latte. Even my small, rarely used conscience is vocal on its thoughts of wasting the barista's efforts and depriving an employee of their daily cup of coffee. Especially one who spent half the night curled up on a chaise in a closet and the other half squished between their boss, a kid and a hairless cat.

Balancing the coffee cups on top of each other, I open the employee-only door and walk to the service elevator.

Alice

. . .

I've yawned three times in the past five minutes.

Tying a piece of twine around one of the hooks I made from a paperclip, I pull it tight. Setting it aside, I stand and survey the twelve butterfly card stock pendants that are now ready to hang above the front display model Deborah and I assembled in an unused space on Moore's inventory floor.

Besides the handmade butterflies that match the various-sized lights that were delivered, we managed to find and assemble the correct number of mannequins that match the display plans.

Deborah had to leave to pick up her work computer and phone from the IT department, but we accomplished quite a bit in the hours after the morning meeting.

I stifle another yawn.

By now the adrenaline from waking up in Thomas's bed and then racing to work has long passed. The excitement over the new light fixtures has waned. And the energy accrued from the extroverted part of my personality (small though it may be) while meeting my new co-workers is depleted.

Smacking my cheeks lightly with the palm of my hands, I attempt to jump-start my energy reserves.

I could really use George's fancy espresso machine right now. Or a run to the café.

But seeing as George was giving off heavy 'I'm annoyed' vibes to Thomas, and I didn't want him to try and extract details over my marriage, I thought giving George space smarter than working without caffeine. My eyes water from yet another yawn.

I may have been wrong.

Physically shaking myself, I brush aside the cons of today

and concentrate on the pros.

In my youth, a foster care family I stayed with used to have movie night on the weekends. Always a Disney movie. *Herbie*, *Bedknobs and Broomsticks* and, one night, *Pollyanna*. It might have been that the main character, Pollyanna, was an orphaned girl who was shipped off to her rich aunt's house, but for some reason that movie stuck with me. And in the movie, the orphan who had nothing, would play the glad game. Naming all the things she was glad about to distract her from all the things she was sad about.

As I drag the ladder in front of the mannequins, I resurrect the game I thought I'd forgotten. I'm glad Thomas did not seem upset after seeing me for the first time since yesterday's dressing room incident. I'm glad that I caught his lips lift in a tiny, but telling, upward direction when he noticed my shoes.

And then there's my new colleagues.

I'm glad that before leaving for the IT department, Deborah showed no signs of annoyance over shadowing someone younger than her. I'm glad that freshly divorced with two boys in high school, Deborah said she feels like a new woman at forty, happy that Bell took a chance on her. I'm glad that is something we have in common.

When I step to the rung needed to reach the fishing line I'd strung over the mannequins, the glad game seems to have worked its magic on my exhaustion.

I should teach it to Mary. She may need it as there still isn't any word from Kayla. I know she isn't a kidnapped child, but I keep thinking about what I heard on the news once, that the first forty-eight hours after a disappearance are critical. That if they don't find or hear from anyone about the kidnapped child in that time, the chances of finding them go down significantly.

My legs start to wobble, and I realize I should've discarded my heels at the base of the ladder. I also should stop thinking about things that counteract the glad game.

Not wanting to climb back down, I tell myself how glad I am that I'm here, working a job I love, making a mock-up display that I designed. An unhelpful voice reminds me that Pollyanna fell out of a tree at the end of the movie and became paralyzed. I'm about to climb back down when a voice startles me.

'Don't move.' Thomas's distinct timbre rings out across the cavern-like inventory floor.

Whereas a second before I'd felt confident enough to climb down safely, Thomas telling me not to move suddenly makes it seem that much harder to keep my legs from shaking.

'What?' Too nervous to even turn my head, I address the wall in front of me. 'What's wrong?'

'What's wrong?' The soles of his shoes slap across the cement floor, getting louder with each step until I can see the shape of him in my peripheral vision.

'What's wrong is that you're on top of a ladder in heels with no one around to help you.'

'Oh.' The tension in my muscles ease now that I know I'm not in imminent danger. Annoyed at his interruption, even more so because he was right and I shouldn't have been on top of the ladder, I snap. 'You're here now, so can you hold the ladder?'

Without waiting, I stretch my arms overhead. From the way the ladder suddenly gets steady, I know Thomas did what I asked. Lifting on the balls of my feet, I snag the line with the hook and lower my arms. Carefully bending down to grab the top of the ladder for balance, I start my slow climb down, though I almost fall when Thomas hands wrap around my waist in an attempt to help me down.

Taking a deep breath – his touch unnerved me more than

climbing the ladder – I pivot to face him. 'I'm fine.'

He's frowning at the jauntily swinging butterfly above us. 'You are not fine.' He thrusts one of the coffee cups he was holding toward me. 'What you are is a worker's comp incident waiting to happen.'

Though extremely doubtful over what Emily said about Thomas not handling his feelings well, I pretend it's true and that he's worried rather than annoyed. 'What's this?' I raise the cup in my hand.

His nostrils flare, but he says no more about the ladder. 'Coffee.'

I decide he's rather cute when I pretend he cares. 'For me?' The look he gives me has me rolling my lips in to keep from smiling. 'Thank you.'

He grunts in reply before taking a sip from his own cup.

I quickly take a long sip, closing my eyes as soon as the liquid touches my tongue. Honestly, I'm more surprised at the coffee than I was about the shoes. The shoes were Thomas's wordless apology. I'm not sure what the coffee means.

When I open my eyes, Thomas is staring at me. 'Where is Deborah?'

'The IT department.'

'Hmmm.' He stares for another beat before taking a sip of his own coffee, looking over the lid at the mock-up display.

'I thought you didn't drink coffee.' I watch his Adam's apple bob as he drinks.

Ignoring my statement, he gestures to the various-sized paper butterflies. 'Are you planning on hanging those?'

'Um...' Pulling my gaze away from his throat, I look back at the one floating butterfly. 'Yes.'

The eyebrow over his good eye twitches.

I glance at my feet. 'But I'll take off my shoes next time I get on the ladder.'

The eyebrow reaches his hairline.

Not sure what will lower that annoying brow of his, I try, 'And wait for Deborah to get back?'

His eyebrow does flatten, but then so does his mouth. 'Deborah will be in IT for the remainder of the workday.'

'Oh.' I rock back on my heels and take another sip of coffee wondering how much longer he's going to stay. I'd planned on getting this done today and it's obvious Thomas isn't going to let me while he's around.

'You're going to continue to hang butterflies as soon as I leave, aren't you?'

I choke on my coffee, wondering if I spoke my thought aloud or if I'm just that predictable.

Sighing, Thomas sets his cup on a nearby stack of boxes. 'Let's get to it, then.'

It isn't until he's plucked one of the butterflies off the ground by its paperclip hook that his actions register.

'Wait. You're going to help me?'

His expression couldn't scream 'duh' any louder than if he was Alicia Silverstone in *Clueless*.

'Yes, well...' Ducking my head, I move forward and reach for the string hanging from the paperclip in his hand. 'At least let me do the climbing.'

'No.' He looks pointedly at my feet. 'You can't climb a ladder in heels.'

I open my mouth, but he cuts me off.

'And you can't take them off because the floor is dirty.' He turns and begins his ascent. 'I'll climb.'

With his own fancy shoes, albeit flat ones, clacking against the metal I almost don't hear him add, 'Red shoes suit you.'

But I do.

22

ALICE

If five days ago you would've told me that I'd be waiting for Thomas to finish work so we could leave together, I would've said you got hit in the head with a dildo one too many times.

Then again, I never would've thought he'd spend two hours going up and down a ladder hanging, rehanging and adjusting paper butterflies while I stood back and assessed the overall look. And yet he did just that four days ago.

Since then, Thomas and I have established a truce of sorts.

He doesn't seem as angry about having agreed to help us and I have made sure to stay out of his way as much as possible – both at work and at home.

Which has been easy considering how early he wakes up and how late he comes home.

Thomas clicks his mouse a few times. 'I'm almost done.'

'Take your time.' I shift in the chair opposite his desk. 'Your mother said she isn't leaving until five.'

Emily informed me over dinner last night that she had a date. Seeing as Thomas wasn't there and hasn't been home for dinner every night this past week, Emily said she'd inform him by phone.

This morning, as I prepped lasagne, she said Thomas agreed to leave work on time today.

I can't imagine Thomas is pleased over his mother making him agree to anything, let alone leaving work on time because his mother has a date with a thirty-year old professional bowler. He didn't even need to, as I'm fully capable of watching Mary on my own, but Emily seems to be annoyed over Thomas's work schedule.

Thankfully, I wasn't there for the conversation between them. I was simply informed to 'collect' Thomas at the end of the day today.

'Maintenance and the electrical team received the updated specs. Everything should be ready for next Friday.'

'Great.' I take a breath to quell my excitement. 'Thank you.'

Not only had Thomas been helpful on the ladder, but he even drew my attention to the fact that the fluorescent glow from the butterfly fixtures would cast light differently depending not only on their height, which is what I had measured out, but also on the depth of their placement.

I wanted to ask him if he learned about light through photography but decided not to chance ruining the truce.

'A courier just dropped this off.' George strides into the room and tosses a large envelope on the desk.

Not looking up from what he's reading on his computer, Thomas hmmms.

Thomas really needs to fix things between George and him. Even from my seat in front of Thomas's desk I can feel tension between them.

'Hi, George.' I give him a small wave as if he can't see me sitting inches from where he stands.

George's eyes soften for a moment – 'Hi, Alice' – before spinning on his loafers and stalking out of the office.

If Chase were here, he'd have already settled their dispute. Sighing, I rack my brain for a way to facilitate an olive branch between the two of them when I catch sight of my name on the envelope. 'What's this?' I spin it around to face me.

Thomas glances away from the computer, his hand freezing over his mouth when he sees the envelope in my hand.

I read the sender's name, 'Fielding & Church Law Firm'.

He nods, as if coming to a decision and swivels his chair to face me. 'Those are the papers I had my lawyer draw up.'

'Oh.' Pulling the metal sides of the closure up, I unfold the opening and slide out the papers. 'Is this the non-disclosure and post-nuptial you talked about earlier?'

Thomas stares at the papers. 'Yes.' He looks uncomfortable. More so than usual.

Confused over his reaction, I grab his fountain pen off the desk. 'I'm actually really glad this came.'

'You are?'

Uncapping the pen, I follow the yellow tabs stuck at various points in the contract to flip through each page. 'Yes. Because even though I can't say that I wouldn't do it again, I still feel really, really bad forcing you into all this.' I sign my name and initial at each indicated line as I talk.

When I finish, I cap the pen, placing it back perpendicular to his desk blotter.

He frowns at the papers. 'You didn't read it.'

Spinning it back around to face him, I slide the contract toward him. 'Should I have?'

His eyes narrow. 'You should always read over any legal document before signing it.'

'You helped me even though I blackmailed you. Out of the two of us, I'm the least trustworthy.'

Thomas scoffs.

'And if signing something that ensures I won't spend money that I had no intention of spending in the first place, or saying things I'd never say will possibly make you less mad at me, then I'll sign my name all day.'

He continues staring at the papers, but his frown is different. More contemplative than angry. 'I'm not mad at you. I haven't been for a few days.'

'Really?' The weight on my shoulders eases. 'You should really tell people those things, you know? I kept freaking out about when Kayla comes back and Mary and I move out how awkward things at work would be with you angry at me.'

Once more his frown changes, but this time I can't define it.

The clock on the wall chimes.

I rise, tapping the desk when he continues to stare. 'Let's get back to the house and celebrate you not being mad at me with lasagne.'

* * *

Thomas

'Let's use this pink brick instead.' Mary holds up a Lego from the bin of pieces my mother bought her at the toy store.

It's been four days since my house was infiltrated by Alice, a tiny dictator and a hairless judgmental rodent. And while my days at Moore's have been surprisingly pleasant what with my employees finding the fact I married their co-worker endearing, I've worked late every night this week to avoid the chaos waiting for me in my previously well-ordered home.

But not tonight.

'We can swap it for that one.' Mary points to the Lego space shuttle instruction booklet in my hands.

Placing the instructions down, I grab a clear, plastic bag of Legos from the box. 'You have a penchant for arbitrarily selecting colors.'

'What's a pinch-ant?'

I pour out the bricks, making sure to keep the bag marked 'one' beneath it to keep the pieces organized. 'A habit or tendency.'

Mary thinks this over while I begin sorting the pieces by color. 'What's ar-bi-tar-lee?'

I point to one of the many pictures she's drawn – pink clouds, blue horses, purple houses. 'Choosing colors for things that don't match real life.'

She plucks the white piece from my hands and gives me the pink one in its place. 'Yeah. That sounds like me.'

I stare long and hard at the pink brick, wondering why I'm not refusing its infiltration into the Lego build. Or that I'm helping at all.

I blame my mother calling me at work today, guilting me about working too much and ignoring my family. 'Something your father would do.'

And as much as I wanted to refute it, to say, 'They aren't my *real* family,' I couldn't. So I agreed to leave work on time to stop further comparisons to the man I once looked up to and then incarcerated, so that Alice wouldn't have to spend the evening alone with Mary while Mother cougared the night away with the sugar-baby version of the Big Lebowski.

Jesus. I rub the hand not holding a brick down my face.

A loud and obnoxious slurp draws Mary's and my eyes to Mike, lounging on his cat condo behind my chair, leg up and licking himself.

Mary, in full dictator mode, puts her small fists on her waist. 'Prince Michael, you know better than that.' She shakes one finger at him. 'Princes don't slurp.'

To my surprise, the devil spawn listens, lowering his leg and stretching out on his high perch.

Mary smiles at me triumphantly. 'I've been giving him eddy-cat lessons like Queenie said she had when she was little.'

I surprise myself by laughing, wondering what my brother would think about his hairless pussy learning etiquette.

Clearing my throat, I drop the pink brick into the pile and point to the instructions. 'First, we need to build the astronauts.'

'Oh!' Mary jumps up and runs over to a different Lego build, this one a castle. It seems buying Alice work clothes was just the tip of the purchases Mother made on both Mary and Alice's behalf. But whereas before I was bothered, today... I'm not.

'Here.' Mary hands me a mini-figure dressed in a medieval gown. 'We'll put a space helmet on her.'

'That's not the figure they outline in the instructions.' I rifle through the pile, pulling out a pair of white legs and a torso with small blue and red patches. '*This* is the astronaut.' I point to the stickers that mimic NASA patches. 'See.' I push more pieces around with my index finger until I find a yellow cylindrical head.

'But that guy's outfit is so *boring*.'

'That's what astronauts wear in real life.'

Mary takes apart the princess figurine, then reconstructs it.

'Look.' She's attached a helmet in place of the side braid to the princess's head and switched out the bodice for the NASA space suit top, leaving the bottom half of the gown in place. 'A princess astronaut.'

My nostrils flare as I war between annoyance at being outmaneuvered and laughter. 'Hmmm.'

I'm saved from further Lego set destruction when the oven timer goes off.

Alice's voice calls down from the kitchen. 'Dinner!'

Groaning as I get up from my seat on the floor, I promise myself to stretch more between workouts.

At least I'm not hindered by a fitted suit. Mary took one look at my outfit after I said I'd build with her and declared I needed to change into 'play clothes'.

The child commander tugs on my arm. 'Come on, Thomas. Dinner.'

'So I heard.' Finding out the hard way that stepping on Legos barefoot hurts like the devil, I carefully maneuver around my once spacious and tidy den now cluttered with toys – for both the feline albatross and Mary.

When we enter the dining room, Alice is adjusting my flat-ware so it's perfectly perpendicular to my plate before looking up.

I've taken quite a few pictures in my lifetime. And in doing so I've come to realize that light is essential to capturing the beauty of the moment. More so than composition or subject matter. It's the light that always draws you in.

For better or for worse, looking at Alice, clad in play clothes of her own – her worn leggings and an oversized T-shirt – standing under the glow of the nineteenth-century, hand-cut crystal chandelier, I'm fixed in the moment, staring long enough, hard enough, that I'm struck with a realization.

I haven't been working late to avoid my home's chaos, I've been staying late to avoid facing the truth. All those times I've taken Alice's picture, I hadn't been trying to capture the light, I'd been trying to capture a *feeling*.

She gestures to the casserole dish and large salad bowl on the table. 'I thought we'd eat family style tonight since it's just us.'

Swallowing past a lump in my throat, I sit. Between Mary and Alice.

And it *feels* right.

* * *

Alice

'Thomas?'

Rubber-gloved and elbow deep in the suds-filled sink next to me, Thomas angles his head to the right. 'Yes?'

Standing beside him, drying the dishes he's washed, I'm suddenly self-conscious. 'Um, thank you for helping with the dishes.'

Thomas scoffs and returns to scrubbing the lasagne pan. 'You would've just waited until I wasn't around to do them yourself.'

The familiarity that's grown between us, whether Thomas was willing or not, has enabled me to look back at the start of our relationship with much clearer eyes. Eyes unburdened by prejudice and nerves.

All those times he scolded me for doing things out of my job description, he was worried about me. And when he pointed out flaws in my displays or reprimanded Chase during the Code Penis bachelorette party planning, he was helping, not criticizing or condescending.

It's amazing how he fools people into thinking he's unfeeling.

And I the biggest fool.

An unfeeling man wouldn't arrange multicolored cocks in a hotel suite for his future sister-in-law's bachelorette party. An unfeeling man wouldn't walk down the aisle in baby blue suede shoes in a ceremony that involved a hairless cat he hates and a fat Elvis. And an unfeeling man wouldn't take in a woman and her niece while extending a marriage he wants no part of.

Still waters run deep, they say. Thomas is as still as it gets.

Ironically, a wave of suds crests the sink after a particular vigorous scrub. He glares down at his soaked T-shirt. 'I pay a housekeeper a perfectly good salary to do dishes, you know.'

Biting my lip, I attempt to swallow back my amusement, but a small bubble of laughter escapes. And when he turns that sardonic raised eyebrow at me, I can't help but giggle.

Instead of glaring, like I expect him to, he smiles, and the shock of it melts my own off my face.

Seeing the sudden change, he frowns. 'What's wrong?'

I twist the tea towel in my hands. 'I just feel really guilty that I'm here, enjoying myself when Kayla...' With a deep breath, I carefully lay the towel on the counter, smoothing the creases out as I try to get a hold of my sudden onslaught of emotion. 'I thought she'd be back by now.' I've called the police station every morning since the hospital. Nothing.

I grab the edge of the counter unable to look at him now that I've started to speak my worries out loud. Without Bell or Leslie to listen, the shame and guilt warring in my chest has built up until I've let hope blind me to the most likely outcome.

To the outcome *I* faced as a child. 'I'll start looking for apartments tomorrow.' I nod to myself. 'Just in case.'

The silence stretches out between us until Thomas, slowly, methodically, lifts his arms from the water and removes his gloves, draping them over the edge of the sink, as if preparing to impart soul-shattering advice that will make everything seem better. 'Stop worrying.'

I bust out laughing, awkwardly long and loud. 'You know that even the great and scary Thomas Moore can't order someone to stop worrying.' The tension coiled inside me eases with each chuckle. 'It doesn't *quite* work like that.'

His brow pinches, the light over the sink illuminating the faint bruise still marking the corner of his eye. 'It should.'

His consternation makes me laugh again. 'Yeah, that would be great.' With the back of my hand I wipe away a few tears that escaped. From sadness or laughter, I'm not sure.

'Aunt Alice?' Mary shuffles into the kitchen dressed in her pajamas. Mike, in a matching set, at her heels. 'I want to sleep by myself tonight, okay?'

* * *

Thomas

My stomach hurts.

Staring at the bathroom door, where, on the other side, Alice is most likely in some state of undress, I rub my abs. Instead of its normal ridges, my stomach feels like an overinflated balloon.

Even with the unexpected, but incredibly delicious carb

load, I doubt it's the large quantity of lasagne that's weighing heavy in my gut.

The memory of Alice's hopeful spirit cracking earlier makes me frown hard enough that my eye, almost pain-free, pinches. Her optimistic, trusting attitude used to grate. Now the threat of it breaking combined with the papers she signed makes me feel ill.

I make a mental note to shred the documents she signed first thing Monday morning. Then I'll call my lawyer to change course. Make the priority Mary's continued safety. All things I should've already done.

Alice emerges from the bathroom, a billow of steam behind her. 'Your turn.' Even though I was the one who offered her another of my T-shirts to wear after she splattered spaghetti sauce on hers at dinner, I still swallow at the sight of her in it.

After putting Mary to bed, which included me reading a story about a mouse, a strawberry and a big angry bear, Alice headed to the guest room.

I stopped her, reasoning that if Mary had a bad dream and came upstairs, it would be best if Alice was waiting for her. Furthermore, I have no idea if my mother plans on returning here after her date. There are some things a son doesn't ask because it's better not to know.

And so here Alice and I are, turning sideways to walk past each other as if afraid to touch, despite the fact that we already know each other intimately. Or because of it.

'Thanks.' I pretend my voice isn't rough and awkward and close the bathroom door behind me.

Shaking off the odd emotions, I make sure the shower is freezing before I step under the water. It takes about three minutes until everything potentially problematic is shriveled and I allow myself to get out.

But the arctic blast is all for naught when I enter the bedroom and find the bed empty. I turn just in time to see the light under the closet door go black.

* * *

Shifting under the sheets for the umpteenth time in the past hour since I climbed in, I stretch my limbs across the large expanse of mattress, my comfort unhindered by a six-year-old, a nut-busting feline, or a former dildo-wielding bridesmaid.

I don't like it.

But I'm not sure how to change it. Or if I should.

The gentleman in me dislikes the thought of a woman sleeping on a chaise while I sleep in a bed. The man in me really dislikes it.

But logically, it's the best thing. For starters, I would not fit on the tiny couch. If I gave Alice my bed, I'd need to move to the living room, and I'd rather not get caught by my mother couch surfing in my own house. Or worse, not get caught by her because she's bed surfing in some bowler's apartment.

The closet door opens and I freeze, pretending to sleep while Alice tiptoes out of the closet and into the bathroom.

Making a decision, for good or bad, I rearrange the pillows on the bed while she's inside.

'Sleep here.' The words emerge as soon as she exits the bathroom. I point to the space on the opposite side of the pillow barrier I made like I'm a toddler who can't be trusted to stay on their own side. Which I can't.

'Oh, no. That's okay.' Alice backs up to the closet. 'I'm fine—'

'I'm not.' I lay back down, dismissing any of her arguments. 'I can't sleep knowing you're in a closet.'

I glare at the ceiling in the following silence.

'Um. Okay.' She steps closer. 'If you're sure.' The bed barely jostles when she gets in.

Silence ticks by, her still as a statute, while I turn one way then another wondering why, after ensuring she isn't on a couch and that I won't cross the line (of literal pillows) I still can't get comfortable.

'Thomas?'

'Yes?'

'You don't have to worry. I'm not going to...' she gestures above her stomach with her hands '... you know.'

My brain fails to connect the dots. 'I don't know.'

'If you need more room, you can take the pillows away. I promise I won't cross the line.'

She won't cross the line?

'In addition to apologizing for forcing your involvement with Mary and Kayla, I should've also apologized for the sexual harassment.'

I almost choke on my next breath. 'The what?'

From across the pillows her face stares solemnly at the ceiling as if making an oath. 'I just want to let you know that I have never been so, um, sexually aggressive before. And I'm sorry that my actions were unwelcome.'

'Alice.' I remove the highest pillow between us. 'I haven't the slightest fuck what you are talking about.'

Her head falls toward me, her eyes wide.

In the small amount of light filtering through the blinds, I watch her tongue dampen her lips.

'Did you just curse?'

'What did you mean sexually aggressive?'

She grabs the next pillow in the line and covers her face

with it. 'Hand in lap... climbed you in Vegas... pasties... kissed you.' It's all mumbled behind the pillow, but I get the gist.

'Alice.'

She pulls back from the pillow enough to be understood. 'But I just want to let you know, on top of being really sorry about everything else, that I'm going to make sure you don't have any other regrets.'

Regrets. Hearing her repeat the word I used in the dressing room gut-punches me in the lasagne.

I tug the pillow out of her hands and toss it aside. 'Alice.'

Her eyes are squeezed shut again.

'Look at me.'

'I'd rather not. I'm super embarrassed right now.'

Fighting a smile, which is the last thing I thought I'd be fighting with Alice in my bed, I strive for an apologetic tone. 'I should not have said what I said in the dressing room. I was angry.'

'At me, I know.'

'No, I—' Exasperated with myself, I wish I was better with words. I'd only said what I said because I hadn't known what else to say that would make it easier to hold her at arm's length. But just thinking that makes me feel as lame as a hairless cat. Not going to even try and say it. 'Don't be embarrassed. I never once felt sexually harassed.' I flare my nostrils to keep the smile at bay. 'Or thought you overly aggressive.'

She opens one eye. 'Really?'

'Really.'

Both eyes now open, I'm suddenly hyper-conscious of the open space between us since I tossed the pillow to the floor.

'Thank you for saying that.' She gives me a small smile. 'It makes me feel better knowing that you weren't uncomfortable while I was having the best sex of my life.' She freezes, as if realizing what she just said.

Surprising me, Alice laughs, rolling onto her back, hands covering her face. 'I really know how to put my foot in it when I'm around you, huh?'

I lose the battle on the smile.

She's an odd combination of smart and naive. She's enchanting and sweet. She's too good for me.

When I remain quiet, Alice lowers her hands, her eyes going wide as she watches me inch closer. Lean in.

'Thomas?'

I brace for the usual internal recriminations. For anger to bubble up. Anger at myself for not being able to control myself. Anger at Alice for making me yearn for things I shouldn't want.

But none of that happens.

When I kiss her, I feel not an ounce of regret.

I just feel Alice.

* * *

Alice

Thomas shifts closer, his lips firm against mine, his tongue tracing the seam of my mouth. And when I open for him, my earlier embarrassment fades as I taste winter fresh toothpaste and his desire.

His kiss softens before he pulls back, his eyes searching mine. 'Am I being too sexually aggressive?'

There's a smile in his voice. But instead of being annoyed or flustered over him repeating my earlier words, it melts my heart.

Thomas Moore is not playful. Yet, he is with me.

I flex my toes under the covers, trying to find the courage I had after too many drinks in Vegas. 'I wouldn't call that aggressive.'

He smiles and even without a light I feel as if the whole room brightens.

'Is that so?' One moment we're face to face, the next I'm on my back, arms stretched overhead, one of his legs thrown over mine, locking me in place. 'How about now?' One side of his mouth kicks up.

On top of being endearing, playful Thomas is very, very sexy.

With the hand not holding my wrists, he pushes my shirt up under my chin. The flirtation-ness fades from his eyes as he gazes at my breasts. I squirm, worried over their size, but his hand and leg hold me in place.

'Beautiful.' Serious Thomas is back.

His fingers trail down between the small peaks, over my stomach and under the elastic waistband of my panties.

Too caught up in feeling to become self-conscious, I undulate against his whisper-like touches sliding easily over the soft skin, wet with my arousal. Closing my eyes, the sound of my desire on his slickened fingers is sharper in the otherwise quiet room. My legs start to shake.

Slowly, Thomas slides one finger inside. The sound of my moan echoes in the room. And when his finger curls inside me, hitting a spot only I've ever been able to find, I whimper.

'Alice.' His thumb circles my clit.

My eyes roll back in my head as the pressure builds inside.

'Thomas.' His name a plea as I rock my hips, my body searching for release.

His mouth finds the pulse at my neck. Small kisses, gentle nibbles all while sensations scream inside my head.

Until it's not inside anymore. Until spasms rack my body. Until I'm near crying from release as he propels the orgasm on and on by holding his palm to my clit while his finger continues beckoning inside me.

When the shaking stops and reality returns, I'm not awkward or embarrassed. I'm not even exhausted or satiated.

I want *more*.

Flickers of the woman I was in Vegas come to life, but this time clear-headed.

Hands now free, I cup the sides of his face, bringing it closer to mine, capturing his lips as he did mine at the start.

Despite my intentions, he holds back. 'We don't need to do anything. It's fine. *I'm* fine.'

Some part of me recognizes that he's trying to be a gentleman. That he's giving me the option of an orgasm without reciprocation. Like he's trying to prove something.

But wanton me doesn't want a gentleman. '*I'm* not.'

His eyebrows jump as I thread my fingers through his hair and tug him the rest of the way down. My kiss isn't as gentle as his. My touch not as patient.

I plant my feet on the mattress and bridge upward, flipping on top of him and whipping his shirt off me in one motion.

'Jesus.' As Thomas gazes at my breasts, I worry about once again being too aggressive.

I pause, bare-chested above him. 'Too much?'

In answer he crunches up, latching his lips to one nipple, his hand pinching the other.

My hands cradling his head, my voice keens as he lavishes attention on each breast. When I raise up on my knees, Thomas yanks his boxer briefs down, both of us falling into a passionate synchronization.

His dick bounces against my backside.

I don't even take the time to pull down my panties. Instead, I tug the gusset to one side and position the tip of his hard-on where I need him.

Thomas grabs my hips and thrusts up from beneath me, the spike of pleasure arching my back.

I undulate, each sway bringing me closer to release. Closer to a man I'd thought out of reach. The man whose grumpy facade hides surprising kindness.

His hands wrap around my waist, his biceps straining as he lifts and slams me down, my knees barely skimming the mattress.

'Oh. My. God.' My words punctuated every time he drops me onto him.

'Fuck. Fuck. Fuck.' Thomas's chant harmonizes with mine.

Until the rhythm turns animalistic, our bodies taking over as release nears.

Thomas drops his shoulders back to the mattress, arches up and thrusts deep inside me, setting off an eruption of pleasure that leaves me soundlessly screaming. His fingers tighten, bruising my hips as he stills, my orgasm having spurred on his own.

After what feels like an eternity, I collapse on top of him, Thomas's hands trailing up and down my back.

'How was that for aggression?' His voice hoarse from exertion.

I huff out a small laugh, thinking that, just as I've only ever acted wanton with Thomas, it'd be nice if he only ever acts playful with me. 'You win.'

The rumble of his own laugh lulling me into oblivion.

Waking only for a moment when Thomas cursed Mike Hunt.

23

THOMAS

If my brother ever knew that I left the arms of a warm, well-spent woman to debate whether or not Cinderella and Prince Charming really loved each other with a six-year-old, I'd never hear the end of it.

Poor Gus-Gus the mouse struggles up the stairs with a key. I gesture to the TV. 'But how can they love each other when they never talked.'

Mary frowns at me from her side of the couch. 'They talked.'

'When?'

She shrugs. 'While they were dancing.'

'Why didn't we hear them?'

'Because it was *private*.' She widens her eyes and shakes her head on the last word, like I'm the one being nonsensical.

And maybe I am. Having been woken up by a flesh-toned gremlin pouncing on my balls, and Mary explaining that she didn't know how to turn on the TV, I left Alice to sleep in and came downstairs. I'd quickly dressed in some workout clothes before coming down but instead of continuing to the basement,

I sat next to her. Even tolerating the aforementioned ball-pouncer lounging on the back of the couch between us.

Usually when I wake, I'm full of restless energy I need to burn off in the gym. This morning I felt... peaceful.

Well, discounting the demon cat's wake-up call.

The evil stepsisters try their best to fit their large feet into the tiny glass slipper while the sniveling duke looks on. 'The prince didn't even search for her himself. He sent the duke.'

'He was busy.' Mary's arms cross, and I wonder if she's reached the end of her patience with me.

Unable to resist, I ask, 'With what?'

'Prince stuff.'

'Hmmm.' It's like arguing with my brother.

The television dims as Gus-Gus reaches the dark attic floor and I can see my reflection in the screen. I'm smiling.

A shadow moves on the left of the screen.

'What are you two doing?' Alice, still clad in my T-shirt but having added her worn leggings and a pair of my workout socks, pads into the room. Her expression hesitant.

Lately, her hair has had a more polished look to it, whether from the bangs growing out or perhaps some hair product my mother foisted on her, but not this morning.

Her hair is wild with the shorter pieces sticking out at random angles on the left, while the right is more matted from her pillow.

I'm oddly pleased, like her hair is evidence of my prowess. I'm also extremely turned on.

Not the time.

Mary gives me a vengeful smile before pouting to Alice. 'Thomas thinks Prince Charming is an idiot.'

Alice's eyes widen and I'm shocked out of my untimely and immature thoughts.

'I never said the word idiot.' I aim a glare at Mary that makes grown men sweat.

She flashes me an unaffected, chicklet-toothed grin.

Alice rolls her lips, as if trying not to laugh.

Ignoring their irritating and easily read expressions, I cross my arms and glare at the evil stepmother who just instigated the shattering of a glass slipper. 'I just don't think that there was adequate time for Prince Charming and Cinderella to get to know each other.'

Mary lets out an exasperated sigh and pats my arm. 'It's true love, silly.'

Alice starts coughing and I raise one eyebrow in her direction.

At least she *attempts* to clear the amusement off her face. 'How 'bout I go make breakfast?'

Glancing down at my stomach, where the lasagne still resides, I stand. When the sudden weight shift causes the cat to slide from its perch in a dramatic combination of flails and hissing, I consider it a happy accident.

* * *

'Breakfast.' I place a glass in front of each of them, feeling as if I accomplished something even if I didn't get to work out this morning.

Alice and Mary exchange looks with each other.

'It's good for you.'

'What's in it?' Mary asks, looking more curious than Alice's queasy.

'Fruit.' Which is not a lie. There's an apple and I even allowed myself to add two chunks of frozen pineapple to sweeten it. I simply don't mention spinach, celery, and various nutritional and protein powders.

Alice's smile looks misshapen. 'Thank you for breakfast, Thomas.'

Taking her cue from her aunt, Mary nods. 'Yes, thank you, Thomas.'

The glasses remain untouched.

Leaning against the cabinets on the other side of the island, I raise my own glass to them and take a long drink. The pineapple is a good addition.

Braver than Alice, Mary grabs her glass with both hands and brings it to her mouth. I can tell the exact moment the liquid hits her tongue because her whole body freezes before she slowly lowers the glass back down to the island – her cheeks full like a chipmunk, her eyes wide in panic.

Sighing, I gesture to her glass. 'You can spit it out.'

Not wasting a second, she does just that – *blah-ing* and *pi-tah-ing* as she tries to get every drop out of her mouth.

Alice, drink still untouched in front of her, pushes off the island counter with an overly cheerful smile on her face. 'French toast?'

* * *

Alice

'Ta-da!' Mary jazz hands with her mittens. Not having joined her, she frowns at me until I feel compelled to do so.

Thomas – his expression back to being impassive as soon as we stepped out of the house – waits for Mary to feel that the surprise has been sufficiently celebrated, which for me and the busy onlookers passing by on the sidewalk was thirty seconds ago.

Finally dropping her hands, which don't meet her sides due to her squishy puffer coat, Mary asks, 'Are you surprised?'

Thomas's brow, the one over his now bruise-free eye, arches. 'At your aunt's lackluster jazz hands?' He nods once. 'Yes. Yes, I am.'

My lips twitch as I don a look of pretend outrage and Mary giggles.

Thomas Moore is funny.

I don't think many people know this because you'd have to know *him* to get his dry sense of humor. Otherwise, he just sounds like an asshole.

But I think I'm starting to. Know him, that is.

And not just because of the sex, or maybe it is the sex. Because sex with Thomas is... the redness on my cheeks has nothing to do with the cold New York breeze whipping through Chelsea.

I'll admit, when I woke this morning to find him gone, I had a little pity party for one while I mentally rehashed everything I said last night before allowing things to get out of hand. For getting too comfortable. For being greedy.

'No, silly.' Mary makes a show of rolling her eyes before grabbing his hand and tugging him to the door. 'Are you surprised about the *photography exhibit*.' She points, or I think she does under the cashmere mitten Emily bought her to go with her puffy purple coat, to the Aperture Gallery sign above the door. 'They have pictures here like the ones you take.'

And then I found him talking trash on Prince Charming and damn near swooned.

Thomas pivots to hold the door open for us and Mary skips inside.

My nerves get the better of me and I pause at the threshold. 'Is this okay?'

His expression gives me nothing.

'In the moment, after we came across your dark room while playing hide-and-seek, this seemed like a great idea, but now I—'

'Alice hid in there!' Mary throws me under the bus, her cheerful voice drawing the eyes of the other patrons.

Thomas ushers me through the door with his free hand. 'As Mary set up a Barbie campsite in the basement under my workout bench, I figured one or both of you would've seen the darkroom.'

Mary looks slightly sheepish. 'I can't set up camp in my bedroom because it's too nice. You need to rough it for camping.' She takes off her mittens, letting them dangle from her coat by the string woven through her coat sleeves. 'I read that in a book.'

'Mary—' I try to sound admonishing while also whispering in the echoing gallery foyer '—you can't just put your toys everywhere. It's Thomas's house.' I remind her to remind myself. 'And you've already taken over his den.' And his bedroom.

'Den?' Mary looks confused.

'The playroom,' Thomas supplies, a wry twist to his lips.

'Oh.' Mary nods in understanding, then tilts her head at me, as if she's talking to someone a little slow. 'That's where Barbie's *regular* house is. I can't set up camp in there.' She scoffs like I'm being ridiculous. 'It wouldn't be much of a vacation if they could walk to it.'

I open my mouth then close it, my mind blanking on what to say next.

Thomas's shoulders lift infinitesimally. 'She may be spending too much time with my mother.'

'Come on, Thomas.' Finished with our discussion, Mary grabs Thomas's hand and tugs him to the counter where she grabs every glossy brochure they have.

I sigh, part in exasperation with Mary and part over the adorable sight of Thomas holding Mary's hand. Even with the return of his stoic countenance, he still seems... softer. Easier this morning.

Maybe it's because it's a Saturday. Maybe it's because he got laid last night. Maybe...

This it isn't permanent, I remind myself. Don't let waking satiated from sex and finding the man who satiated you watching cartoons with your niece do things to you.

Like put tingles in your panties and your heart. Save that for your next romance novel.

Shaking myself, I try to stay realistic. Happy, but realistic.

I'm glad Thomas accepted my apology. I'm glad the attraction wasn't one-sided. I'm glad Mary and I could take him on a surprise outing to thank him for—

'Ooo, look at this one.' Mary points to a photo of a woman chopping down a tree. A nude woman.

My mouth drops open and I stare. First at *the* bush in a forest and then at the other photos in this particular showing.

They're all people in the forest. And they're all nude. And while I've always been a believer that the human body is beautiful and art is art, my new, parental-like inner voice screams, *don't let her see the penises!*

Thomas must feel the same because he slides a hand over Mary's eyes.

* * *

Thomas

I scan the park we came to after ushering Mary blindly out of the 'Getting Back to Nature' exhibit. 'Thank you for taking me to the gallery.'

'I really don't think you need to be thanking me for our ten-second visit.' Alice shakes her head, her arms and legs crossed as she sits on the bench beside me. 'So much for our thank you gift.'

Her need to thank me rubs. Probably because where she thinks my actions to home Mary were altruistic, in reality I was being a selfish ass. Something the papers she signed drove home yesterday.

My eyes pause on Mary making friends with a girl in a pink coat, while my mother, who joined us at the park, holds their place in line for the swings. 'Never had so much fun in a gallery.'

'Ha ha.' Alice's breath puffs out in the cold air. While cold, it's still relatively sunny for a late afternoon in February.

'No, really.' I shift my weight toward her. Even wearing my overcoat, I wish I'd added a sweater over my button-down. 'While I respect and appreciate photography as an artform, I mostly just enjoy taking the photos.'

Alice leans the rest of the way into me until our shoulders touch. 'Because it makes you feel a part of what it is you're taking pictures of?'

The surprise must register on my face because she leans back quickly, hands out. 'Ah, sorry. Don't mind me.'

I clear my throat, gesturing toward the playground. 'I started taking pictures when I was Mary's age.'

We watch Mary, nose red from the cold, run around playing with other kids.

'Who taught you?' Alice looks pointedly at my mother, looking like a cover model of AARP *Vogue*, still waiting in line for the swings. 'Emily?'

'No.'

When I don't elaborate, Alice turns to me, the question in her eyes.

Annoyed with myself for bringing it up, I grumble, 'I did.'

'Huh.' Settling back on the bench, she leans against me once more. And just when enough time has passed that I think we're finished with the conversation, she asks, 'Why do you keep it a secret?'

'I don't.' I shrug. 'Not really. I just...'

'Just what?' Alice asks.

Not having the words, but also not wanting to disappoint Alice, I stand. 'Wait here.'

'What?' She jerks forward. 'Where are you going?'

I close my coat against the breeze, judging the distance between here and my house across an expanse of frost-crisped grass. 'I'll be back soon.'

Unlike mine, Alice's expressions are easy to read. And whereas I don't often feel the need to explain myself, with her I do. 'I'm going to retrieve something.'

'Okay.' She elongates the word as if she doesn't believe me.

I walk fast across the frost-crisp grass of Central Park. To keep warm, but it takes me a few minutes longer than I'd judged.

Once home, I had trouble making up my mind on which one to take. Thankfully, I get back just in time.

'We're next!' Mary shouts from across the playground, having joined my mother in line, both of them with their arms wrapped around each other.

I wave with my free hand, then pass what I'm carrying to Alice.

She frowns at my prized possession. 'A camera?'

'A Pentax K100. It's the camera I learned on.' I shrug feigning nonchalance. 'If you don't count the old, disposable cameras.'

She holds it carefully, like she knows how much it means to me. '*You* used a disposable camera?' Her exaggerated surprise is cute. 'The great and mighty Thomas Moore?' She laughs. 'How very pedestrian of you.'

'Yes, well.' I clear my throat. 'They were the easiest to buy and conceal from my father. Before my high school offered a photography elective that required me to purchase this.'

Her smile dims and I move on before she can ask follow-up questions.

'Here.' I help her stand then move behind her, guiding her hands around the camera with my own. 'I already set the aperture and shutter speed.' I point the camera at Mary who has just started to pump her legs on the swing. 'Now press this button.' I point to the shutter release.

Click.

It's a sound I've heard thousands, maybe even millions, of times since I started taking pictures. Yet this click sounds different. The familiar noise is almost lost in the unfamiliar cacophony of children around the park, their parents trying to wear their kids out before dinner and bedtime.

A place where I never thought I'd be, let alone taking pictures.

'Do you think it came out, okay?' She pulls the camera back, pouting when she realizes there isn't a digital screen to show her the photo.

'That's part of the fun.' I raise her hands once more. 'Getting to see the pictures developed. Figuring out if you captured the moment correctly or not.'

Pulling free, Alice turns to me, smiling. 'That sounds very unlike you. Didn't you just say not too long ago that you hate surprises?'

I grimace, not having an answer for that. 'Well, I guess Chase is right then.'

'And what does your brother say?'

'That I'm a frustrating enigma with no sense of humor.'

She frowns on my behalf. '*I* think you're funny.'

That surprises a laugh out of me.

'Aunt Alice!' Mary swings high, then back low, her legs working in tandem. 'Thomas!' She lets go of the chains with one hand to wave, causing Alice to grab my hand – *hard*.

I wave with my free hand, then tuck Alice's hand and mine into my coat pocket. Keeping it there even after Mary grabs hold of the chain again.

24

THOMAS

'Do you know why I love romance novels?' Alice peers at me over the edge of her phone. We're in the living room. Me sitting at the end of the sofa, Alice laying down next to me, her feet in my lap.

It's what we've done the past three nights since the infamous gallery excursion. With my mother deciding to go on a dating spree with every ineligible thirty-year-old bachelor in the city, Alice has taken to cooking dinner – this time a carb load that included chicken, rice and two cans of condensed soup – then Alice and I put Mary to bed and retreat to the living room to read.

Dipping my chin down, I look over my reading glasses at her. 'Why is that?'

Alice giggles, the one glass of wine she had at dinner, from a bottle my mother left for us, making her tipsy enough that I no longer question the convenient blanks in her mind from Vegas.

I frown, realizing that I've stopped questioning a lot of things about that night that I shouldn't have in the first place.

Like how all my clothes were neatly arranged by the side of the bed or how the rings—

'Sex.'

I cough out a laugh, the newspaper in my hands creasing.

Alice beams, as if getting me to laugh was her goal.

Over the past few days, I suspect she and Mary are keeping a running tally on who can get me to laugh the most.

Mary just might have the edge, because one, after work while Alice cooks dinner, I've found Mary's efforts to make me color 'are-bit-tear-lee' amusing rather than perturbing. And two, I like to do *other* things with Alice rather than laugh.

Case in point. 'Sex, hmmm?' I shake out my paper to fold it. 'And here I thought it was the romance.'

Her sly smile jump-starts the warm-up to us eventually burning off the calories from dinner. 'Oh.' She feigns innocence. 'Actually, what I was *going* to say before you sidetracked me with those sexy reading glasses of yours, is that my *favorite* thing about romance novels is that they're happy.' She gets a glazed look that I'm not sure is 100 percent cabernet related. 'And the absolute *best* part is when there's an epilogue into the future featuring them doing something simple like eating dinner or gathering around the Christmas tree with their growing family.' She blinks a few times, the pinch between her brows forming, as if wondering why she's suddenly getting emotional.

Knowing what I know about her childhood, I get why the epilogue would be her favorite part. But I can't speak to that even if I wanted to. While things are exponentially better between my mother, brother and I now that Father is in jail—though the same can't be said for Liz—I don't think myself capable of more than this temporary truce Alice and I have forged over the last few days.

I'm smart enough to know Alice and Mary will be better off without me. They just need the security I can give them until they're able to move on.

'Sexy reading glasses?' I toss my paper aside, content to distract her – and myself – the best way I know how.

Grabbing one foot, I raise it to move it behind me, making room to shift between her legs. I may not be good with words or promises that don't involve contractual obligations but I can... I pause, body turned toward her, a sudden realization distracting me.

I *still* haven't shredded the papers Alice signed. They're in my desk drawer, right where I put them that day in my office, buried under an ever-growing pile of drawings from Mary.

I've been distracted. Lawyers and investigator reports, working with Human Resources on the new employee hand-book, the unexpected hours I spent with Alice creating the mock-up display. Unexpected tasks on top of work responsibilities, that honestly, I haven't been doing the best job of keeping up with.

I'm dropping the ball. Making small mistakes that I knew I would if I ever let myself be derailed by my fascination with Alice Truman.

'Thomas?' The concerned tone in Alice's voice brings me back to the moment. 'What's wrong?'

'Nothing.' And it *is* nothing. I'll simply do it tomorrow. Stay late to ensure I'm caught up on everything as we near the retail season change.

'Are you sure?'

Sliding my hands up the inside of her legs, I push them farther apart. 'Yes.' A delicious blush spreads across her cheeks. 'You know what *my* favorite part about romance novels is?'

The smile is back in her eyes. 'You have a favorite part? What?'

I drag my knee up, bracing it on the cushion. Lowering my body on top of hers, making sure to support my weight on my forearms beside her. 'They give you *ideas*.'

She wiggles under me, rubbing against my dick, obviously hard under my play clothes joggers. 'Seems like you're the one with ideas.'

I press my pelvis down. 'True. I remember reading a particularly inspiring passage from your book on the plane.'

Her mouth drops open. 'You did *not*.'

I circle my hips, the shock of what I read having ingrained the words in my brain – both my big and small ones. '"His cock swelled, throbbing. With a roar, he found his"—'

Her hands cover my mouth. 'Oh my God.' She laughs, the contractions doing great things to the place we're pressed together. '*Stop*.'

'You want me to stop?' My cheeks tighten, the muscles still unused to smiling so often.

Alice slow blinks. She likes it when I smile as much as when I laugh.

'No.' Her hands tunnel into my hair and she pulls me closer. 'Don't stop.'

Kissing Alice is ever-changing. Sometimes fast, sometimes slow. But always addictive.

I rock my hips as we kiss, the friction building the heat between us.

Not wanting to crush her, but definitely wanting to touch her, I rest most of my weight on my right forearm, leaning against the back of the couch so I can lift my left.

My core tightens as I balance and I'm thinking I need to add some yoga into my workouts.

Just as my fingers trail down her side, slipping into the waistband of her panties – my phone rings.

Startled, my balance fails and I collapse.

'Ooof.' Alice's breath expels across my ear...

'Damn it.' It takes me a minute to leverage up from the thick couch cushions, reminding me of my age. 'You okay?'

Alice, having gotten her breath back, giggles.

Grabbing my phone off the side table, I almost smile with her until I see my lawyer's number on the screen. Silencing the call, I lean over and kiss Alice's cheek. 'Why don't you head to bed?'

Face falling, she struggles up on her elbows. 'I—'

'I'll be up in a minute.' I stride out of the room before Alice can say anything else, turning toward the back stairs. The basement is closer than my office on the second floor and will give me more privacy.

A few steps from the bottom, I slide my thumb across my phone's screen. 'Henry.' I flick on the overhead pot lights, blinking as my eyes adjust. 'What's wrong?'

Henry, used to working past office hours by now, doesn't even grumble or apologize for the late call. 'I got a call from the state today, right before closing, saying they couldn't find yours and Alice Truman's marriage license.'

'Shit.' I glare at myself in the floor-to-ceiling mirror behind my bench press cage.

'I suggested there might have been a clerical error and they seemed okay with it, but now they want a copy of your and Ms Truman's marriage license.'

Pivoting on my heel, my foot slicing across something sharp. 'Fuck.'

'I've already procured the apartment we talked about earlier. The one in the contract. I know you said you didn't want to use it, but it would ensure Alice could continue fostering the child.'

Even staring in the mirror at a man I don't recognize, a man in sweats and socks with hair tousled, still half-hard from Alice, I don't want to concede his point.

I stare at the Barbie camper, now parked under my dumb-bell rack.

No. It's better for Mary to have to stay here. She hasn't had any nightmares the past few nights and moving might mess with her sense of security.

'Mr Moore?'

Turning away from the mirror, I begin the climb upstairs. 'I have a better option.'

25

ALICE

'Hi, George.' Walking beside Mary, who's struggling under the weight of Thomas's briefcase that she *insisted* on carrying, I approach the executive assistant's desk.

He looks up from his keyboard, a wide grin shifting his glasses.

'Hi, George!' Mary lets go of the handle with one hand, nearly dislocating the other shoulder, so she can wave. As if George could possibly miss her in her bubble gum pink Dolce & Gabbana children's faux-fur coat, citron tutu, and black Doc Martens.

Punk princess chic, Emily had called it, looking on proudly at Mary's self-styled outfit as I met them at Moore's main entrance, before she then hustled over to Susan in women's luxury. Something about picking up a new outfit for her date tonight.

I take hold of the briefcase Thomas forgot this morning before Mary really does injure herself.

'Hello there.' George gets up from his desk, buttons his suit jacket. 'And who might this be?'

'I'm Mary.' She curtseys.

'Well now.' George lifts his eyes to mine, and I have to twist my lips to keep from laughing.

Emily created a monster.

'Nice to meet you, Mary.' George bows at the waist 'I'm George.'

Mary giggles.

'Moore's wouldn't be in business without him,' I add, still feeling guilty about keeping so much from my friend.

To my relief, George winks at me.

'I'm gonna give Thomas his briefcase.' Mary rocks back on her thick-soled boots. 'He forgot it this morning.'

By the way George's eyebrows soar, I can tell he has a host of questions, but thankfully he doesn't ask any of them. 'Sorry, Mary, but Mr Moore left a little while ago.'

Mary deflates. 'Oh.'

I feel the same way, a small niggling of doubt since that phone call last night. Thomas never did come to bed to finish what we started on the couch. At least, not before midnight which was the last time I looked at the clock. And like usual he was up before I was to work out.

I'd been hoping to reassure myself that everything was okay. 'Meeting?'

'I'm actually not sure.' He sniffs, his posture stiffening, making it obvious he and Thomas have yet to make up. 'He didn't bother to say. Just told me to hold all his appointments.'

Mary shifts back and forth on her feet.

'Mary, do you have to go to the bathroom?'

She crosses one boot over the other. 'I gotta tinkle.'

George grins. 'Why don't you use the bathroom in Thomas's office.' He points to the door behind him. 'You can leave his briefcase on his desk.'

'Thanks!' She takes off like a shot.

I hustle after her, worried about tutu removal. 'Thanks, George.'

A few minutes later, accident averted, Mary skips out of the bathroom and over to Thomas's desk.

I follow her out, closing the private bathroom door behind me. 'What are you doing?'

'I drew Thomas another picture.' Mary struggles with the brass closure on the leather attaché case. 'I want to put it on his desk for him.'

'Hold on, now.' I remove her hands before she starts yanking and open the case myself. 'Here.' The bright blue horse drawing easy to spot. 'We'll leave this—'

'He kept them!' Mary smiles at me over Thomas's open desk drawer.

'Mary, you do not open other people's—'

'But look!' She reaches her tiny hands into the drawer and comes up with a stack of papers. 'He kept them.'

I can't even finish reprimanding her. Because in her hands is the reassurance I was looking for when I agreed to walk Mary to Thomas's office. A thick stack of Mary's drawings, probably every one she's managed to sneak in his briefcase in the mornings and then some are clasped in her hands.

'We should hang them up for him.' Mary looks around the office. 'But where?' Spinning on her boots, she knocks into the side of the desk, papers fluttering to the ground. 'Ow!'

'Oh, sweetie.' I grab her hand she knocked. 'Are you okay?'

She's pouting, but not crying.

Turning her hand one way and then the other, I kiss each side. 'All better.'

She makes sad eyes at the floor. 'I dropped them.'

'That's okay.' I brush the wisps of hair off her face. 'What do we do when we make a mess?'

'We clean it up.' There is far less enthusiasm in her voice than a minute ago.

Showing her pity, I nudge her with my shoulder. 'Why don't you ask George if he has any tape? We can hang your pictures on the window. Thomas will be sure to see them when he gets back.'

My answer is the quick pounding of size two Doc Martens racing out the door.

Moving around the desk, I bend to collect drawings. Black and white rainbows, a purple rocket ship, various technicolored Mike Hunts...

My hand stills over a clipped stack of papers recognizing the header. It's the contract I signed for Thomas just last week.

I move to put them back in the drawer, when another non-drawing catches my eye. A rush of heat flows under my skin, the sound and lights of the office dimming.

'Got the tape!' George walks in next to a skipping Mary. His excitement jarring me back to the moment. Catching sight of my expression, which is probably as shell-shocked as I feel, he stops. 'Everything okay?'

Swallowing past my sudden dry mouth, I finish gathering the papers. Making one stack of drawings, one of the contract and copies of... whatever these are. Not looking at them, I feigned normalcy. 'George, would you help Mary?'

Standing, I place the drawings on the desk and carry the other documents to the couch.

Probably sensing that I need a minute, George nods. 'Sure.'

He distracts Mary by having her organize how she wants her pictures displayed while I sit down, staring at a document I never thought I'd have to look at again – my state-issued birth certificate. The 'unknown' mother and father glaring at me.

I take a deep breath, and shuffle it underneath the stanch, leaving the contract on top.

Given the fact that no marriage occurred on the eighteenth
of February…

Mary giggles at something George said, but their voices fade as I continue to do what I promised Thomas – read the things I sign. With shaking hands, I turn each page after I've read it.

Mr Thomas Moore, henceforth known as the first party, will ensure the safety of one Miss Mary Roger, with the understanding that Miss Alice Truman, henceforth known as the second party, will therefore forfeit any employment status at Moore's Clothier Inc.

Under the contract are pages of information about Kayla and me. Kayla's last known jobs, her ex-boyfriend's police report. A compilation of a private investigator's report that my birth certificate must have been a part of.

'Look, Aunt Alice!' Mary calls.

I don't raise my head, worried my blurry vision might spill over. I clear my throat, holding a hand to my chest. 'One sec, sweetie.'

Blinking my vision clear, I read the last document. It's a list of all the foster homes I ever stayed in from age six to eighteen.

And now I know that Thomas Moore's Central Park mansion is just another for the list.

* * *

Thomas

When Mason called my office almost as soon as I arrived to tell me he found Kayla, I was apprehensive. And not at all prepared for what we found when we got there.

'Hey, boys, welcome.' The ponytailed waitress drops two cocktail napkins on the dark-stained, resin-covered table with a smile. 'I'm Kayla and I'll be taking care of you.' She grabs a pen from her front apron. 'Can I get you guys something to drink?'

My brain does not compute how this healthy, untroubled, clear-eyed young woman serving drinks in a tavern restaurant on Staten Island could be capable of abandoning her injured child at a hospital.

'Kayla Rogers?' Mason asks, sounding very much like the police officer he used to be.

Kayla's smile fades, her eyes shifting between us. 'Yes?'

'I'm Private Investigator Mason.' Mason tips his chin toward me. 'This is my client, Thomas Moore.'

I nod at her.

'I'll give you two some time to talk.' He points to the bar in the middle of the restaurant where a few of the early lunch crowd are watching this past weekend's sports highlights. 'I'll just be over there.'

Kayla takes a step back, as if preparing to run.

I reach out and grab her wrist, holding her in place. 'It's about Mary.'

She stiffens, then, as if giving in to the inevitable, sinks into the chair Mason left.

I wait while a group of men wearing polo shirts and lanyards laugh at some shared joke. While a mother lays a highchair cover down before sitting her baby into it. While a couple sit on the same side of a booth sharing fries. Still, Kayla says nothing.

She plays the silent game better than I do.

'Aren't you going to ask how she is?'

Concern flashes in her eyes, then fades just as fast. 'She's with Alice, she's fine.'

My suit slides across the heavy wood seat of my chair. 'How do you know?'

She gives me a look to rival that of any teenager. 'Because Alice wouldn't let anything happen to her.'

'No.' I lean forward, invading her space and wiping the smart-ass look off her face. 'How did you know Mary was with Alice? You left before Alice arrived.'

'Oh.' She picks up the cocktail napkin in front of her, making small tears along the edges. 'I listened to the voicemails she left before I cancelled my phone.'

'I see.' And I do. I see that she's a woman who took the time to give herself peace of mind about her daughter but didn't care enough to return the calls to give Alice the same.

'Who are you anyway?' Head still down, she peers at me from under her lashes. It reminds me of Mary. As does her olive skin and chestnut hair.

But it's obvious in these few minutes that everything smart, caring and kind Mary got from Alice.

'I'm Mary's...' I'm at a loss to explain anything. I settle for, 'I'm Alice's boss.'

'Oh, *that* Thomas Moore.' She smirks like she knows something I don't.

I really don't care for Kayla Rogers.

'Yes, that Thomas Moore.' I can only imagine what stories she must've heard from Alice back before, well, before Vegas. Before lasagne and Lego and a nude photo exhibit. 'I'm here to talk about the mess you handed Alice to fix.' I look around the worn but serviceable restaurant. 'All for this.'

'Don't judge me.' She adopts more of that teenage attitude. 'I did what I did for Mary.' She gives me a once-over. 'You can't tell me that Mary isn't happier now.'

I don't return the favor. 'Compared to eviction and shelters, yes, I suppose she is happier.'

Kayla flinches. Then, acting self-righteous, she tosses the napkin on the table. 'What do you care, anyway? You're just Alice's boss.'

'Yes, I am. And Alice is also good friends with my brother and sister-in-law. And seeing as they are out of town at the moment, I stepped in.'

'Good for you then Richie Rich, but I have a job I need to get back to.' She moves to stand.

'Getting back to work isn't one of your two choices.' Having had enough of her unapologetic attitude, I let the menace in my voice give her pause.

She recovers by crossing her arms, as if she believes otherwise. 'I guess you're about to tell me what my choices are?'

I nod. 'The first choice is waiting for the police to arrive.'

Her arms and mouth drop. 'What for?'

'Believe it or not, it's illegal to abandon your child.'

She rolls her eyes. 'It's not like I left her on the side of the road like Alice's parents did. I left Mary at a *hospital*.'

I swallow back the rage I feel on Alice's behalf at Kayla's casual comment about her past. 'Child abandonment is child abandonment no matter where the abandonment takes place.'

Hers eyes shift to the exit sign at the back of the restaurant.

I lean back, wanting her to choose the first choice, but needing her to choose the second for Mary and Alice's sake. '*Or*, you can sign over guardianship to Alice and make your abandonment legal, which will ensure Mary's safety. If you do that, I'll make sure you don't get jail time.'

'The second.' She answers fast. 'I choose the second.'

'Good choice.' I don't even care what reasons she had, or what she went through. All I know if that she doesn't *want* to be Mary's mother, then she *doesn't* deserve to be Mary's mother.

I flag Mason, his cue to call my lawyer, waiting in his car outside.

Kayla continues to shred the napkin.

The Statue of Liberty cuckoo clock on the wall ticks away. When I see Mason lower his phone, I wonder how long this is going to take.

The drive from the office to the ferry took far longer than it should've with how skittish my lawyer is behind the wheel of his too-big-for-city-driving Bentley.

I never appreciated Brian more. I make a mental note to give my chauffer a raise.

'Listen, I'm going to get fired if I don't finish my shift.' Kayla looks at her phone. 'I'm off in an hour.'

'No.' I watch Henry hustle in with his briefcase from the safety of his car he parked three blocks down. I've waited long enough. Mary and Alice have waited long enough.

Kayla stands. 'I need this job, okay?' She looks more serious than she did about leaving her daughter. 'I was lucky to get—'

'I don't care.' I don't even have to try to remove every ounce of emotion from my face to show her how much I sincerely don't give one flying fuck about inconveniencing her.

From the way she swallows, it must translate.

Henry arrives at the table, briefcase with notary stamp inside clamoring on top of the table. 'Give me a minute to get everything in order.'

I can feel a headache brewing between my eyes. 'Why isn't it already?' All I heard on the ride was him rehashing the process of voluntary relinquishment of parental rights, as if studying before a test. Which, it probably was for him seeing as he usually just deals in business law.

'Honestly?' Henry glances at Kayla. 'I didn't think she'd sign it.'

Kayla flushes. 'I'm going to check on my tables. Flag me down when you're ready.'

Lady Liberty chimes two more times before we leave, Mary's safety secured in Henry's briefcase.

'Now all we need is Ms Truman's signature and everything will be legal.' Henry begins his legal rambling as soon as we leave the restaurant.

Mason wisely takes a cab to the ferry.

My body thrums with restless energy, like I missed my morning workout when in fact, I spent an extra fifteen minutes this morning with heavier weights than usual.

As the ferry gets closer to Whitehall terminal with real Lady Liberty on my left, I begin rehearsing all the reasons Alice should sign the guardianship papers so we can settle this *before* the lack of marriage license becomes an issue.

Alice

Thomas strides into the office, a man with bad hair plugs trailing behind him. He does a double take when he notices me sitting on the couch. 'Alice.' The small lift at the corner of his mouth, for once, doesn't make my heart pound.

'Thomas.' I'm quite proud of how calm I sound.

Thomas's lips flattened.

'I'm Henry Farrier.' Bad Hair Plugs offers me his hand. 'From Fielding & Church law firm.'

I take it. 'The same name on nearly every page of these documents.' I slide my hand out from his to pick up the stack of papers on the coffee table in front of me.

Thomas stills.

We stare into each other's eyes for a beat.

'Henry.' Thomas talks to his lawyer while looking at me.

The lawyer looks from the contract to Thomas. 'Yes, Mr Moore?'

'Leave.'

'Yes, Mr Moore.' With a nod he retreats the way he came.

Thomas waits for the door to close before speaking. 'I was going to shred those.'

'But you didn't.' I stand, holding the stack of papers upright and facing him, the copy of my birth certificate on top. 'Did you have these drawn up before or after you found out about my childhood?'

He frowns at it. 'What does that have to do with anything?'

My voice threatens to crack, but I clench my fingers around the edge of the papers to keep me focused. 'What other possible reason did you have to think I was so lacking, so out of place at my job that you wanted to get rid of me?' I feel my lip curl as I glare at him. 'Wanted it badly enough to use my worry about Mary against me?'

He runs a hand through his hair, the gesture so out of place it's jarring. With a yank, he drops it. 'I couldn't stop thinking about you.' The last word echoes in the office. He blinks, as if he startled himself. Taking a beat, all emotion clears from his expression as he exhales. 'And it was interfering with my work.'

I stare at him wondering if he knows how asinine that excuse sounds. 'If that were true you simply would've asked me out on a date.'

'You're an employee.'

I point at the papers with my free hand. 'Was.'

He moves to grab them, but I pull back.

'Oh no. I'm keeping this. And I've sent a copy to my lawyer.'

'Your lawyer?'

'Leslie.'

His renewed stoicism breaks. 'Goddamnit.' Another breath. 'All right let's table *that*—' he points to the contract '—for a second.' He takes a step forward, carefully, as if approaching a wounded animal.

I have to admit, I *feel* like one.

'The state knows we aren't married.' He holds up a hand, hurrying to add, 'But the good news is I found Kayla.'

My hold on the documents loosens. 'You did?'

Thomas nods. 'Yes.'

'Is she okay?' I remember what the report said about her boyfriend having once been arrested for drugs. 'Does she need help?'

'She's fine.' He pauses, as if gauging my reaction. 'I had her sign over guardianship of Mary to you.'

I blink three times before what he said registers, anger burning hotter than the pain from my reopened childhood wounds. 'You don't get to decide that.'

'Alice—'

'Honestly, who do you think you are?' The rage hits hard and fast. 'You hire a private investigator to dig into our lives, and then, when you find Kayla, you don't tell me? You just tell her to give up her daughter?' My voice rises with each question.

'Alice...' He pauses, as if waiting to see if I'm going to talk over him again. 'This is a good thing.' He points to the papers in my hand. 'You read about her ex-boyfriend, her inability to hold a job.'

I curse as a tear falls. 'You think just because you have some facts about someone's past that you know everything there is to know about them?'

He sighs. As if *I'm* putting him out. 'Alice, Kayla signed the guardianship papers like *that*.' He snaps his fingers.

I flinch.

'She doesn't deserve Mary.' He runs another hand through his hair, the usually combed, standard business cut in disarray. 'And since the state has realized we're not married, it's best if you sign the guardianship papers now.'

'I'm not going to sign away Mary's mother because you think it's more convenient.'

'Fine.' He snaps, pinching the bridge of his nose. 'If you won't see reason about Kayla then we'll just make your legal address my address. That way in case the social workers raise a fuss about not finding our marriage license, at least your registered address will meet fostering standards.'

His presumption exhausts me.

I never wanted anything from him. But if what he said about the state knowing is true, then Mary's at risk again.

Flipping to the second page of the contract I read, 'The first party, as compensation for any emotional and/or financial distress of the second party, will purchase and bestow upon the second party a place of residence which meets all New York State fostering requirements. This place of residence will also reside in a top five rated New York City school zone.'

I'm trembling. As if I'm about to burst from all the emotion warring inside me. For being disappointed in myself for not searching for a place to live from the start. For being gullible enough to believe Kayla would come back. For wanting what was happening between Thomas and I to mean something.

My fingertips curl, creasing the stack of papers.

I hadn't realized just how much I wanted to believe until now.

Reining all of that in, I stare at an anomaly – Thomas Moore's stricken face. 'The second party would like her residence.'

'But I'm telling you, you don't have to. You and Mary can stay with me.'

'Why would I do that?' I hate myself for asking this question.

His eyes cut from mine. 'Moving would be too disruptive for Mary. It'll be better she stays until—'

'Until what? You get bored? You decide you want your house back? You want to start your own family?' I laugh unkindly. 'I've been through all of that before. Many times. It's best Mary leaves now before she gets too attached.' Like I did.

'That's not...' His eyes burn with intensity, but I can't read them. I can't read *him*. But I can read a contract.

'Mr Farrier,' I call out, my voice as broken as I feel.

The lawyer scrambles in.

Eyes on Thomas, I ask, 'Is my compensation residence move-in ready?' From the corner of my eye I see him glance at Thomas.

Not breaking eye contact, Thomas gives a small slow nod. His face inscrutable.

'Uh, yes. It's a lovely fully furnished, two-bedroom in Greenwich.'

'I'd like to move in today please.'

26

'Hello, Thomas.'

'Jesus.' I'm scared back a step when I'm greeted by my mother, calling out from the kitchen under the pendant light over the island.

Shrugging out of my overcoat, I drape it over the banister, a sign of my exhaustion, before joining my mother in the kitchen. 'I thought you had a date.'

'Who wants to go on a date when their son has managed to make a complete cluster-fuck of their life?'

Vulgarity out of Emily Elizabeth Moore's mouth would pull anyone up short. I pause reaching for a high ball glass. 'I take it you talked to Alice.'

'Yes.' She takes a sip of her wine.

I grab a bottle of Scotch from the liquor cabinet. 'She made her choice.'

'Oh?' She scrutinizes me over the rim of her glass.

I pour more than I should, and drink almost all of it. 'I don't even know how this all started.'

'With you following her around the store like a lost puppy?'

I cough on my next sip. 'What?'

She tilts her head, considering. 'Maybe not a puppy. You're too old for that. Perhaps circling her like a vulture is better.'

'Jesus, no.' Ignoring the rare burn of embarrassment for having been so obvious about my interest in Alice, I pour more Scotch in my glass. 'I meant the marriage. For all we know Alice and I *are* married, but the paperwork is under a bed somewhere.'

She stares at me, as if only just realizing something. 'You really didn't know?'

I frown at my mother's amused tone. 'Know what?'

'Liz put those rings on you as a joke.'

I glance at the amber liquid, wondering exactly how much I've had.

'I honestly thought you knew.' She lifts her glass, then puts it back down. 'I mean, after this afternoon when Alice came back and moved out, I realized *she* didn't know, but when she mentioned the contract I thought *you* did.'

'I'm going to need you to explain.' I take another deep swallow.

My tone has Mother releasing her glass to adjust her diamond bracelets. 'Well, don't get mad. I'm sure there's an explanation to why she didn't tell you.'

'Mother.'

Sighing, she gives in. 'Liz had planned on swapping out Bell and Chase's custom Harry Winston bands with the tacky dice ones before the ceremony as a joke, *however* when she got to her hotel suite and saw Alice's and your clothes strewn all over the place and you two in bed together, she thought putting them on you would be funnier.'

I wait for anger. Or annoyance. Or some negative wave of emotion to hit me. It doesn't. But I feel like it should. 'And this is the child you want to let wander around, unchecked, when this is the kind of stuff they do while "finding themselves"?'

Mother raises her glass once more and tips it in my direction. 'You think you're doing much better?'

Thinking of Alice's stricken face as she held up her birth certificate, I don't answer. Instead, I ask my own question. 'Why didn't you say something then, if you knew we weren't really married?'

'When you arrived with a little girl and a social worker, I played along because I thought you were doing Alice a favor.' She laughs as if she can't believe the shit show that has become my life.

Me either.

'I didn't know your plan was to fire a woman who had done nothing wrong but capture your attention.' There's more judgment in her tone than when she handed my father divorce papers.

'I was angry when I made that plan. I wasn't going to do it.'

She takes another sip of her wine. 'And then later, when neither of you said anything, I didn't either because I was enjoying being Queenie.' She stares at the white countertop.

'I shouldn't have lied to you.'

Mother raises her head, a small smile on her face. 'I'm glad you did.' She touches her palm to my cheek. 'It made me happy getting to see my serious boy smile so much.' She drops her hand and we both stare into our glasses, thinking.

'How was she?' I finally ask, sliding my drink across the countertop between my hands. 'Alice, I mean. When she came home?'

Mother thinks this over. 'Sad.' She nods. 'She seemed sad and resigned.'

I take another sip. 'And Mary?'

She leans down and slides something out of her purse. 'She left you this.'

It's a picture of the park. Birds, grass, trees. It takes me a second to figure out what's different. 'All the colors are right.'

'I think she thought you'd like it.'

I hate it.

She gets up and I follow her to the foyer where she pulls out a purple puffy coat from the closet. A perfect match to the one Mary has and I wonder if she had been planning on wearing it with her on their next park outing.

'You know—' she turns so I can help her with her coat '— you were always so worried about becoming your father. Still are.' She turns to face me, somehow the monstrous jacket looking chic and not ridiculous. 'Staying in control, keeping your distance, toeing the line. But where has that gotten you?' She raises her arms to gesture around us, the move hindered by the heavy sleeves. 'You're all alone, in a prison of your own making. You couldn't be more like your father right now if you tried.'

The liquor in my gut turns. And something stabs at my chest. 'I told her not to go.'

'Why?'

I sigh, running a hand through my hair. 'She asked the same thing.'

Another sad smile. 'And let me guess, you said something about Mary, or about work or about anything except the truth.'

'What truth?'

She doesn't answer, just raises one eyebrow at me as if telling me I should already know.

It's annoying and probably karma.

'You better figure it out. Because if you don't, you're going to lose the family you always wanted before you ever really had them.' She swishes her way to the door, pausing once she opens it. 'Oh, and don't forget to feed the cat.' She points behind me.

When the door shuts, like rubbing salt on a wound, the flesh-colored albatross hisses from his perch on the landing.

* * *

Alice

'But *why* did we have to leave Thomas's house?' Mary's eyes implore me from across the large table in the brightly lit kitchen of the new apartment.

Besides Thomas's house, I've never lived somewhere so nice. Thankfully the homeowner fees were part of the contract. Leslie made sure of that.

The apartment door opens into small foyer with a closet, before transitioning into a living room to the right and a kitchen on the left, both sharing an entire wall of windows. With two bedrooms opposite the living room wall, each with their own bathroom.

Even the building itself is charming. Brown brick with black trim on a quiet road.

Outside, a car honks.

Well, quiet for New York City.

'I told you, there was an accident. Thomas and I aren't really married.'

Mary hadn't said much when we left Thomas's yesterday. She'd been playing dress up with Mike when I got home and talked with Emily, so thankfully she doesn't know the details.

But now, after the sleepover adventure at a new apartment is over, she has questions.

'So?' Mary pokes at her pancakes, for once completely uninterested in the overload of chocolate chips that I'd hoped would lift her spirits. 'Mom lived with Jack and they weren't married.'

I pause, my coffee mug halfway to my lips at Mary's first mention of her mother. 'Um, yes. She did.' I haven't brought up the fact that I know where she is, too worried to disappoint her if... well, if something doesn't go right. 'Do you want to talk about your mom?'

She shrugs and pokes her pancakes some more. 'She left.'

I take a sip of coffee, trying to feel my way through what to say next. 'Do you miss her?'

'Not really.'

I wonder if that's true or just something she's told herself. I make child counseling a priority in my ever-growing list that involves job searching, home schooling and getting the courage to go visit Kayla.

Thomas's lawyer gave me his card, telling me to call him if I needed anything. He seemed quite troubled about how everything played out and a little too infatuated with Leslie after their too long, hashed-out phone call.

I should've called Leslie sooner. I should've done a lot of things. And not done some others.

Mary lowers her fork to the table. 'Does that make me a bad kid?'

'No.' My coffee mugs lands hard on the table. 'You could never be a bad kid.'

'Are you sure?'

I get up to drop to my knees in front of her, pulling her into a hug. 'Positive.'

We hug a minute, and I wait for more questions. But only one comes.

'Can Queenie come play?'

* * *

Alice

The ferry ride over was cold even though I sat inside. I blame it for the chill I can't seem to shake as I sit on Kayla's apartment stoop, waiting.

When I called Emily on Mary's behalf for a play date, she was more than happy to come over. Elated even. And happy to watch Mary so I could make my way over to Staten Island.

After twenty minutes with only my burning anxiety keeping me warm, I spot Kayla walking toward me. She's talking on her phone, holding her nails out under the sun as if inspecting them.

Like a normal twenty-six-year-old without a care in the world.

I don't think I've ever seen her so happy. The time I spent researching rehabilitation centers seems a waste. My worrying a waste.

'I'm telling you. You have to go to the nail salon on First, they do the best job with—' Kayla sees me, her smile fading. She says something into the phone and hangs up. 'What are you doing here?'

Annoyed that she even has to ask, I stand up. 'I'm here to—'

'Never mind.' She looks left then right. 'Let's go inside.'

She hustles to use her key to open the security door and then speed-walks a few feet down to the first-floor apartment.

She ducks her head into what appears to be one of two bedrooms and breathes a sigh of relief. 'Angela's gone.' She turns, dropping her purse on the four-seat kitchen table. 'My roommate.' She shrugs off her jacket and drapes it over the back of a chair. 'But it's her day off so you need to be gone before she gets back.' She stands back, crosses her arms over her chest. 'You can't stay.'

I stare at the perfectly applied make-up, the copper high-lights in her hair, the fresh flush of health on her cheeks. I've imagined her gaunt and dirty. Helpless and forlorn. But never this. 'Are you... Are you serious right now?'

'Hey, I signed the papers your boss wanted me to.' She holds up her hands, freshly manicured. 'I thought that was that. I thought we could all move on.'

'Move on?' I almost choke on the words. 'You want to *move on* from abandoning your daughter without an explanation?'

Her eyes cut to the side but her mutinous expression remains unchanged.

'Do you know how worried I've been?' Shock is wearing off, giving way for the emotions I've suppressed these two weeks. 'The police mentioned your ex and drugs and then there was the alcohol that the doctor smelled on Mary at the hospital.'

'I never did drugs.' She recrosses her arms. 'And I told Jack to keep it out of the house. But I didn't know that he was using our rent money to buy them.' She juts her hip. 'And the alcohol was just rubbing alcohol the shelter gave me for Mary's cut.' She waves that misunderstanding away, like it's the shelter's fault for the misunderstanding.

Having not been invited to sit down, I settle for leaning back against the kitchen counter, needing a moment to process this diatribe of unapologetic excuses. I pinch the bridge of my nose, but the gesture makes me think of Thomas, so I drop my hand.

'And then I was laid off all because I missed a few shifts.' She rolls her eyes. 'So I had to use the money you sent for Mary's school for rent but it—'

'Stop. Just stop.' I take a deep breath. 'Why didn't you tell me? Ask me for help?'

Kayla pops her other hip. 'You would've loved that, huh?'

'What are you talking about?'

'Martyr Alice, coming to save the day.' Kayla's hands drop to her sides, her fists clenching. 'Do you know how annoying it is to be around you all the time?'

I press my hand to my chest, dropping my chin. 'Me?'

She thrusts a perfectly polished nail at me. '*You* were the one that told me when I was pregnant that being a mother would be great. That having a family was the best thing. And I believed you.' She drops her arm as if suddenly tired. 'But I was never meant to be a mother. At least not so young.' Her eyes cut away. 'I never should've had Mary.'

I brace my hands on the counter behind me. 'Kayla...'

'It's true, okay?' She paces to the side. 'And the fact that I can say it is proof I did the right thing when I left her.' She stops, looking out the barred window facing the street. 'When I stood in that hospital and the nurse asked Mary if she wanted her mommy to hold her hand, Mary asked for you instead.'

Guilt hits me, making it hard for me to meet her eyes when she faces me. 'I never—'

'I knew right then that you were more her mom than I ever was or would be.' She shrugs. 'And I wasn't even mad.' She steps closer, for once not looking accusatory. 'I was *relieved*.'

Silence fills the space as her words sink in. Words I understand but can't relate to.

I wonder if this is why Thomas saw Kayla without me. Because he knew it would hurt.

'She's happy, isn't she?'

I can tell Kayla's asking the question, not because she cares, but because she thinks the answer will prove her right.

And maybe it does.

I think of Mary's drawings. Her lack of nightmares. Her ready smiles. How she's found family in Queenie who showed up to play with her even after I left her son's house so I could come see Kayla. 'Yes. Mary is happy.'

She nods once, hard. And for a brief moment, real emotion peaks through before disappearing with a wave of her spiked manicure hand. 'I knew it. You're her mom.'

The door opens and a girl I assume is Kayla's roommate walks in, a grocery bag in each hand. 'Hey, Kayla, I got mixers for tonight's—' She stops when she spots me.

There's an awkward moment as Kayla shifts anxiously on her feet and the roommate's gaze shifts between Kayla and me.

I put on my best fake smile, determined that it will be my last. 'It was good to see you again, Kayla.' I step around the roommate to the still open door. 'Just remember you can always call, okay?' My voice nearly cracks on the last word but I keep it together.

Kayla nods.

Leaving her to her new life, I catch a ferry to get back to mine.

27

THOMAS

I can't sleep.

Last night I thought it was the alcohol. Too much to keep me awake, not enough to put me under. Tonight, it's the silence. Or what the silence means.

No Alice. No Mary. No discussions of which princess rules them all (always Cinderella) over breakfast (sugar-filled). No shy smiles and passionate kisses.

The silence makes me *ache* in a way exercising never does.

It also makes it too easy to keep asking myself the question both Alice and my mother asked – *why?* Why did I want them to stay when I made it so easy for them to leave?

Apparently, I only fooled myself using Mary's safety as the answer.

Mary is safe right now, just like my lawyer said she and Alice would be in the apartment I purchased. And as long as she has Alice, she'll be fine.

I even made sure to send them groceries, complete with chocolate chips, worried Alice would use her savings for food.

She's determined to follow the damn contract to the letter having emailed her resignation this afternoon.

And while I feel guilt, if I'm honest with myself, which I hate doing when it comes to feelings, guilt isn't the answer to *why*.

The why is Alice.

Her smile. Her shy strength. Her warmth. I miss her because I love her. Her and Mary.

I hadn't thought myself capable of it. Especially not in such a short amount of time.

I pause, remembering my mother's opinion on my having been circling Alice for the past year. As much as I wanted to deny it, for fear of it making me seem predatorial like my father, there is truth to it.

Mary simply came in like a kaleidoscope wrecking ball to the heart.

The sheets pull across my legs and I stiffen.

My existential crisis may be the prime reason I can't sleep, yet I can't ignore legitimate concern that my brother's flesh-toned Beelzebub is planning something. I've opened my eyes multiple times in the last few hours to find him glaring at me. Each time he seemed a little closer than the last.

To say he's displeased would be an understatement.

He spent all of last night watching me drink and flip through the pictures on my phone after Mother left. And all today meowing from outside my dark room door. I came out multiple times on the rare chance he was having a Lassie moment and was trying to alert me to some kind of disaster. But each time I was met with a hiss.

Just as sleep seems to find me, I feel movement on the bed. I open my eyes just in time to see Mike's wrinkled ass coming toward me.

'That's it.'

Climbing out of bed, I get dressed and head to the basement.

'Is he dead?' George's voice seeps into my consciousness.

'Don't say that.' A woman's southern twang.

'Sorry, Ms King.'

'It's Mrs Moore now, George. And I don't think he's dead.' My brother's soft laughter. 'This is totally worth coming home from Hawaii early.'

Someone sniffs.

'He smells awful.' Mother's tone implying that my odor is on par with matricide.

'Do you think he's just been exercising this whole time?' Bell asks.

'That is the lamest form of heartbreak ever.' Chase sneers. 'Honestly, who exercises when they're sad?'

Someone grunts.

'Chase, dear. You'll give yourself a hernia.'

'Thanks for the vote of confidence, Ma.'

'I'm fully confident in the strength of your charm. Your biceps, not so much.' There's a pause. 'And don't call me Ma, it's so...'

'Pedestrian?'

'Yes, that. Thank you, George.'

The more I hear the less I want to wake.

I'm hit with an arctic blast that shocks both my brain and body into full working order in seconds. Sitting up from my prone position on my workout bench, I sputter and cough. 'Fuck.'

'There.' My mother, holding my empty water jug, smiles at me like she hadn't just tried to drown me. 'Now we can figure out what's going on.' She hooks the jug handles on the bench press cage where I left it.

'Yo, T-money.' Chase holding Mike, lifts the cat's front paw and waves.

'Good morning, Mr Moore.' George straightens his glasses.

'You need a shower,' Mother says.

'What are you all doing here?'

'You didn't think we'd leave you to your own devices, did you?' Chase asks, resting a hip on the dumb-bell rack.

'We're here to help.' Bell collects the cat, who looks much happier in her arms rather than my brother's. 'But—' she levels me a look '—as Alice's friend, I have to first say that you're a complete asshat who doesn't deserve her.'

A drop of water slides off the bridge of my nose. 'Noted.'

'Really, dear.' Mother's nose twitches. '*Shower.*'

* * *

Twenty minutes later, at the vehement urging of my mother, I'm showered and dressed in clean clothes. My choice of play clothes surprising everyone by the look on their faces.

'Okay,' Chase asks as I enter the living room, eyeing my Under Armour track pants, 'what's the plan?'

'Yes.' George stares at me expectantly. 'Please tell me there's a plan and that I'm part of it.'

I walk past them toward the back stairs.

'He's not going to exercise again?' Mother asks the room.

'Is that why he dressed like that?' George asks.

'He's coming back, right?' Chase asks.

'I'm coming back,' I call as I reach the stairs.

'Oh. Cool.'

A minute later, I lay what I'd been working on since I woke hungover yesterday on the coffee table.

Chase is nearest. He flips it open, turning it to make sure everyone can see.

As they all lean over and look, it feels as if ants are crawling up my spine.

Chase straightens. 'The pictures are... great.' He bares his teeth in a grimace. 'But I'm not gonna lie. This could either come off very sweet or extremely creepy.'

Bell smacks his arm. 'I think it's sweet.' Her smile wavers. 'I mean, as long as you know Thomas, it's not creepy.'

George bites his lower lip. 'I vote it's creepy.'

I drop my chin to my chest. After Mother told me to find what I'm good at, the only thing I could come up with was photography. I went through all my archives, putting together an album with all the pictures I ever took of Alice. I was astounded by the amount of them. They aren't all of just her, like Chase said, that would be creepy. There are group shots. Work shots. Some she isn't even in, they're just pictures of some of the floor displays she designed that I told myself would make a good picture. But when you put them all together – it's overwhelming.

Mother collects the album. 'I'll make sure she gets it.'

'You?' Chase asks. 'I'm not sure this is the time Thomas should be delegating. This is groveling time.'

'This will work to soften her up. Think of it as your dancing Elvises.'

Chase looks like someone insulted his cat. 'You're comparing my flash mob of Elvises in a honky-tonk bar to a stalker—'

Bell elbows him in his gut.

'Okay, okay.' Chase rubs his stomach. 'What else you got?'

I stare at them.

'Anything?' Bell asks, looking hopeful.

'I...' Sweat breaks out on my brow. 'I love her.'

Their expressions all shout 'duh'.

'That's a great start, dear,' Mother says. 'Now try to sound as if it isn't killing you to say it.'

Chase flops on the sofa. 'What Thomas needs is a way to say something without saying something. Like the photo album but less creepy.'

'But it needs to be something important to Alice,' Bell adds. 'It can't just be about Thomas.'

'And what about Mary?' George asks. 'Should she be a part of this too?'

As they bounce ideas back and forth, an idea forms, but it's... I shift in my seat, uncomfortable at the thought.

Ignoring it, I power through. 'George.'

'Yes?'

'I need you to call Human Resources and do three things for me.'

'You got it.'

'One, tell them to accept Alice Truman's resignation.'

Bell's mouth drops open.

'And have them send her a request to come to the store for a formal outboarding meeting. Make sure she calls to make an appointment so we know what time she's coming.'

'Ahhh.' Bell nods.

George smiles. 'And the third?'

'Have the HR manager call me about removing your formal warning from your file.'

'Aw, Mr Moore.' He touches a palm to his chest.

I point to my sister-in-law whose cat has taken a deep-dive

into her cleavage. 'Bell, I'll need your help with the front display.'

She salutes me with one hand, trying to unearth Mike with the other.

Chase helps her, retaking the animal before jumping around like a boxer before the bell.

'And me?' The beast's four legs and nether region dangles as he jumps. 'What about me?'

I resign myself for the most painful part of my plan. 'You come with me. But for God's sakes leave the cat.'

28

ALICE

'Do you think the prince loved Cinderella?' Mary grabs a handful of popcorn from the bowl between us.

Watching Mary's favorite movie for the second time today, I glance up from my laptop. 'Of course, sweetie.' I've been looking for remote work. Even if it's just clerical stuff. That way I can homeschool Mary to help catch her up for next year.

'But he doesn't talk to her.'

'He scours her kingdom to find her though.' An email notification pops up from my work account. 'Sometimes actions speak louder than words.'

'What's sours?'

Noting the email is from Moore's human resource department, I click on it. '*Scours* – means to search.'

'Oh.' She watches Cinderella and the prince dance.

Outboarding. They want me to come in to formally resign and take an accounting of all equipment I was given in my role as lead visual merchandiser.

My savings account takes a mental hit when I realize I'll need to replace both my phone and my laptop. Then my stress levels take a hit at the thought of going back to Moore's. I check the soonest meeting time offered. Tomorrow. Better to get it over with.

'Yeah, but he didn't look for her himself.' Mary continues. 'He sent his soldiers.'

I stare at her, wondering why she's suddenly so down on her favorite movie. 'He's a prince. He can't be everywhere at once. He has other responsibilities.' I frown, now wondering why I'm suddenly thinking about Thomas though I've been working very hard not to.

'Hmmm.' She glares at the TV in a perfect imitation of the man who broke my heart.

I've been careful not to let Mary see me cry. But it's obvious from her questions and expression that mine isn't the only heart that misses Thomas Moore.

Ding dong.

Sliding my laptop to the side, I pad over to the door. Emily called earlier, wanting to take Mary to the library.

'Hello, dear.' Emily bustles in, a large box in her arms. 'Mary, are you ready?' Emily walks over to the kitchen table and sets the box down. 'I thought we'd stop at Serendipity after, if that's okay with your aunt.' She shoots me a sly smile, knowing full well I won't say no to Mary having ice cream if she asks in front of her.

'Yay!' Mary races to her room to get her shoes.

I turn to Emily, lips pursed. 'Sneaky.'

She waves away my comment. 'Yes, yes, I know.'

I point to the box. 'What's that?' Suspicion laced in my voice.

'A gift.' She holds up a hand before I can argue. 'I didn't spend a single penny on it.'

I frown, still uncomfortable with receiving anything from

her after all she's already spent. Especially knowing that we aren't family. Not legally, anyway.

'Ready!' Breaking records on getting ready now that ice cream is on the table, Mary hustles over and grabs her matching purple puffer jacket from the closet.

The two of them look so adorable together, I tear up.

It's nice having someone who cares. For me and Mary.

Even if every time I see her it hurts.

'Okay, then.' Emily ushers Mary out the door. 'Off we go.'

I stare at the closed door, wondering why Emily seemed in such a rush. Eyes still narrowed, I turn my attention to the box.

It looks like a shirt box, but larger, more substantial. The yellow Post-it note glaring on top of the shiny black cardboard.

Tentatively, I walk over and read it.

BECAUSE SOMETIMES WORDS FAIL ME.

It's Thomas's handwriting. Large, all-cap print, slightly slanted to the left.

Swallowing, I lift the lid. It's a photo album.

I tell myself not to open it. That only added sadness is between the pages, pages I'm sure are filled with the photos Thomas and I took that day in the park. And yet I grab the bottom right corner and lift.

It's not the pictures from the park. It isn't even pictures from Mary and my time living with Thomas. It's me, almost a year ago, at Moore's. Me with my unattractive blunt bang haircut and slightly baggy salesman uniform.

When did he take this?

Each page following is a timeline of my work at Moore's starting just before Chase and Thomas took control from their father. First pictures of me in the shoe department all the way up to the Valentine's displays I created. Not all pictures have me in them. But they're somehow about me.

And on the last few pages are the pictures of our time with him. Mary on the swing. Emily and me laughing in the kitchen. Mike Hunt laying on a bed of Barbie clothes.

Thomas's face might never show up in the photos, but he's there in all of them. I *feel* him.

On the last page, there's another Post-it note.

I'M SORRY. PLEASE COME HOME.

* * *

'We're just going in and out, okay?' I lean down so Mary can hear me over the city noise.

Holding my hand, Mary skips up the last step of the subway a block away from Moore's. 'Okey-dokey.'

'No shopping,' I add. 'No dawdling.'

I don't know if I'm reminding her or me.

'Got it.'

Even as a cold wind blows down the street, whipping my cheeks, I'm sweating. I don't know if I'm hoping to see Thomas, or to avoid him.

I'M SORRY. PLEASE COME HOME.

But *why*? Even if I forgive him for the contract, the private investigator, meeting with Kayla without me, which, annoyingly, I think I already have, it doesn't make any sense for Mary and me to move back in with him.

He's already provided us with a place to live. But it would have been nice if he'd offered me my job again. My heart races faster the closer we get to the store, but my feet slow as the foot traffic increases.

I pull Mary's hand in closer. 'Don't let go.'

After a minute of weaving through the crowd, I realize it's the windows flanking Moore's entrance that's creating the crowds.

I knew the butterfly lights and the tableaus of mannequins enacting spring activities were eye-catching, but these crowds are more like the ones drawn by the annual Christmas displays. Dread pools when I think Thomas might have hired another display company after I left. That my design was never used.

But the dismay only lasts a moment until I see the soft lavender glow emanating from the top of the window.

Weaving through the crowd, my relief is quickly followed by shock as I peek into the first window – and freeze.

It's my design, but it's also not.

The high-gloss, wigless, white mannequins are the perfect canvas for the purple neon glow of the butterfly lights suspended from above – just as I'd planned. But beyond that, it's different.

Instead of two mannequins dressed in tennis clothes holding rackets, they're in office apparel. The female mannequin, wearing a Moore's salesperson's uniform, is standing next to a shoe display, while the male, in a three-piece suit, is standing behind her, his phone in hand. The name tag on the salesperson reads 'Alice'.

'Aren't those your shoes?' Mary points to the table where a duplicate of my red bowed shoes sit.

I barely hear her, her voice and the noise of the crowd nearly drowned out by my heartbeat. 'I *think* so.'

We move along with the crowd to the next scene. Where instead of a father and son flying a kite, it's once again a female and male couple. This time in formal wear. The female wearing a deep-V, sky-blue Vera Wang slip dress and the male a garish black and blue paisley tux and blue suede shoes. The male mannequin is holding his hand over his left eye that has been colored with purple marker.

People jostle to take pictures, stepping in front of the man and opening my line of sight to the woman.

'Oh. My. God.' I stare, open-mouthed at the woman's hand. Not the one holding a bouquet of flowers, but the other – holding Trusty Thrusty. A hysterical laugh erupts as I stare at the extra-large purple dildo that doesn't even fit in the mannequin's hand. I can see fishing line cutting into the thick silicone, holding the dildo in place.

Women hold out their hands as if measuring its size, smiling appreciatively. Guys snicker. An elderly woman rolls her eyes but doesn't stop looking.

Mary gasps and points and I nearly cover her eyes before realizing she's pointing to the next scene. 'That's Mike Hunt!'

People next to us on the sidewalk startle and turn to us as Mary jumps up and down in front of the third tableau. It's a mannequin cat, wearing the collar Thomas bought him, sitting on its haunches next to a man and girl mannequin building a rocket ship out of Legos. The Lego bricks are multicolored.

'This is so cool.' Mary skips in place, waiting for the crowd to move.

Finally, we reach the entrance to Moore's.

'Alice!' Bell shoots her hand into the air and waves, as if we're much farther than three people away.

'Bell?' I watch my friend bob and weave past the three bystanders before she envelops me into a hug.

'I'm so happy to see you!' Her smile as bright as it was on her wedding day suddenly blurs and I realize I'm crying.

'Oh, Alice. No, don't cry.'

'I'm sorry I left your wedding. I should've—'

'Stop. Please.' She glances behind her as if afraid someone might see. 'I beg of you. I am *not* mad.'

'Aunt Alice?' Mary's worried looks smacks some sense into me.

'Ah, sorry.' Clearing my throat, I smile. And while slightly forced due to circumstances, I'm genuinely happy to see my friend. I knew I missed her but hadn't realized how much I needed her. Especially now.

'Do you know what—' I gesture behind me to the window '—this is?'

'Maybe.' From her smile I know instantly that she not only knows but was involved.

'What do you mean, "maybe"?'

Ignoring me, Bell leans down to Mary, her hands resting on her thighs. 'And you must be Mary.'

'Yep.' Mary curtseys. 'Did Aunt Alice call you Bell? Like the princess?'

'Yes, she did.' She curtseys in return. 'I'm your Aunt Bell.'

Mary's eyes go wide. 'Really?'

While surprised at Bell calling herself Mary's aunt, I don't argue. I mean, technically I'm not Mary's aunt either so if Bell wants to…

'Shall we see the rest of the display?' Bell straightens and reaches out a hand to Mary who grabs it.

'Oh, I don't know…' Glancing back at the display I just saw, I'm apprehensive about what lies on the other side.

Thomas's apology. The groceries I'm pretty sure he had delivered. The photo album. And whatever this… I look back to the display I've just seen, then ahead to the one I haven't… whatever this is.

If I simply enter Moore's now, if I turn in my equipment and leave without seeing what's beyond this point, I could go back to the life I planned.

'Come on, Aunt Alice.' Mary grabs Bell's hand and tugs on mine. 'I want to see what happens next.'

And since I do too, I let Mary guide me past the entrance to the window on the other side, holding her hand a little tighter than before.

Just around the corner of the entrance alcove, three butterfly lights hang from the ceiling of the display. Underneath them, three mannequins stand next to a stop sign. The man and woman mannequin, each dressed in suits, stand on either side of a child mannequin – a girl based on its purple dress, glitter high-tops and sequined backpack. Like they're waiting for a school bus.

'That's not us, is it?' Mary tilts her head, her brow pinched.

I frown with her, unsure of the answer.

This time Bell leads us along.

At the next scene, three mannequins are at the beach. A male mannequin in swim trunks holds a girl mannequin on his hip, pointing out beyond the glass, as if to the ocean. Slightly behind them to the left a female mannequin lounges in a beach chair –reading.

I can just make out *Demon's Lust* on the front cover of the paperback. The same book I was reading on the plane to Vegas. The one Thomas quoted while kissing me.

While the memory brings tears to my eyes, it's the last tableau that makes my breath catch.

It's a Christmas scene. The man, woman and child from the other scenes are sitting around the tree. But there are others too. More adults. More children. I give a watery laugh at not one, but two cats. It's the mannequins' family.

'It's the epilogue,' I whisper, understanding dawning.

'What's a-pee-log?' Mary asks.

'It's what happens after the story ends.' I dab at my cheeks with my coat sleeve. 'But even if I'm right, it doesn't make sense. It's missing the whole part where—'

'Thomas!' Mary lets go of Bell's and my hands, dodging between the crowd to get to Thomas, noticeable by his height and his general aura of self-confidence. He catches her as she launches herself at him, hiking her on his hip just like in the beach scene.

Two hands on my back, Bell gives me a push to get me going. My path made easy as the people gathered to look at the display pull back, as if subconsciously aware that something is about to happen.

With each step, my previous understanding turns to uncertainty, then aggravation, then fear. Finally, anger emerges. Anger at the man who has once more made me afraid. Afraid to hope. To take a chance.

And then I'm a foot away, staring up into Thomas's dark eyes. His hair perfectly styled, his bespoke three-piece suit under a camel cashmere blend topcoat.

And the jerk smiles. He smiles like he's happy to be holding Mary in his arms. As if he's happy to see me. 'Alice, I—'

'You never said you loved me.' I cringe as I blurt the real reason I'm angry. The reason why I can't trust anything he does, no matter how sweet.

Thomas's head tips back at the force of my words. People around us stop looking at the windows and start looking at me.

But before Thomas can speak, Mary pipes up. 'Sometimes actions speak louder than words, Aunt Mary.' She drops her head to the side, touching Thomas's. 'Isn't that what you said?'

I did. I did say that. And I meant it. But even though all of

Thomas's actions – the illogical desire for Mary and me to stay with him, the album with the pictures going back almost a year, the display featuring all the things Thomas, Mary and I could be – add up to love, I still can't shake my doubt.

'That can be true,' Thomas answers for me. 'But sometimes a person needs words, and if someone truly cares for them, they'll stop being a pathetic coward and say them, even if they've never said them before. Even if they aren't sure they deserve to say them.'

Mary's eyes ping-pong between us. 'I don't think true love is supposed to be so complicated.'

A few people laugh, including Bell, who steps around me. 'Mary honey, would you like to meet your Uncle Chase?' She holds up her hands ready to take her. Mary doesn't look tempted until Bell adds, 'He has Mike with him.'

She perks up. 'Prince Michael?'

At Bell's nod, Mary struggles to get down.

Thomas lets her, making sure she's securely on her feet before letting go. Just as she reaches the door, Mary turns, peeking around Bell. 'Don't forget to kiss when you're done!'

Bell follows Mary inside, mumbling something about her getting along great with Uncle Chase.

Leaving me alone with Thomas.

And a crowd full of curious New Yorkers.

'First I'd like to say I'm sorry.' Thomas's fierce expression, now that Mary is gone, would be frightening if I wasn't 99.9 percent sure his anger is directed at himself. 'There's no excuse for having that contract writ—'

'I blackmailed you.' I step closer, eager for the words I'm hoping will follow. 'I get it.'

He shakes his head, the open side of his overcoat brushing against me. 'But then the private detective—'

I grab the edges of his coat, the contact reassuring. 'It helped you find Kayla before the police did.'

He settles his hands on my shoulders, bracing himself against my getting closer as I attempt to slide my hands around his waist. 'Yes, but I should've told you when—'

'It's okay, I forgive you.' My fingers tighten around the fabric of his suit jacket. Nerves of self-doubt starting to build with every sentence that isn't the one I need hitting my ears.

'You know—' one brow surges up in tandem with a slight uplift to the corner of his mouth '—for someone who wants words, you sure interrupt a lot.'

I open my mouth to respond, then snap it closed when someone in our audience chuckles.

The other corner of his mouth lifts.

'You asked me why in my office. Why Mary and you should continue living with me. Why I would want you to.' One of his hands on my shoulders slides up my neck, cradling my jaw. 'I couldn't answer. Probably because every answer I told myself was a lie. And I didn't want to lie to you anymore.' His thumb caresses my cheek. 'The truth is I don't deserve you. You're stronger than I am. You're smarter than I am. And you are much better at words than I am.'

Someone in the crowd sniffles.

'But I love you.' His hands drop away, as if now that he's admitted his crime, he's awaiting a final verdict.

A group of women collectively sigh.

Meanwhile I can't help but think he's so stupid. That *I'm* so stupid. Him for a variety of reasons and me for needing the words. Because now that I've heard them, they only serve to underline what my heart already knew. My head just needed to catch up.

'Thomas?' Holding his gaze, I slide my arms fully around his waist.

I watch his Adam's apple bob. 'Yes?'

I lift onto my tiptoes, my body flush against his. 'I—'

'Aunt Alice!'

There's a collective groan from the crowd as Mary bursts out of the doors. 'Thomas bought me a cat!' She races out, throwing herself at Thomas, and therefore me.

Thomas staggers back a step but manages to keep us from falling.

'Thank you, Thomas, thank you.' Mary squeezes us tight.

Chase peers out the door, Mike Hunt in his teddy bear suit strapped to Chase in a baby carrier. 'You guys done out there, or what? Mary and I want to take Mike back to T-money's house for a play date with the new kitten.'

Mary looks up from her hug. 'Can we?'

Thomas looks at me, his eyes full of hope.

I shrug, struggling to feign nonchalance. 'Seeing as my new apartment doesn't allow pets, I guess Mary and I have no choice but to move back in with you.'

Thomas's brow furrows.

I reach out, smoothing the space between his eyes, trailing my fingers down the bridge of his nose, tracing the flat line of his lips. 'So it's a good thing I love you too.'

Under my index finger, Thomas's smile grows.

And there, in front of a crowd of strangers, customers and an audience of family and employees, Thomas Moore kisses me.

People cheer.

Slightly panting, Thomas and I come up for air. A wealth of wordless promises in his eyes.

Mary bows to the crowd. 'And they lived happily ever after.'

EPILOGUE
THOMAS

'Admit it.' Chase smirks at me from one end of my living room sofa. 'You love Dick.'

I raise one eyebrow at my brother, peering over the vacant cushion between us, Elvis's Christmas album playing softly from the surround sound. 'His name is King Richard.' I pet Mary's Bengal cat who purrs contently. 'And he is ten times the cat yours is.'

I take pleasure in my brother's fallen expression.

I specifically bought Mary a Bengal – a large, stately, easily trained breed with a lush, spotted coat – to ensure that the feline living in my house wasn't anything like my brother's follicularly challenged demon cat.

And then Mary named him King Richard Moore.

Aka King Dick Moore.

My brother, initially put-out when I didn't buy another sphynx, was beyond pleased.

'Hey.' Chase cuddles said demon – who's wearing a Christmas sweater – to his chest. 'Be nice.' Mike's wrinkly skin collects under his neck as my brother pulls him closer.

'You're not bullying Uncle Chase, are you, Daddy?' Mary, wearing a red and green plaid princess dress, comes into the room holding a plate of Christmas cookies.

'He is, Mary.' Chase nods, overly serious over Mike's bald head. 'Your daddy is a great big bully.'

While it never ceases to please me every time Mary calls me Daddy since Alice and I officially adopted her this past summer, I could do without the close bond she's forged with her mischievous uncle.

Alice jingle jangles into the room with yet another plate of cookies, Bell close behind with a tray of glasses and a pitcher of milk.

My first thought is that I'm going to need to up my cardio this week.

My second, as my eyes lock onto Alice's green apron with red fur and jingle bell trim worn over her red Victoria Beckham dress, is that I must've been a very good boy.

Alice's eyes light up as she surveys the room. Family and a Christmas tree. Just what I promised her in the display I made ten months ago.

The substantial down payment I made to the best Christmas tree farm in New York was worth it for the look on Alice's and Mary's faces when not one, but four Christmas trees were delivered to the house on the first of the month. One in the foyer for Alice to see as soon as we get home from work together. One to sit by in the living room at night as we read. And two small ones for our bedroom and Mary's.

Making love to Alice by Christmas tree light has been the highlight of the holiday season.

Mother swoops in behind Alice, a large, wrapped box in her hand. 'Who's ready for Christmas presents?'

'Me!' Mary jumps up and down. 'Me!'

'Mom, it isn't Christmas yet.' Alice shakes her head at my mother, who beams at her in return. Both are equally ecstatic at Alice calling her mom.

'Just one, dear.' Mother holds up a French-tipped nail. One with a Christmas tree painted on it, a la Mary's suggestion. 'A Christmas Eve tradition.'

Alice looks at me. 'Is that true? You normally open a gift on Christmas Eve?'

'No.' I ignore my mother's harsh stare. 'But it could be a new tradition.'

Mother's buoyant again. 'Yes, a new tradition.' She places the wrapped box in front of Mary before Alice can object. 'Here, Mary, open this one.' Mother looks at each of us. 'This is for the family, but I thought Mary could open it.'

Mary tears through the paper only to find another box. And then another, and then another. She's waist high in boxes and wrapping paper before she finally reaches an envelope.

Watching her try and fight her disappointment at the sight of such a small gift would be hilarious if I also wasn't extremely nervous over what the hell my mother has done this time.

'Go on,' Mother urges, her eagerness making me even more nervous.

Mike motorboats Bell, who struggles to control her perverted pet from slithering into her dress.

King Richard drops his head on my chest and purrs, calming me down.

There is no question over whose cat is superior.

'What is it, sweetie?' Alice asks when Mary opens the envelope.

Mary frowns at the strips of paper in her hand. 'A boat?'

Alice's jaw drops. 'Mom...'

'Not a boat!' Mother raises both hands. 'Not a boat.' She

hustles around all the boxes and points at the paper in Mary's hand. 'Tickets.' She beams at the room. 'For a Disney Cruise.'

'No way.' Mary's whisper overflows with awe.

'And—' Mother adopts a smug expression '—we'll be having dinner in Cinderella's banquet hall.'

'No way!' Mary throws herself at Mother. 'You're the best, Queenie. Thank you, thank you, thank you!'

Alice drops onto the arm of the sofa. 'So much for the new bike Santa got her,' she murmurs to me, a look of loving exasperation on her face.

King Richard places one paw on her lap, making Alice smile.

Seriously, he is the most intelligent of beasts.

* * *

Alice

A few hours later, with Mary in bed and everyone else gone home for the night, Thomas and I are alone and surrounded by tall stacks of wrapped presents.

'I thought you told me you were done buying gifts after the Barbie Dream House?' I eye the presents Thomas gathered from all our various hiding places around the house. 'That looks like a significant amount more than when I last counted.'

'Most of those are from Santa.'

'Uh-huh.' I roll my eyes. 'Mary is so spoiled.'

He shrugs. 'It's good for her.'

'Yeah.' I sink back into the sofa next to him enjoying the multicolored glow from the Christmas tree. 'I guess it is.'

He shifts beside me, reaching behind him. 'It's good for you too.' Thomas hands me a long, cylindrical tube.

'How long have you had this shoved under the couch cushion?'

'Never mind that.' He gestures to the carboard tube with a squashed red bow on it. 'Open it.'

'Hold on.' Leaning forward, I slide my present for Thomas out from under the sofa. 'Turns out we had the same hiding place.' Hefting the large, heavy but slim wrapped box, I drop it in his lap. 'You open this first.'

Knowing Thomas, the tube he gave me probably contains the Hope Diamond. There's no way I'm following that.

I grimace at the box, nervous. 'It's just something small, really.'

He kisses my cheek. 'Thank you.'

Thomas is one of those annoyingly slow gift openers. Sliding his finger under the tape, peeling it back as if the wrapping paper is made of gold.

By the time he finally gets to my present I'm too relieved to be anxious. Even more relieved when a slow smile spreads over his normally serious face.

It's a framed black and white picture from our wedding this past summer.

It took Thomas four months after Mary and I moved back in with him to convince me to get married. For real this time. Though I was confident Thomas loved me, *loved us*, I was still skittish as paperwork between Kayla and the state was finalized and Mary started therapy to deal with the knowledge that her mother gave her up.

When I finally said yes, Thomas hadn't wanted to wait. So we eloped – this time to Hawaii, not Vegas.

Actually, it turned into more of a destination wedding than

elopement when Thomas's family tagged along. Which was fine by me. Because they're my family now too.

Bell being Bell still hums Elvis's 'Blue Hawaii' every time Thomas and I kiss.

She hums it a lot.

'Who took this?' Thomas stares at the picture, still smiling.

It captures the moment after our vows when Thomas and I took Mary by the hand, swinging her in her grass skirt between us as we walked down the beach.

'I had someone from the resort take it.' I look over the frame, nervous about giving a photograph to a photographer.

Everyone in the family, plus George, Susan and even Raymond, hold sparklers around us. Everyone save Chase who has Mike Hunt in one arm, King Richard in the other – both cats in bow ties, hissing. I'd like to think they were unhappy over their close proximity to the sparklers, but I rather think they were hissing at each other.

'I love it.'

I let out a sigh of relief. 'Yeah?'

'Yes.' He leans over, kissing me.

When he straightens, far too soon, his smile is more thoughtful. 'This will be the first picture of me in my house.'

'I know.' Standing, I take the frame from him and walk over to where all eight stockings are hung. 'That's why I think this is the best place for it.' I lean it on top of the painting, which probably cost more than a car, that hangs above the mantel.

He nods, smile still in place. 'Perfect.'

My sigh has a more dream-like quality this time. Because this – Christmas trees, family gatherings and Thomas Moore – is my life. 'Yeah, it is.'

'But I think next year will be even better.'

Laughing, I step around piles of presents back to the sofa.

'This Christmas isn't even over yet, and you're already thinking of next year.'

He picks the tube back up from the couch. 'Open.'

Wondering what in the world he could fit in a twenty-inch, narrow cardboard tube, I pause. 'It isn't a dildo, is it?' I shake it, remembering the weight of Trusty Thrusty all those months ago, and realize it's much too light.

I'm rewarded with a trademark Thomas Moore eyebrow lift. 'Just because Moore's is now in the sex toy business, does not mean my house will be inundated with dildos.'

I bite my lip to keep from laughing. Thomas is still a bit flabbergasted by the overwhelming outcry from Moore's patrons demanding their own Trusty Thrusty after he placed one in the front window display.

Turns out our customers like their Gucci and Chanel with a side of dick.

Moore's now has its own sex toy department next to women's lingerie.

Chase's business cards now read 'CEO & dildo runner'. He had some made for Thomas, but he burned them.

'Yes, sorry.' I duck my head to keep Thomas from seeing my amusement. 'Of course not.'

Popping the plastic top off one end of the tube, I slide out a rolled piece of paper. I unfurl it and spread the large paper out on the coffee table in front of us, next to the plate of cookies for Santa.

Blueprints.

'I don't get it.' I squint closer to the page, the lines hard to see under the Christmas tree lights. 'What's this?'

If I didn't know better, I'd think Thomas is nervous by the way his eyes shift to the side and his throat works to swallow. 'Plans for our new fifth floor.'

I tilt my chin up, staring as if I can see through the ceiling. 'You're going to add a floor to the house?' I'm pretty sure the city will have something to say about that.

'No, I'm going convert the attic. Which is currently unused.' He leans forward and taps the paper. 'This will make it useful.'

Trying to ignore the delicious waft of his cologne, I read the words in the middle of the boxes drawn out on the blueprints that I can now see are rooms. 'You want to build two bedrooms up there? And a bathroom?' I frown at Thomas, still not getting it. 'Why?'

He shrugs, the small movement at odds with his anxious expression. 'More bedrooms mean more kids we can foster.'

Elvis croons about being home for Christmas. The antique grandfather clocks ticks. My heart beats double time. Everything but what Thomas just said is suddenly crystal clear. Until I feel a tear sliding down my cheek and Thomas's eyes go wide.

Then the *only* thing I can think is, 'You really love me, don't you?'

My vision blurs, but I see Thomas's shoulders sag in relief before he gathers me to him, kissing away my tears. 'Yes, I do.' Then his lips find mine.

Sinking into his embrace, we make love by tree light, Thomas having perfected couch sex months ago.

And when we're spent, happy and tear free, Thomas spoons me from behind, both of us enjoying the sight of Christmas before us and the feel of our naked bodies laying together.

'I take it you like the gift?' Thomas's voice rough and still just a touch anxious.

'Love it.' Smiling, I twist back to touch my lips to his once more. '*So* much better than a dildo.'

* * *

Want to find out what happens when Thomas meets Chase at the local cat cafe? Find out that and Moore (as in Liz!) in the bonus epilogue....

Sign up to Sara L. Hudson's mailing list for news, competitions and updates on future books.

ABOUT THE AUTHOR

Sara L. Hudson is a bestselling romantic comedy author living in Houston, whose books include the hilarious Space series, featuring the men and women of NASA and their panty-melting happily-ever-afters.

Sign up to Sara L. Hudson's mailing list for news, competitions and updates on future books.

Visit Sara's website: www.saralhudson.com/

Follow Sara L. Hudson on social media here:

facebook.com/SaraLHudsonWriter

twitter.com/_SaraLHudson

instagram.com/sara_l_hudson

ALSO BY SARA L. HUDSON

Anyone But You Series

Anyone But The Billionaire

Anyone But The Boss

Boldwood

Printed in Great Britain
by Amazon

48561667R00188